More praise for *THE WATCHMAN*

"Packed with whiplash plot twists and taut dialogue, *The Watchman* deftly reveals the taciturn, damaged Joe Pike. . . . As good a psychological test case as it is a thriller."
—*Entertainment Weekly*

"Crais writes in a taut, muscular style tailored to the lethal moves of this romantic mercenary soldier. . . . A story that cannily exploits the sexual dynamic of violence and danger. . . ."
—*The New York Times*

"A stunningly emotional thriller."
—*Booklist* (starred review)

"*The Watchman* is a true achievement, deftly combining a whirlwind of action with moments so moving they'll take your breath away."
—*Chicago Sun Times*

"Crais digs deep to let Joe Pike's persona rule *The Watchman.*"
—*Sun-Sentinel* (FL)

"[A] first-rate thriller . . . the tension never slackens."
—*Library Journal*

"Storytelling that is both intricate and sturdy. . . ."
—*Los Angeles Times*

"The resolution is touching as well as just."
—*Pittsburgh Post-Gazette*

"Can one get addicted to crime fiction? . . . I'm now hooked, and I have Robert Crais to blame."
—*Dayton Daily News*

ALSO BY ROBERT CRAIS

The Two Minute Rule
The Forgotten Man
The Last Detective
Hostage
Demolition Angel
L.A. Requiem
Indigo Slam
Sunset Express
Voodoo River
Free Fall
Lullaby Town
Stalking the Angel
The Monkey's Raincoat

ROBERT CRAIS

THE WATCHMAN

POCKET STAR BOOKS
NEW YORK LONDON TORONTO SYDNEY

Pocket Star Books
A Division of Simon & Schuster, Inc.
1230 Avenue of the Americas
New York, NY 10020

This book is a work of fiction. Names, characters, places, and incidents either are products of the author's imagination or are used fictitiously. Any resemblance to actual events or locales or persons, living or dead, is entirely coincidental.

Copyright © 2007 by Robert Crais

First Pocket Star Books paperback edition February 2008

POCKET STAR and colophon are registered trademarks of Simon & Schuster, Inc.

For information about special discounts for bulk purchases, please contact Simon & Schuster Special Sales at 1-800-456-6798 or business@simonandschuster.com.

Cover design by Tom Tafuri
Cover photos: L.A. scene © Corbis, man © Superstock

Manufactured in the United States of America

10   9   8   7   6   5   4   3   2   1

ISBN-13: 978-1-4165-1497-8
ISBN-10:   1-4165-1497-X

for Lauren

no sacrifice too great
no love so dear
no parents more proud

ACKNOWLEDGMENTS

Aaron Priest, the Joe Pike of literary agents, put it together and made it happen.

Pat Crais, the most feared copy editor in publishing, picked up my slack with devotion and zeal.

My publishers, Louise Burke and David Rosenthal, inspired me with their support, advocacy, and strength.

My editors, Marysue Rucci and Kevin Smith, provided insights that added dimension and depth, and more than a few laughs. Jon Wood, my UK editor at Orion, must also be acknowledged for his unwavering support under the adverse conditions of last-minute publishing deadlines.

Laura Grafton, my director at Brilliance Audio, contributed enormously.

Clay Fourrier of Dovetail Studio designed and maintains my website at www.robertcrais.com. Carol Topping manages the site and creates our newsletters. Clay and Carol make possible the amazing relationship I have with readers around the world.

Create in me a clean heart, O God;
and renew a right spirit within me.

—PSALMS 51:10

Hush! my dear, lie still and slumber.
Holy angels guard thy bed!

—ISAAC WATTS

pike—n.; a long-bodied, predatory fish
known for its speed and aggression.

—OXFORD AMERICAN DICTIONARY

CITY OF ANGELS

City of Angels

THE CITY was hers for a single hour, just the one magic hour, only hers. The morning of the accident, between three and four A.M. when the streets were empty and the angels watched, she flew east on Wilshire Boulevard at eighty miles per hour, never once slowing for the red lights along that stretch called the Miracle Mile, red after red, blowing through lights without even slowing; glittering blue streaks of mascara on her cheeks.

Accounting for her time before the accident, she would later tell police she was at a club on Yucca in Hollywood, one of those clubs du jour with paparazzi clotted by the door. She had spent an hour avoiding an aging action star while seeing her friends (trust-fund Westsiders and A-list young Hollywood; actors, agents, and musicians she had no problem naming for the police), all taking cell-phone pictures of each other, blowing air-kisses and posing with rainbow drinks. The police sergeant who interviewed her would raise his eyebrows when she told him she had not been drinking, but the Breathalyzer confirmed her story. One Virgin Cosmo which she did not finish.

Three was her witching hour. She dropped a hundred on the valet for her Aston Martin, and red-lined away. Five blocks later—alone—she stopped in the middle of Hollywood Boulevard, shut the engine, and enjoyed a cashmere breeze. The scents of jasmine and rosemary came from the hills. The engine ticked, but she listened to find the silence. The stillness of the city at this hour was breathtaking.

She gazed up at the buildings and imagined angels perched on the edge of the roofs; tall slender angels with drooping wings; standing in perfect silence, watching her without expectation as if in an eternal dream: We give you the city. No one is watching. Set yourself free.

Her name was Larkin Conner Barkley. She was twenty-two years old. She lived in a hip loft downtown in an area catering to emerging painters and bicoastal musicians, not far from the Los Angeles River. Her family owned the building.

Larkin pushed the accelerator and felt the wind lift her hair. She bore south on Vine, then east on Wilshire, laughing as her eyes grew wet. Light poles flicked past; red or green, it didn't matter and she didn't care. Honking horns were lost in the rush. Her long hair, the color of pennies, whipped and lashed. She closed her eyes, held them closed, kept them shut even longer, then popped them wide and laughed that she still flew straight and true—

—85—
—90—
—101—

—a two-hundred-thousand-dollar Tuxedo Black convertible blur, smudged by alabaster skin and Medusa copper hair, running wild and free across the city. She flashed over the arch at MacArthur Park, then saw the freeway coming up fast, the Pasadena; a wall guarding downtown. She slowed, but only enough, just barely enough, as cars appeared and streets narrowed, flying over the freeway into the tangle of one-way downtown streets—Sixth, Seventh, Fourth, Ninth; Grand, Hill, and Main. She turned where she wanted, went the wrong way, ran hard for the river; slowing more, finally, inevitably, as everything rippled and blurred—

She told herself it was the dry night wind and lashing hair, the way her eyes filled when her lonely race finished, but it was always the same whether the air was dry or not, whether her hair was down or up, so she knew. For those few minutes running across the city, she could be and was herself, purely and truly herself, finding herself in those moments only to lose herself once more when she slowed, falling behind as her true self ran free somewhere ahead in the empty night—

She lurched across Alameda, her speed draining like a wound.

—65—

—60—

—55—

Larkin turned north on an industrial street parallel to the river. Her building was only blocks away when the air bag exploded. The Aston Martin spun sideways to a stop. White powder hung in the air like haze; sprayed over her shoulders and arms. The other car had been a *flashing shape, no more real than a shadow in the sea, a flick of gleaming movement broken by the prisms of her tears, then the impact.*

Larkin released her belt and stumbled from the car. A silver Mercedes sedan was on the sidewalk, its rear fender broken and bent. A man and a woman were in the front seat, the man behind the wheel. A second man was in the rear, closest to the impact. The driver was helping the woman, whose face was bleeding; the man in back was on his side, trying to pull himself up but unable to rise.

Larkin slapped the driver's-side window.

"Are you all right? Can I help?"

The driver stared at her blankly before truly seeing her, then opened his door. He was cut above his left eye.

Larkin said, "Ohmigod, I'm sorry, I'm so sorry. I'll call 911. I'll get an ambulance."

The driver was in his fifties, well dressed and tan, with a large gold ring on his right hand and a beautiful watch on his left. The woman stared dumbly at blood on her hands. The backseat passenger spilled out the rear door, fell to his knees, then used the side of the car to climb to his feet.

He said, "We're okay. It's nothing."

Larkin realized her cell phone was still in her car. She had to get help for these people.

"Please sit down. I'll call—"

"No. Let me see about you."

The man from the backseat took a step but sank to a knee. Larkin saw him clearly, lit by the headlights of her car. His eyes were large, and so dark they looked black in the fractured light.

Larkin hurried to her car. She found her cell phone on the floor, and was dialing 911 when the Mercedes backed off the sidewalk, its rear fender dragging the street.

Larkin said, "Hey, wait—!"

Larkin called after them again, but they didn't slow. She was memorizing their license plate when she heard the man from the backseat running away hard up the middle of the street.

A tinny voice cut through her confusion.

"Emergency operator, hello?"

"I had a wreck, an auto accident—"

"Was anyone injured?"

"They drove away. This man, I don't know—"

Larkin closed her eyes and recited the license number. She was scared she would forget it, so she pulled out her lip gloss—Cherry Pink Ice—and wrote the number on her arm.

"Ma'am, do you need help?"

Larkin felt wobbly.

"Ma'am—?"

The earth tilted and Larkin sat in the street.

"Ma'am, tell me where you are."

Larkin tried to answer.

"Ma'am, where are you?"

Larkin lay back on the cool, hard street. Dark buildings huddled over her like priests in black frocks, bent over in prayer. She searched their roofs for angels.

The first patrol car arrived in seven minutes; the paramedics three minutes later. Larkin thought it would end that night when the police finished their questions, but her nightmare had only begun.

In forty-eight hours, she would meet with agents

from the Department of Justice and the U.S. Attorney's. In six days, the first attempt would be made on her life. In eleven days, she would meet a man named Joe Pike.

Everything in her world was about to change. And it began that night.

STAY GROOVY

1

THE GIRL was moody getting out of the car, making a sour face to let him know she hated the shabby house and sun-scorched street smelling of chili and *episote*. To him, this anonymous house would serve. He searched the surrounding houses for threats as he waited for her, clearing the area the way another man might clear his throat. He felt obvious wearing the long-sleeved shirt. The Los Angeles sun was too hot for the sleeves, but he had little choice. He moved carefully to hide what was under the shirt.

She said, "People who live in houses like this have deformed children. I can't stay here."

"Lower your voice."

"I haven't eaten all day. I didn't eat yesterday and now this smell is making me feel strange."

"We'll eat when we're safe."

The house opened as the girl joined him, and the woman Bud told him to expect appeared: a squat woman with large white teeth and friendly eyes named Imelda Arcano. Mrs. Arcano managed several apartment houses and single-family rentals in Eagle Rock, and Bud's office had dealt with her before. He hoped she wouldn't notice the four neat holes that had been punched into their fender the night before.

He turned his back to the house to speak with the girl.

"The attitude makes you memorable. Lose it. You want to be invisible."

"Why don't I wait in the car?"

Leaving her was unthinkable.

"Let me handle her."

The girl laughed.

"That would be you all over it. I want to see that, you *handling* her. I want to see you *charm* her."

He took the girl's arm and headed toward the house. To her credit, the girl fell in beside him without making a scene, slouching to change her posture the way he had shown her. Even with her wearing the oversize sunglasses and Dodgers cap, he wanted her inside and out of sight as quickly as possible.

Mrs. Arcano smiled wider as they reached the front door, welcoming them.

"Mr. Johnson?"

"Yes."

"It's so hot today, isn't it? It's cool inside. The air conditioner works very well. I'm Imelda Arcano."

After the nightmare in Malibu, Bud's office had arranged the new house on the fly—dropped the cash and told Mrs. Arcano whatever she needed to hear, which probably wasn't much. This would be easy money, no questions part of the deal, low-profile tenants who would be gone in a week. Mrs. Arcano probably wouldn't even report the rental to the absentee owner; just pocket Bud's cash and call it a day. They were to meet Mrs. Arcano only so she could give them the keys.

Imelda Arcano beckoned them inside. The man hesitated long enough to glance back at the street. It was narrow and treeless, which was good. He could see well in both directions, though the small homes were set close together, which was bad. The narrow alleys would fill with shadows at dusk.

He wanted Mrs. Arcano out of the way as quickly as possible, but Mrs. Arcano latched onto the girl—one of those female-to-female things—and gave them the tour, leading them through the two tiny bedrooms and bath, the microscopic living room and kitchen, the grassless backyard. He glanced at the neighboring houses from each window, and out the back door at the rusty chain-link fence that separated this house from the one behind it. A beige and white pit bull was chained to an iron post in the neighboring yard. It lay with its chin on its paws, but it was not sleeping. He was pleased when he saw the pit bull.

The girl said, "Does the TV work?"

"Oh, yes, you have cable. You have lights, water, and gas—everything you need, but there is no telephone. You understand that? There really is no point in having the phone company create a line for such a short stay."

He had told the girl not to say anything, but now they were having a conversation. He cut it off.

"We have cell phones. You can hand over the keys and be on your way."

Mrs. Arcano stiffened, indicating she was offended.

"When will you be moving in?"

"Now. We'll take the keys."

Mrs. Arcano peeled two keys from her key ring, then left. For the first and only time that day he left the girl alone. He walked Mrs. Arcano to her car because he wanted to bring their gear into the house as quickly as possible. He wanted to call Bud. He wanted to find out what in hell happened the night before, but mostly he wanted to make sure the girl was safe.

He lingered at his car until Mrs. Arcano drove away, then looked up and down the street again—both ways, the houses, between the houses—and everything seemed fine. He brought his and the girl's duffels into the house, along with the bag they had grabbed at the Rite Aid.

The television was on, the girl hopping through the local stations for news. When he walked in, she laughed, then mimicked him, lowering and flattening her voice.

" 'Hand over the keys and be on your way.' Oh, that charmed her. That certainly made you forgettable."

He turned off the television and held out the Rite Aid bag. She didn't take it, pissed about him turning off the set, so he let it drop to the floor.

"Do your hair. We'll get something to eat when you're finished."

"I wanted to see if we're on the news."

"Can't hear with the TV. We want to hear. Maybe later."

"I can turn off the sound."

"Do the hair."

He peeled off his shirt and tossed it onto the floor by the front door. If he went out again or someone came to the door he would pull it on. He was wearing a Kimber

.45 semiautomatic pushed into the waist of his pants. He opened his duffel and took out a clip holster for the Kimber and a second gun, this one already holstered, a Colt Python .357 Magnum with the four-inch barrel. He clipped the Kimber onto the front of his pants in the cross-draw position and the Python on his right side. He hadn't chanced the holsters with Mrs. Arcano, but he hadn't wanted to take the chance of being without a gun, either.

He took a roll of duct tape from his bag and went to the kitchen.

Behind him, the girl said, "Asshole."

He made sure the back door was locked, then moved to the tiny back bedroom, locked the windows, and pulled the shades. This done, he tore off strips of duct tape and sealed the shades over the windows. He taped the bottoms and sides to the sills and jambs, all the way around each shade. If anyone managed to raise a window they would make noise tearing the shade from the wall and he would hear. When the shades were taped, he took out his Randall knife and made a three-inch vertical slit in each shade, just enough for him to finger open so he could cover the approaches to the house. He was cutting the shades when he heard her go into the bathroom. Finally cooperating. He knew she was scared, both of him and of what was happening, so he was surprised she had been trying as hard as she had. And pleased, thinking maybe they would stay alive a little while longer.

On his way to the front bedroom he passed the bath. She was in front of the mirror, cutting away her rich copper hair. She held the hair between her fingers, pulling it straight from her head to hack it away with the cheap Rite Aid scissors, leaving two inches of jagged spikes. Boxes of Clairol hair color, also fresh from the Rite Aid, lined the sink. She saw him in the mirror and glared.

"I hate this. I'm going to look so Melrose."

She had peeled down to her bra but left the door open. He guessed she wanted him to see. The five-hundred-dollar jeans rode low on her hips below a smiling dolphin jumping between the dimples on the small of her back. Her bra was light blue and sheer, and the perfect color against her olive skin. Looking at him, she played with her hair, which now stuck out in uneven spikes. She fluffed the spikes, shaped them, then considered them. The sink and floor were covered with the hair she had cut away.

She said, "What about white? I could go white. Would that make you happy?"

"Brown. Nondescript."

"I could go blue. Blue might be fun."

She turned to pose her body.

"Would you love it? Retropunk? So totally Melrose? Tell me you love it."

He continued on to the front bedroom without answering. She hadn't bought blue. She probably thought he hadn't been paying attention, but he paid attention to everything. She had bought blond, brown, and black. He locked and taped the front bedroom windows as he had done in the rest of the house, then returned to the bathroom. Now the water was running and she was leaning over the sink, wearing clear plastic gloves, massaging color into her hair. Black. He wondered how long it would take for the red to be hidden. He took out his cell phone, calling Bud Flynn as he watched.

He said, "We're in place. What happened last night?"

"I'm still trying to find out. I got no idea. Is the new house okay?"

"They had our location, Bud. I want to know how."

"I'm working on it. Is she okay?"

"I want to know how."

"Jesus, I'm working on it. Do you need anything?"

"I need to know how."

He closed the phone as she stood, water running down the trough of her spine to the dolphin until she wrapped her hair in a towel. Only then did she find him in the mirror again and smile.

"You're looking at my ass."

The pit bull barked.

He did not hesitate. He drew the Python and ran to the back bedroom.

She said, "Joe! Damnit."

In the back bedroom, he fingered open a slit in the shade as the girl hurried up behind him. The dog was on its feet, squinting at something he could not see.

She said, "What is it?"

"Shh."

The pit was trying to see something to their left, the flat top of its head furrowed and its nubby ears perked, no longer barking as it tested the air.

Pike watched through the slit, listening hard as the pit was listening.

The girl whispered, "What?"

The pit exploded with frenzied barking as it jumped against its chain.

Pike spoke fast over his shoulder even as the first man came around the end of the garage. It was happening again.

"Front of the house, but don't open the door. Go. Fast."

The towel fell from her head as he pushed her forward. He hooked their duffels over his shoulder, guiding her to the door. He checked the slit in the front window shade. A single man was walking up the drive as another moved across the yard toward the house. Pike didn't know how many more were outside or where they were, but he and the girl would not survive if he fought from within the house.

He cupped her face and forced her to see him. She had to see past her fear. Her eyes met his and he knew they were together.

"Watch me. Don't look at them or anything else. Watch me until I motion for you, then run for the car as fast as you can."

Once more, he did not hesitate.

He jerked open the door, set up fast on the man in the drive, and fired the Colt twice. He reset on the man coming across the yard. Pike doubled on each man's center of mass so quickly the four shots sounded like two—*baboombaboom*—then he ran to the center of the front yard. He saw no more men, so he waved out the girl.

"*Go.*"

She ran as hard as she could, he had to hand it to her. Pike fell in behind her, running backwards the way cornerbacks fade to cover a receiver, staying close to shield her body with his because the pit bull was still barking. More men were coming.

When Pike reached the bodies, he dropped to a knee and checked their pockets by touch. He was hoping for a wallet or some form of ID, but their pockets were empty.

A third man came around the corner of the house into the drive, saw Pike, then dove backwards. Pike fired his last two shots. Wood and stucco exploded from the edge of the house, but the man had made cover and the Python was dry. The third man popped back almost at once and fired three shots—*bapbapbap*—missing Pike, but hitting his Jeep like a ball-peen hammer. Pike didn't have time to holster the Python. He dropped it to jerk free the Kimber, pounded out two more shots and dropped the man at the edge of the house. Pike ran for the car. The girl had the driver's door open, but was just standing there.

Pike shouted, "Get in. *In.*"

Another man appeared at the edge of the house, snapping out shots as fast as he could. Pike fired, but the man had already taken cover.

"*In.*"

Pike pushed the girl across the console, jammed the key into the ignition and gunned his Jeep to the corner. He four-wheeled the turn, buried the accelerator, then glanced at the girl.

"You good? Are you hurt?"

She stared straight ahead, her eyes red and wet. She was crying again.

She said, "Those men are dead."

Pike placed his hand on her thigh.

"Larkin, look at me."

She clenched her eyes and kneaded her hands.

"Three men just died. Three more men."

He made his deep voice soft.

"I won't let anything happen to you. Do you hear me?"

She still didn't look.

"Do you believe me?"

She nodded.

Pike swerved through an intersection. He slowed only enough to avoid a collision, then accelerated onto the freeway.

They had been at the house in Eagle Rock for twenty-eight minutes. He had killed three more men, and now they were running. Again.

He was sorry he lost the Colt. It was a good gun. It had saved them last night in Malibu, but now it might get them killed.

2

BLASTING NORTH on the 101. Pike gave no warning before horsing across four lanes of traffic to the exit ramp. They fell off the freeway like a brick dropped in water.

Larkin screamed.

They hit the bottom of the ramp sideways, Pike turning hard across oncoming lanes. Horns and tires shrieked as Pike turned again up the opposite on-ramp, back the way they had come. The girl was hugging her legs, hunched into a knot like they tell you to do when an airplane is going to crash.

Pike pushed the Jeep to the next exit, then pegged the brakes at the last moment and fell off again, checking the rearview even as they fell.

The girl moaned.

"Stop it. Stop—Jesus, you're going to get us killed."

They came out by USC, busy with afternoon traffic. Pike cut into the Chevron station at the bottom of the ramp, wheeling around the pump islands and office, then jammed to a stop. They sat, engine running, Pike pushing bullets into the Kimber's magazine as he studied the cars coming down the ramp. This time of day the ramp filled fast. Pike studied the passengers in each vehicle, but none acted like killers on the hunt.

"Did you recognize the men at the house?"

"This is insane. We're killing people."

"The one in the front yard, you passed him. Have you seen him before?"

"I couldn't—God, it happened—no."

Pike let it go. She hadn't seen the two he killed earlier, either; just dark smudges falling. Pike himself had barely seen them: coarse men in their twenties or thirties, black T-shirts and pistols, cut by bars of shadow and light.

Pike's cell phone vibrated, but he ignored it. He backed from the end of the building, then turned away from the freeway, picking up speed as he grew confident they weren't being followed.

Ten blocks later, Pike eased into a strip mall, one of those places where the stores went out of business every two months. He turned past the end of the mall into a narrow alley and saw nothing but dumpsters and potholes.

Pike shut the engine, got out, circled the Jeep, and opened her door.

"Get out."

She didn't move fast enough, so he pulled her out, keeping her upright because she would have fallen.

"Hey! What—*stop it!*"

"Did you call someone?"

"No."

He pinned her against the Jeep with his hip as he

searched her pockets for a cell phone. She tried to push him away, but he ignored her.

"Stop that—how could I call? I was with you, you freak. Stop—"

He snatched her floppy Prada bag from the floorboard and dumped the contents onto the seat.

"You *freak*! I don't have a phone. You took it!"

He searched the pockets in her purse, then pulled her duffel from the backseat.

"I didn't call anybody. I don't have a phone!"

Pike finished going through her things, then stared at her, thinking.

"What? Why are you staring at me?"

"They found us."

"I don't know how they found us!"

"Let me see your shoes."

"What?"

He pushed her backwards into the Jeep and pulled off her shoes. This time she didn't resist. She sank back onto the seat, watching him as he lifted her feet.

Pike wondered if they had placed a transponder on her. Maybe she had been bugged from the beginning, which was how the U.S. Marshals and Bud Flynn had almost lost her. Pike checked the heels of her shoes, then looked at her belt and the metal buttons that held her jeans. She drew a deep breath as he pulled off her belt.

She said, "Like that?"

Pike ignored her smile. It was nasty and perfect.

"Want me to take off my pants?"

Pike turned to her duffel, and she laughed.

"You are such a freak. These are my things. They haven't been out of my sight since I went with the marshals, you freak! Why don't you *say something*? Why don't you *talk to me*?"

Pike didn't believe he would find anything, but he had to check, so he did, ignoring her. Pike had learned this with the Marines—the one time a man didn't clean his rifle, that's when it jammed; the one time you didn't tape down a buckle or secure your gear, the noise it made got you killed.

"Are we just going to stay here? Is it even *safe* here? I want to go home."

"They almost killed you at home."

"Now I'm with you and they've almost killed me twice. I want to *go home*."

Pike took out his cell phone and checked the messages. The three incoming calls were from Bud Flynn. Pike hit the send button to return the calls and wondered if they were being tracked by his phone, the signal triangulated between cell stations. To track him they would have to know his number, but Bud had it. Maybe if Bud knew it, they knew it, too.

Bud answered immediately.

"You scared the hell out of me. I thought you were done when you didn't answer."

"They found us again."

"Get outta here. Where are you?"

"Listen. She wants to come home."

Pike was watching the girl when he said it, and she was staring back.

Bud didn't answer right away, but when he did his voice was soft.

"Now let's take it easy. Let's everybody calm down. Is she safe? Right now, is everything good?"

"Yes."

"I want to make sure I understand—are you talking about the Malibu house or the house I just sent you to, the one in Eagle Rock?"

Bud had sent them to a safe house in Malibu the night before, then put them onto the Eagle Rock house when the shooters hit Malibu.

"Eagle Rock. You gave me two bad houses, Bud."

"Not possible. They could not have known about this house."

"Three more men died. Do the feds have me covered on this or not? I have to know, Bud."

Bud already knew about the two in Malibu. The feds had screamed, but promised to cover for Pike and the girl with the locals.

Now Bud didn't sound confident.

"I'll talk to them."

"Talk fast. I lost one of my guns, the .357. When the police run the numbers, they'll have my name."

Bud made a soft hiss that sounded more tired than angry. Pike didn't press him. Pike let him think.

"All right, listen—she wants to come home?"

"Yes."

"Put her on."

Pike held out the phone. The girl put it to her ear, but now she seemed uncertain. She listened for several minutes, and then she spoke once.

She said, "I'm really scared. Can't I come home?"

Pike knew the answer even before she gave back the phone. Here they were in an alley in southeast Los Angeles, temperature in the mid-nineties, and this girl looked cold. She flew over places like this in her family's private Gulfstream, but here she was, all for being in the wrong place at the wrong time and, for likely the first and only time in her life, trying to do the right thing. And now the right thing meant being with him.

Pike took back the phone even as a car turned into the far end of the alley. He immediately put himself between the girl and the oncoming car, then saw the driver was a young Latina, so short she drove with her head tilted back to see over the wheel.

Pike lifted the phone.

"Me."

"Okay, listen—she's good to stay with you. I think that's best and so does her father. I'll line up another house—"

"Keep your house. Did you ID the men in Malibu?"

"We have to get you safe. I'll line up another house—"

"Your houses are bad."

"Joe—"

"They had us twice at your houses. I'll get us a house."

"You can't cut me out like this. How will I know—"

"You gave her to me, Bud. She's mine."

Pike shut off his phone. The girl was watching him there in the angry heat of the alley.

She said, "Now I'm yours? Did you really say that?"

"If you want to go home I'll take you home. That's up to you, not them. That's all I meant. I'll take you back if you want."

Pike knew she was thinking about it, but then she shrugged.

"I'll stay."

"Get in."

Pike helped her into his Jeep, then studied both ends of the alley. He wanted to start moving, but his Jeep was now a liability. The police would eventually know he was involved because of his gun, but if a witness in Eagle Rock had his license plate, the police might already be looking for a red Jeep Cherokee. Pike wanted to avoid the police, but he couldn't just sit. When you weren't moving you were nothing but someone's target.

The alley was clear. Right now, at this moment and in this place, Pike and the girl were invisible. If Pike could keep it that way, the girl would survive.

3

PIKE TURNED into the Bristol Farms on Sunset at Fairfax, and parked as far from the intersection as possible, hiding their Jeep.

She said, "What are we doing?"

"I have to call someone. Get out."

"Why don't you call from the car?"

"I don't trust my cell. Get out."

"Can't I wait here?"

"No."

Pike was concerned she might be recognized even with the new hair and sunglasses, but she might change her mind about staying with him, take off running, and get herself killed. They had known each other for exactly sixteen hours. They were strangers.

Larkin hurried around the Jeep to catch up.

"Who are you calling?"

"We need new wheels and a place to stay. We need to learn something about the people who are trying to kill you. If the police are after us, it changes our moves."

"What do you mean, moves? What are we going to do?"

Pike was tired of talking, so he didn't. He led her past the flower stand at the front of the market to a bank of pay phones, and pushed quarters into a phone.

Larkin hooked her arm around his, as though the Santa Anas would blow her away if she wasn't anchored. She glanced into the market.

"I want to get something to eat."

"No time."

"I could get something while you're talking."

"Later."

Pike owned a small gun shop in Culver City, not far from his condominium. He had five employees: four men and one woman—two who were full-time and three who were former police officers.

A man named Ronnie answered on the second ring.

"Gun shop."

Pike said, "I'm calling in two."

Pike hung up.

Larkin squeezed his arm.

"Who was that?"

"He works for me."

"Is he a bodyguard, too?"

Pike ignored her, watching the second hand circle his Rolex. Ronnie would be walking next door to the laundromat for Pike's call.

While Pike waited, two men in their late twenties passed by on their way out of the market. One of them looked Larkin up and down, and the other stared at her face. Larkin looked back at them. Pike tried to read if the second man recognized her. Out in the parking lot they goosed each other before climbing into a black Audi, so Pike decided they hadn't.

Pike said, "Don't do that again."

"What?"

"Make eye contact like you did with those guys. Don't do it."

Pike thought she was going to say something, but instead she pressed her lips together and stared into the market.

"I could have gotten something to eat by now."

At the two-minute mark, Pike made his call and Ronnie picked up. Pike sketched the situation, then told Ronnie to close the shop and send everyone home. The men who wanted Larkin dead had almost certainly known Pike's identity when they hit the safe houses, but hadn't needed it to find the girl. Now that Pike had disappeared with her, they would try to find Larkin by finding him, and this knowledge would give them the people in Pike's life like overlapping ripples, one ripple leading to another, each ripple breaking the next.

Ronnie said, "I hear you. What do you need?"

"A car and a cell phone. Get one of those prepaid phones they sell at Best Buy or Target."

"Okey-doke. You can use my old Lexus, you want. That okay?"

Ronnie's Lexus was twelve years old. Ronnie's wife had handed it down to their daughter, but his daughter was away at law school, so mostly the car sat parked. It was dark green.

Pike told Ronnie to leave the Lexus at an Albertsons

they both knew in thirty-five minutes, just leave it and walk away. Thirty-five minutes would give Pike time to hit his condo before ditching the Jeep.

Pike said, "Ronnie. Turn on the security and surveillance cameras when you guys lock up. Then don't go back. Nobody go back until you hear from me."

"Might be better if we stayed open. If your friends roll around we could sort'm out."

"LAPD might come around, too."

"I hear you."

Pike hung up and immediately walked the girl back to his Jeep. He felt the passing minutes like a race he was losing. Once you engaged the enemy, speed was everything. Speed was life.

She pulled at his arm.

"You're walking too fast."

"We have a lot to do."

"Where are we going?"

"My place."

"Is that where we're going to stay?"

"No. The shooters are going there, too."

Pike lived in a sprawling condominium complex in Culver City, less than a mile from the sea. A stucco wall surrounded the grounds, with gates that required a magnetic key. The condos were arranged in four-unit pods laid out around two tennis courts and a communal pool which Pike never used. Pike's unit was set in a far back corner, shielded from the others.

Pike drove directly to his complex, but didn't enter the property. He circled the wall, looking for anyone who might be watching the gates or watching out for his Jeep. Pike hated bringing the girl to his condo, but he believed the window of time through which he could enter was shrinking.

Pike circled the complex once, then turned into the rear drive and waved the gate open with his key.

Larkin looked around at the buildings.

"This isn't so bad. I thought you probably lived in some grungy rat hole. How much money do bodyguards make?"

Pike said, "Get on the floor under the dash."

"Can I get something to eat at your place? You gotta have something to eat, don't you?"

"You won't be getting out of the car."

Pike knew she rolled her eyes even without seeing it, but she slithered down under the dash.

"When men ask me to go down like this, it's usually for something else."

Pike glanced at her.

"Funny."

"Then why don't you smile? Don't bodyguards ever smile?"

"I'm not a bodyguard."

Pike drove to the small lot where he normally parked. Only three cars were in the lot, and he recognized all three. He stopped, but did not take the Jeep out of gear or shut the engine. The grounds were landscaped with palm trees, hibiscus, and sleek birds-of-paradise. Concrete walks wound between the palms. Pike studied the play of greens and browns and other colors against the stucco walls and Spanish roofs.

Larkin said, "What's happening?"

Pike didn't answer. He saw nothing out of the ordinary, so he let the Jeep drift forward and finally shut the engine. He could take the girl with him, but would move faster without her.

Pike held out the Kimber.

"I'll be thirty seconds. Here."

She shook her head.

"I hate guns."

"Then stay here. Don't move."

Pike slipped out of the Jeep before she could answer and trotted up the walk to his door. He checked the two dead-bolt locks and found no sign of tampering. He let himself in and went to a touch pad he had built into the wall. Pike had installed a video surveillance system that covered the entrance to his home and the ground floor.

Pike set his alarm, let himself out, and trotted back to the Jeep. Larkin was still under the dash.

She said, "What did you do?"

"I don't know anything about these people. If they come here, we'll get their picture and I'll have something to work with."

"Can I get up?"

"Yes."

When they passed back through the gate, no one appeared in the rearview mirror. Pike turned toward the Albertsons.

Larkin climbed out from under the dash and fastened her seat belt. She looked calmer now. Better. Pike felt better, too.

She said, "What are we going to do now?"

"Get the new car, then a safe place to stay. We still have a lot to do."

"If you're not a bodyguard, what are you? Bud told my father you used to be a policeman."

"That was a long time ago."

"What do you do now? When someone asks what you do, say you're at a party or a bar, and you're talking to a woman you like, what do you tell her?"

"Businessman."

Larkin laughed, but it was high-pitched and strained.

"I grew up with businessmen. You're no business-man."

Pike wanted her to stop talking, but he knew the fear she had been carrying was heating the way coals will heat when you blow on them, and the chatter would only get worse. This was a quiet time, and the quiet times in combat were the worst. You might be fine when hell was raining down, but in those moments when you had time to think, that's when you shook like a wet dog in the wind. Pike sensed she was feeling like the dog.

Pike touched the side of her head. When he touched her, her lips trembled, so he knew he was right.

"Whatever I am, I won't hurt you, and I won't let anyone else hurt you."

"You promise?"

"Way it is."

He smoothed the spiky hair still coarse with fresh color, but that's when she spoke again.

"You think I'm oblivious, but I know what you're doing. We could leave Los Angeles right now and hide someplace like Bisbee, Arizona, but that isn't what you want. You don't want to hide; you want to get them

before they get us. That's why you want their pictures.
You're going to hunt them down."

Pike concentrated on driving.

"Told you. I'm not a bodyguard."

She didn't say anything more for a while, and Pike
was thankful for the silence.

4

THE GREEN Lexus was waiting in the third row in the parking lot, just another car in a sea of anonymous vehicles. Pike parked the Jeep in the nearest available space, but didn't shut the engine. He fished under the dash, found the nylon web with practiced efficiency, and dropped a holstered .40-caliber Smith & Wesson into Larkin's lap.

"Put this in your purse."

"I'm not touching it. I told you, I hate guns."

He reached under the passenger-side dash and came out with a .380 Beretta pocket gun. He reached again and found a plastic box containing loaded magazines for the Smith and the Beretta. He dropped them into her lap, too.

She said, "Ohmigod, what kind of freak are you?"

He went back under the dash a last time for a sealed plastic bag containing two thousand dollars and credit cards and a driver's license showing his face in the name of Fred C. Howe. He put the bag into her lap with the guns.

"This one has money. Maybe it'll fit your purse better."

Pike finally shut the engine and got out without waiting for her. He carried their bags to the Lexus, then went to the left front tire where Ronnie had hidden the key. Pike loaded their bags into the Lexus, then locked the Jeep and left the key in the same place under the tire. Ronnie would return for the Jeep later and leave it behind the gun shop.

Larkin watched Pike with her arms crossed.

"What are we going to do now?"

"First step, get in the car."

"How about, second step, get something to eat?"

"Soon."

Pike wedged the Kimber under his right thigh, butt out, ready to go. He started the engine for the air, then picked up the new phone. Ronnie had left the phone, two extra prepaid phone cards, and a note on the driver's-side floorboard. Along with the phone was a charger Pike could plug into the car, a second charger for use in a house, and an earbud for hands-free driving. Ronnie had already activated the phone and registered two thousand minutes of calling time, so the phone was good to go. He had written Pike's new cell phone number on the note.

Larkin said, "I am *so* starving. Could we *please* get something to eat?"

Pike studied the phone to figure it out, then fired up the Lexus and backed out, already thumbing in the number of a real estate agent he knew.

Larkin said, "Thank God. *Finally.* I'm so hungry my stomach is eating itself."

"Not yet."

Larkin colored with irritation.

"Oh, *fuck* this! This is *absurd*! I'm *hungry*. I want *food*."

Pike had to get them a place to hide. He had considered a motel, but a motel would increase their contact with people and contact was bad. They needed privacy in a neighborhood where no one was likely to recognize the girl. They needed immediate occupancy with no questions asked, which meant Pike could not do business with strangers. He had once helped the real estate agent deal with an abusive ex-husband, and had since bought and sold several properties through her.

When Pike had her on the line he described what he needed. Larkin was slumped against the door on her side of the car, arms crossed and sullen.

She said, "Help! Help! He's raping me! Help!"

Loud.

The real estate agent said, "Who's that?"

"I'm babysitting."

Larkin glared harder—

"You've never sat a baby like me."

—then leaned closer to the phone.

"I gave him a blow job!"

Pike's friend said, "Sounds nice."

Larkin shouted, "I blew him and now he won't feed me! *I'm starving to death!*"

Pike cupped the phone so he could continue.

"Can you find a house for me?"

"I think I have something that will work. I'll have to get back to you."

Pike gave his friend his new number, ended the call,

then glanced at the girl. She was slumped back against her door again, glaring at him through her dark glasses as if she was waiting to see what he would do. Testing him, maybe. Everything Pike knew about this girl had been told to him by Bud Flynn and the girl's father less than seventeen hours ago, and now he knew that Bud's information could not be trusted.

Pike glanced over at her again.

"What's your name?"

She took off her glasses and frowned at him as if he were retarded.

"What are you talking about?"

"What's your name?"

"I don't get it. Is this some kind of game we're playing, truth or dare, what?"

"Your name."

"I don't get why you're asking my name."

"What is it?"

Her face flattened in frustration and she pulled at her shirt.

"I'm hungry. When are you getting me something to eat?"

"Name."

"LARKIN CONNER BARKLEY! Jesus Christ, what's *YOUR* FUCKING NAME?"

"Your father?"

"CONNER BARKLEY! MY MOTHER IS DEAD! HER NAME WAS JANICE! I'M AN ONLY FUCK-ING CHILD! FUCK *YOU*!"

Pike checked the rearview, then pointed at her purse on the floor under her feet.

"License and credit cards."

She snatched up her purse, dug out her wallet, and threw it at him.

"Use the cards to buy me some lunch."

Pike fingered open the wallet and thumbed out her driver's license. It showed a color picture of her along with the name Larkin Conner Barkley issued by the California Department of Motor Vehicles. Her address showed as a high-rise in Century City, but both Bud and her father had described a home in Beverly Hills.

Pike said, "You live in Century City?"

"That's our corporate office. Everything goes to that address."

"Where do you live?"

"You want to go to my loft? I got a great loft. We own the building."

"Where?"

"Downtown. It's in this great industrial area."

"That where they came for you the first time they tried to kill you?"

"I was with my father. In Beverly Hills."

"When was that?"

"I don't know. Jesus!"

"Think."

"A week. Not even. Six days, maybe."

"Who is Alex Meesh?"

She sank back, her angry confidence gone.

"The man who's trying to kill me."

Pike had already heard it from her father and Bud, but now he wanted it from her.

"Why does he want you dead?"

She stared out the windshield at oncoming nothingness and shook her head.

"I don't know. Because I saw him that night with the Kings. When I had my accident. I'm cooperating with the Justice Department."

Pike fingered through her credit cards, reading their faces between glances at the road. The cards had all been issued to Larkin Barkley, sometimes with the middle name and sometimes not. Pike pulled out an American Express card and a Visa. The AmEx was one of those special black cards, which indicated she charged at least two hundred fifty thousand dollars every year. He tossed her wallet back onto the floorboard at her feet, but kept the two credit cards and her driver's license. He wedged them under his leg along with the gun.

Pike knew what Bud and her father had told him, but now he wanted to identify the players and find out for himself what was true. He would need help to find out those things, so he dialed another number.

Larkin glanced over, but this time her heart wasn't in it. She made a weak smile.

"I hope you're calling for reservations."

"I'm calling someone who can help us."

The phone rang twice, and then a man answered.

"Elvis Cole Detective Agency. We can do anything."

"I'm coming up."

Pike closed the phone and turned toward the mountains.

5

THIRTY-TWO HOURS earlier, on the morning it began, Ocean Avenue was lit with smoky gold light from the street lamps and apartment buildings that lined Santa Monica at the edge of the sea. Joe Pike ran along the center of the street with a coyote pacing him in the shadows bunched on the bluff. It was three fifty-two A.M. *That early, the Pacific was hidden by night and the earth ended at the crumbling edge of the bluff, swallowed by a black emptiness. Pike enjoyed the peace during that quiet time, running on the crown of the empty street in a way he could not when light stole the darkness.*

Pike glanced again into the shadows and saw the coyote pacing him without effort, sometimes visible, other times not as it loped between the palms. It was an old male, its mask white and scarred, come down from the canyons to forage. Every time Pike glanced over, the coyote was watching him, full-on staring even as it ran. The coyote probably found him curious. Coyotes had rules for living among men, which was how they flourished in Los Angeles. One of their rules was that they only came out at night. Coyotes probably believed the night belonged to wild things. This coyote probably thought Pike was breaking the rules.

Pike hitched up his backpack and pushed himself faster. A second coyote joined with the first.

Joe Pike ran this route often: west on Washington from his condo, north on Ocean to San Vicente, then east to Fourth Street, where steep concrete steps dropped down the bluff like jagged teeth. One hundred eighty-nine steps, stacked up the bluff, interrupted four times by small pads built to catch the people who fell. Without the pads, anyone who stumbled could be killed. One hundred eighty-nine steps is as tall as a nine-story building. Running the steps was like running up nine flights of stairs.

This morning, Pike was wearing a surplus rucksack loaded with four ten-pound bags of Gold Medal flour. Pike would run the steps twenty times, down and up, before turning for home. Around his waist, he wore a fanny pack with his cell phone, his ID, his keys, and a .25-caliber Beretta pocket gun.

Pike was not expecting the call that morning. He had known it would come, eventually, but that morning he was lost in the safe ready feel of sweat and effort when his cell phone vibrated. He had a nice rhythm going, but the people who had his unlisted number were few, so Pike heeled to a stop and answered.

The man said, "Bet you don't know who this is."

Pike let his breathing slow as he shifted the ruck. The weight only grew heavy when he stopped running.

The man, confused because Pike had not answered, said, "Is this Joe Pike?"

Pike had not heard the man's voice since an eight-year-old boy named Ben Chenier was kidnapped. Pike and his friend Elvis Cole had searched for the boy, but they had needed help from the man on the phone to find the kidnapper. The man's price was simple—one day, the man would call with a job for Pike and Pike would have to say yes. The job might be anything and might be the kind of job Pike no longer wanted or did, but the choice would not be his. Pike would have to say yes. That was the price for helping to save Ben Chenier, so Pike had paid it. That word. Yes. One day the man would call and now he had.

Pike said, "Jon Stone."

Stone laughed.

"Well. You remember. Now we find out if you're good at your word. I told you I would call and this is the call. You owe me a job."

Pike glanced at his watch, noting the time. A third coyote had joined the first two, staring at him from the shadows.

Pike said, "It's four A.M."

"I've been trying to get your number since last night, my man. If I woke you, I'm sorry, but if you stiff me I have to find somebody else. Hence, the uncomfortable hour."

"What is it?"

"A package needs looking after, and it's already hot."

Package meant person. The heat meant attempts had already been made on the target's life.

"Why is the package at risk?"

"I don't know and all I care about is you keeping your word. You agreed to let me book you a job, and this is it. I gotta tell these people whether you're in or not."

Grey shapes floated between the palms like ghosts. Two more coyotes joined with the first three. Their heads hung low, but their eyes caught the gold light. Pike wondered how it would be to run with them through the night streets, moving as well as they, as quietly and quickly, hearing and seeing what they heard and saw, both here in the city and up in the canyons.

Stone was talking, his voice growing strained.

"This guy who called, he said he knew you. Bud Flynn?"

Pike came back from the canyons.

"Yes."

"Yeah, Flynn's the guy. He has some kinda bodyguard thing with people who have so much dough they shit green. I want some of that green, Pike. You owe me. Are you going to do this thing or not?"

Pike said, "Yes."

"That's my boy. I'll call back later with the meet."

Pike closed his phone. Brake lights flared a quarter mile away where San Vicente joined with Ocean. Pike watched the red lights until they disappeared, then hitched his ruck again. Eight or ten coyotes now waited at the edge of light. Three more appeared in an alley between two restaurants. Another now stood in the street a block away and Pike had not even seen it approach. Pike breathed deep and smelled the sage and earth in their fur.

The older coyote did not turn for the canyon. It circled wide of Pike, then crossed Ocean Avenue and continued up Santa Monica Boulevard. The other coyotes followed. The city was theirs until sunrise. They would hold it as long as they could.

Pike unslung the ruck and let it drop. He took a deep breath, then lifted his hands high overhead, stretching. His muscles were warm and his weak shoulder—the shoulder that had almost been destroyed when he was shot—felt strong. The scars that laced his deltoid stretched, but held. Pike bent forward from the hips until he easily placed his palms on the street. He let his hands take his weight, then lifted his feet until he was standing on his hands in the middle of Ocean Avenue.

Pike felt peaceful, and held his balance with a perfect center.

He lowered himself straight down until his forehead touched the street, then pushed upright again, doing a vertical pushup, not for the effort but to feel his body working. His shoulder tingled where the nerves were damaged and would always be damaged, but Pike lifted himself without strain.

He lowered his feet and stood, and saw that the coyotes were back, watching, street dogs at home in the city.

Pike shouldered the ruck and continued with his run. In fourteen hours, he would be driving north to pick up the girl and see Bud Flynn for the first time in twenty years, a man he had deeply and truly loved.

Fifteen hours later, Pike arrived at the remains of a church in the high desert.

The church had no doors or windows and now was broken stucco walls with empty eyes and a gaping mouth a mile off the Pearblossom Highway thirty miles north of Los Angeles. Years of brittle winds, sun, and the absence of human care had left it the color of dust. Graffiti marked its walls, but even that was old; as much a faded part of the place as the brush and sage sprouting from the walls. It was a lonely place, all the more desolate with the lowering sun at the end of the day.

A black limousine with dark windows and an equally black Hummer were parked nearby, as out of place as gleaming black jewels. They had been unseeable when Pike turned off the highway, here at the edge of the desert.

Pike braked his Jeep facing the two vehicles. Blacker shapes moved behind the tinted Hummer glass, but Pike saw nothing within the limo. Pike was settling in to wait when Bud Flynn and another man appeared in the church door. This man was overweight, with a face like a block and lank hair he pushed from his eyes. He appeared nervous, and went back inside the church as Bud, smiling, came out, stepping into the dwindling sun across twenty years and two lifetimes.

Pike had not seen Bud since the day in the Shortstop Lounge when Pike resigned from the LAPD and wanted Bud to hear it man-to-man, them being as close as they were. Bud had asked if Pike had another job lined up, and Pike told him, but Bud had not approved. He reacted like a disappointed father angered by his son's choice, and that had been that. Pike had signed on with a professional military corporation out of London. He was going to work as a professional civilian soldier, he said— a security specialist. Bullshit, Bud said—no better than a goddamned criminal: a mercenary.

Now, seeing Bud, Pike felt the warm touch of earlier, better memories, and climbed out of the Jeep. Bud was older now, but still looked good to go.

Bud put out his hand.

"Good to see you, Officer Pike. Been too long."

Pike pulled Bud close and hugged him, and Bud clapped Pike on the back.

"I'm in corporate investigations now, Joe. Fourteen years; fifteen this March. Business is good."

"You use mercenaries as investigators?"

Bud looked uncomfortable and maybe embarrassed, both of them thinking about that day in the Shortstop, but he plowed on.

"Sometimes the investigation part leads to security work. A friend gave me Stone's name. Stone has former Mossad and Secret Service agents on tap—people experienced with high-risk clients. I was looking for someone like that when he floated your name."

Pike glanced at the Hummer. The low carriage showed the weight penalty that came with armor and bullet-resistant glass.

"The girl in there?"

Jon Stone had explained the bare bones of it when he called back with the directions: A young woman from a well-to-do family had survived three murder attempts and Bud Flynn had been hired to protect her. Period. Stone knew nothing else because—correctly, Pike thought—Bud Flynn felt Stone did not need to know more. It was enough for Stone to know the girl was rich. A person with Pike's resumé could command top dollar, and Stone would bleed these people for every cent he could get.

Flynn ignored Pike's question about the girl and turned toward the church.

"Let's go inside. You can meet her father and I'll

explain what's going on. If you decide you want to do this, we'll meet the girl."

Pike followed him, thinking, it's already been decided.

The church smelled of sage and urine. Beer cans and magazines dotted the concrete floor, filthy from the sand blown through the broken walls, and faded by time. Pike guessed the urine smell was left by animals. The man with the lank hair was standing beside a lean man with the intelligent eyes of a businessman and a mouth cut into a permanent frown. A cordovan briefcase sat on the ground by the door. Pike wondered which owned the briefcase and which was the girl's father. He positioned himself away from the windows.

Bud nodded toward the man with the lank hair.

"Joe, this is Conner Barkley. Mr. Barkley, Joe Pike."

Barkley squeezed out an uncomfortable smile.

"Hello."

Barkley was wearing a silk short-sleeved shirt that showed his belt bulge. The frowning man was tieless in an expensive charcoal sport coat. Pike was wearing a sleeveless grey sweatshirt, jeans, and New Balance running shoes.

The frowning man took folded papers and a pen from his coat.

"Mr. Pike, I'm Gordon Kline, Mr. Barkley's attorney and an officer in his corporation. This is a confidentiality agreement, specifying that you may not repeat, relate, or in any way disclose anything about the Barkleys said today or while you are in the Barkleys' employ. You'll have to sign this."

Kline held out the papers and pen, but Pike made no move to take them.

Bud said, "Gordon, why don't we push on without that, considering."

"He has to sign. Everyone has to sign."

Pike watched Conner Barkley staring at the blocky red arrows inked across his deltoids. Pike was used to people staring. The arrows had been scribed into his arms before his first combat tour. They pointed forward. People stared at the tats and Pike's faded sweatshirt with the sleeves cut off, and saw what they wanted to see. Pike was good with that.

When Barkley looked up from the tats, his eyes were worried.

"This is the man you want to hire?"

"He's the best in the business, Mr. Barkley. He'll keep Larkin alive."

Kline pushed out the papers.

"If you'll just sign here, please."

Pike said, "No."

Barkley's eyebrows bunched like nervous caterpillars.

"I think we're all right here, Gordon. I think we can press on. Don't you, Bud?"

Kline's frown deepened, but he put away the papers, and Bud continued.

"Okay, here's what we have: Mr. Barkley's daughter is a federal witness. She's set to offer testimony before the federal grand jury in two weeks. There have been three attempts on her life in the past ten days. That's three deals for the black ace in a week and a half, and all three were close. I have no choice but to think outside the box."

"Me."

Pike shifted just enough to see the limo. The desert had filled with red light from the settling sun. He felt the temperature dropping. At night up here, the air would be sharp and clean.

"Why isn't she in a protection program?"

Barkley spoke up, pushing the hair from his eyes.

"She was. They almost got her killed."

Gordon Kline crossed his arms as if the entire United States government was a waste of taxpayer money.

"Incompetents."

Bud said, "Larkin was in a traffic accident eleven days ago—three A.M., she T-boned a Mercedes—"

Barkley interrupted again.

"You don't expect to run into these kinds of people driving your car—"

Gordon Kline said, "Conner—"

"Look where we are—up here in these ruins running for our lives. A traffic accident—"

Barkley pushed his hair from his face again, and this time Pike saw his hand tremble. Bud went on about the Mercedes.

"There were three people onboard. A married couple, George and Elaine King, it was their car; with a male passenger in the rear. You know the name, George King?"

Pike shook his head, so Bud explained.

"A real estate developer, squeaky clean, no wants, warrants, or priors. George was bleeding, so Larkin got out to help. The second man was hurt, too, but he left the scene on foot. Then George pulled himself together enough to drive away, but Larkin got their plate. Next *day, the Kings told the police a different story—they say they were alone. A couple of days later, agents from the Justice Department contacted Larkin with a sketch artist. A couple of hundred pictures later, Larkin ID'd the missing man as one Alexander Liman Meesh, an indicted murderer the feds believed to be living in Bogotá, Colombia. I have an NCIC file on him I can give you."*

Pike glanced at the limo again.

"How did a traffic accident become a federal investigation?"

Kline moved between Pike and the limo, but no longer seemed upset that Pike hadn't signed the papers.

"The red flag was King. The DOJ told us they've been investigating him for laundering cash through his real estate company. They believe Meesh returned to the States with cartel money to invest with King."

Bud nodded, arching his eyebrows.

"Upwards of a hundred mil."

Kline darkened even more, then glanced at the girl's father.

"The government needs Larkin to link King with a known criminal. With her testimony, they believe they can get an indictment and force him to open his books. Her father and I were against it. We've been against her involvement since the beginning, and look at this mess."

"So King wants her dead?"

Bud said, "King is a money man. He has no criminal background, no history of violence, no connection with anyone in the business short of Meesh. The Justice people think Meesh is trying to protect the cash he's invested in King's projects. If King is indicted, his projects will be frozen along with his assets, so Meesh doesn't want King *indicted. King might not even know that Meesh is after the girl. King might not even know where the money actually comes from."*

"Anyone asked the Kings?"

"They've fled. Their office says they're away on a scheduled vacation, but no one at Justice believes it."

Conner Barkley raked at his hair again.

"It's a nightmare. This entire mess is a nightmare, and now we're—"

Bud interrupted him.

"Conner—would you give me a minute with Joe? We'll meet you at the car. Gordon, please—"

Barkley frowned like he didn't understand he was being asked to leave, but Kline touched his arm and they left. Bud waited until they were gone, then sighed.

"These people are going through hell."

Pike said, "I'm not a bodyguard."

"Joe, listen, the first time they came for her, the kid was at home. That place they have, the Barkleys, it's a fortress—four acres in Beverly Hills north of Sunset, full-on security, a staff. These people are rich."

"I get that."

Bud opened the cordovan briefcase and took out several grainy pictures. The pictures showed three hazy figures in dark clothes moving past a swimming pool at night, then in a courtyard, then outside a set of French doors.

"These were taken by their security cams. You can make out the faces in this one and this one, but we haven't been able to identify them yet. They grabbed a housekeeper, trying to find Larkin. They beat her bad—choked her out and broke three of her teeth and her nose."

The housekeeper was in one of the pictures. Her eyes

looked like eggplants. Her lip was split so badly you could see her gums. Pike figured whoever beat her had enjoyed it. Had probably kept hitting her even after she was unconscious.

"How close did they get?"

"They made a clean break when the police showed. That first time, the attempt on her life came as a surprise, but then she went into federal protection. The marshals brought her to a safe house outside San Francisco that evening—that was six days ago. The next night, they came for her again."

"At the safe house."

"One U.S. Marshal was killed and another wounded. Those boys hit hard."

Pike heard a car door slam and once more shifted to the window. Larkin Conner Barkley had gotten out of the limo to meet her father and Kline. She had a heart-shaped face with a narrow nose that bent to the left. Copper-colored hair swirled around her head like coiling snakes. She was wearing tight shorts that started low and finished high, a green T-shirt, and had a small dog slung in a pink designer bag under her arm. It was one of those micro-dogs with swollen eyes that shivered when it was nervous. Pike knew it would bark at the wrong time and get her killed.

He turned away from the window.

"The same men?"

"No way to know. Larkin called her father and was back in Beverly Hills by sunrise. They were done with federal protection. Mr. Barkley hired me later that day. I moved her out of their house and into a hotel, but they hit us again in a matter of hours."

"So they knew her location all three times."

"Yes."

Pike looked back at the limo. The dimming light in the church had taken on the color of smoke.

"Your feds have a leak."

Bud clenched his jaw, like that's what he was thinking though he didn't want to say it.

"I have a house in Malibu. I want you to take her there tonight—just you. I don't want to bring her back to the city."

"How do the feds feel about that?"

"I cut them out. Pitman, he's the boss over there, he thinks I'm making a mistake, but this is the way the Barkleys want it."

Pike looked back at Bud Flynn.

"Did Stone tell you our setup?"

Bud stared at him, not understanding.

"What setup?"

"I don't do contract work anymore. I owe the man a job. The one job. This is his payoff."

"You're costing a fortune."

"I'm not taking it. That's not the way I want it or why I'm doing it."

"He didn't say anything about that. If your heart isn't in it, I don't want you to—"

Pike said, "Officer Flynn—"

Bud stopped.

"Let's meet the girl."

Her father and Gordon Kline were talking when Pike and Flynn stepped from the church. Bud gestured to the Hummer, where two men in Savile Row suits began off-

loading suitcases and travel bags. The girl put her hands on her hips to study Pike as if she had buyer's remorse. The little dog, hanging beneath her arm in its pouch, watched him approaching with vindictive eyes.

When they reached the car, Flynn nodded at Gordon Kline—

"We're good to go."

—then turned to the girl.

"Larkin, this is Joe Pike. You'll be going with him."

"What if he rapes me?"

Barkley didn't look at his daughter; he glanced at Gordon Kline.

Kline said, "Stop it, Larkin. This is what's best."

Barkley nodded, and Pike wondered if Kline's job was telling Barkley's daughter what to do.

Larkin took off her sunglasses, making a drama of measuring Pike before she looked at her father.

"He's kinda cute, I guess. Are you buying him for me, Daddy?"

Barkley glanced at Kline again as if he wanted his lawyer to answer his daughter. Barkley seemed afraid of her.

She turned back to Pike.

"You think you can protect me?"

Pike studied her. She was pretty and used to it, and the clothes and the hair indicated she liked being the center of attention, which would be a problem. The Savile Row suits were still piling up bags.

Larkin frowned at Flynn.

"How come he isn't saying anything? Is he stoned?"

Pike made up his mind.

"Yes."

Larkin laughed.

"You're stoned?"

"Yes, I can protect you."

Larkin's grin fell away, and now she considered him with uncertainty shadowed in her eyes. As if all of it was suddenly real.

She said, "I want to see your eyes. Take off your glasses."

Pike tipped his head toward the growing pile of bags.

"That your stuff?"

"Yeah."

"One bag, one purse, that's it. No cell phone. No electronics. No iPod."

Larkin stiffened.

"But I need those things. Daddy, tell him I need those things."

The little dog's eyes bulged spastically and it snarled.

Pike said, "No dog."

Conner Barkley raked at his hair, and Gordon Kline frowned even more deeply, but no one looked at the growing pile of bags or the dog.

A bad hour later, Pike and the girl were on their way.

Four and a half hours later, the fourth attempt on Larkin Barkley's life was made in Malibu. Then they were running.

6

Elvis Cole

"JOE—?"

Cole realized Pike had hung up. That was the kind of call you got from Joe Pike. You'd answer the phone, he'd grunt something like *I'm coming up*, and that was it. Polite communication had never been one of Pike's strong points.

Cole put down his portable phone and went back to waxing his car—a yellow 1966 Sting Ray convertible. He was wearing gym shorts and a Harrington's Café T-shirt from a great little café in Baton Rouge. The grey shirt was black with sweat and he wanted to take it off, but he wore it to cover his scars. Cole lived in a small A-frame house perched on the edge of a canyon off Woodrow Wilson Drive in the Hollywood Hills. It was woodsy and quiet, and his neighbors often walked their dogs past his house. Cole figured they didn't need to see the liver-colored stitching that made him look like a lab accident. He figured he didn't need them to see it, either.

Cole hated waxing his car, but the night before he had watched one of his favorite movies, *The Karate Kid*, that scene where Pat Morita trains Ralph Macchio in kung fu blocking techniques by having Macchio wax his car—wax on, wax off. Cole, watching the movie, thought maybe waxing the car would be good therapy.

Thirteen weeks earlier, a man named David Reinnike shot Cole in the back with a 12-gauge shotgun. The pellets had shattered five ribs, broke his left humerus, collapsed his left lung, and, as he later told people in a way that grated on everyone's nerves, ruined a fine day. Fourteen weeks earlier—a week before he was shot—Cole could bend at the waist, rest his chest on his thighs, and wrap his arms around his calves; now, he moved like a robot with rusty joints. But twice a day every day he pushed past the pain, working himself back into shape. Hence, wax on, wax off.

Cole was still working on the car when a dark green Lexus stopped across his drive. Cole straightened, and was surprised to see Pike and a young woman with ragged hair and big sunglasses get out. The girl looked wary, and Pike was wearing a long-sleeved shirt with the sleeves down. Pike never wore long-sleeved shirts.

Cole limped out to meet them.

"Joseph. You should have told me we had guests. I would have cleaned up."

Cole smiled at the girl, spreading his hands to show off his gym shorts, bare feet, and wax on, wax off T-shirt. Mr. Personable, making a joke of his sweat-soaked appearance.

"I'm Elvis. This is me, doing my Ralph Macchio impersonation."

The girl painted him with a smile that was smart and sharp, and jerked a thumb at Pike.

"Thank God you have a personality. Riding around with him is like riding with a corpse."

"Only until you get to know him. Then you can't shut him up."

Cole noticed how Pike touched her back without familiarity, moving her into the carport.

Pike said, "Let's go in."

Cole glanced at the Lexus, already sensing this wasn't a social visit.

"The four-door sedan is bad for your image, m'man. What happened to the Jeep?"

"Let's go in."

Cole led them into his house through the carport, and then into the living room, where glass doors opened onto his deck and filled his house with a view of the canyon. The girl looked out at the view.

She said, "This isn't so bad."

"Thanks. I think."

The money vibe came off her like heat—the Rock & Republic jeans, the Kitson top, the Oliver Peoples shades. Cole was good at reading people, and had learned—over time—that he was almost always right. The trouble vibe came off her, too. She looked familiar, but Cole couldn't place her.

Cole said, "I'm sorry. I didn't catch your name."

The girl glanced at Pike.

"Can I tell him?"

Pike said, "This is Larkin Barkley. She's a witness in a federal investigation. She was in a program, but that didn't work out."

Larkin said, "Ha."

"We could use something to eat, maybe a shower, and I'll tell you what's up."

Cole sensed Pike didn't want to talk in front of the girl, so he gave her the smile again.

"Why don't you use the shower while I make something to eat?"

Larkin glanced back at him, and Cole read a new vibe. She gave him the same crooked smile she had made in the drive, only now she was telling him he could say and do nothing that would surprise her, affect her, or impress her, here in his little house that wasn't so bad. Like a challenge, Cole thought; or maybe a test.

She said, "Why don't I eat first? The Pikester won't feed me. He only wants sex."

Cole said, "He's like that with me, too, but we've learned to adjust."

Larkin blinked once, then burst out laughing.

Cole said, "One point, me; zero, you. Take the shower or wait on the deck. Either way, we don't want you around while we talk."

She chose the shower.

Pike brought in her bag and showed her to the guest bathroom while Cole went to work in the kitchen. He sliced zucchini, summer squash, and Japanese eggplant the long way, then drizzled them with olive oil and salt, and put on a grill pan to heat. After a few minutes Pike joined him, but neither of them spoke until they heard the water running. Then Cole settled back against the counter.

"The Pikester?"

Pike dealt out a driver's license and two credit cards.

The DL picture showed the girl with spectacular red hair. The credit cards showed her name. The AmEx card was black. Money.

Pike said, "I met her for the first time yesterday, but I don't know anything about her. I need you to help me with that."

Pike followed the credit cards with what appeared to be a text-only criminal-history file from the FBI's National Crime Information Center.

"This is the man who's trying to kill her. His name is Alex Meesh, from Colorado by way of Bogotá, Colombia."

Cole glanced over the cover page. Alexander Meesh. Wanted for murder.

"South America?"

"Went down to flee the murder warrants. The feds gave Bud his record, but I didn't see much that would help. Maybe you'll see something different."

Cole listened as Pike described Larkin Barkley's situation in the flat, declarative sentences of a patrol officer making a report. Pike described how the girl had found herself in a Justice Department investigation involving a suspected money launderer named George King and how her agreement to testify had led to the attempts on her life. Cole listened without comment until Pike described the shootings in Malibu and Eagle Rock. Then the skin on his back prickled and he stepped away from the counter.

"Wait. You shot someone?"

"Five. Two last night, three this morning."

Pike, standing there in his kitchen without expression, saying it like anyone else would say their car needed gas.

"Joe. Jesus, *Joe*—are the police after you?"

"I don't know. Malibu was last night and Eagle Rock was only a couple of hours ago. But if not now, then soon—I lost a gun in Eagle Rock."

Cole felt a momentary lightness, like when the earth drops in a temblor. Ten minutes ago, he had been waxing his car. Three days ago, he and Pike had spent the evening planning a backpacking trip.

"This was self-defense, right? You were defending your life and the life of a federal witness. The feds are with you on that."

"I don't know."

"You fled the scene in fear for your life and reported what happened to the Justice Department. All of this happened with the full knowledge of the Justice Department. These people are good with that?"

"I never met them."

Cole stared at his friend. Pike stood on the opposite side of the kitchen with his back to the wall, so effortlessly he might have been floating. His dark glasses were black holes, as if part of him had been cut away.

Pike said, "Either way, we have a bigger problem than the police. The shooters knew our location at both safe houses. They had her when she was with the marshals and again when Bud took her to a hotel. You see how it is?"

Even with the water, Cole lowered his voice. Now he understood why Pike wouldn't talk in front of the girl.

"Someone on her side is giving her up."

"I took her. I cut Bud and the feds out of the loop. I figure as long as no one knows where she is, I can protect her."

"What are you going to do?"

"Find Meesh."

Cole glanced at the printout again. *Currently believed to be residing in Bogotá, Colombia.*

"Meesh might not even be in Los Angeles. He might be back in Colombia."

"He's tried to kill this girl five times. You don't want someone dead that badly, then go away and hope it gets done—you make sure it happens."

Pike went to the pad and pen Cole kept by his phone and scribbled something.

"I dropped the Jeep and got a new phone. This is the number."

Cole's insides felt queasy, but he felt that way often since he was shot. The doctors said it would take time. They said it might never be better.

"You have any idea who's giving her up?"

"Bud is working on it, but who can I trust? Might be one of his people. Might even be one of the feds."

Cole put the number aside. He turned back to the pan and laid in the vegetables. The pan was too hot, but he loved the smell when they hit the hot steel.

Cole and Pike had been through a lot. They had been friends a long time. When Cole woke from his coma, Joe Pike had been holding his hand.

Cole put down the fork and turned.

"I don't like this. I don't like you getting involved in something and not knowing who you're involved with. This guy Meesh. These feds you haven't met. Your friend Flynn you haven't seen in twenty years. It is not up to our standards."

Pike was as still as a statue, as if parts of the story were hidden by shadows.

"Well?"

"I didn't come just for your help. If these people know who I am, they might try to find me through you."

An unexpected sadness emanated from behind the black glasses.

Pike said, "I'm sorry."

Cole felt a sudden flush of embarrassment and turned back to the food.

"Those clowns show up here, I'll kick their bitch asses."

Pike nodded.

Cole said, "I'll see what I can find out about your boy Meesh. We'll start with Larkin when she's done with the shower. Maybe she knows more than she thinks."

Pike shifted against the wall.

"We can't hang here, Elvis."

Cole understood. If the shooters or the police showed up, Pike wanted the girl gone.

"Then you talk to her. But one more thing. When I'm looking into Meesh, I'm going to check out your friend Bud Flynn, too."

Pike's mouth twitched, and Cole wondered if Larkin had noticed that Pike never laughed or smiled. As if the part of a man who could feel that free was dead in Pike, or buried so deep that only a twitch could escape.

Pike said, "Whatever."

Cole was building the sandwiches when Pike's cell phone rang, and Pike brought the phone out to the deck.

Cole layered the vegetables onto whole wheat bread, spread the layers with hummus, then placed the sandwiches back in the grill pan to crisp the bread.

The running water suddenly stopped and its absence was loud in the silence. A few minutes later, the girl came down the hall. Pike was still outside with his phone.

The girl said, "That smells incredible."

"Would you like a glass of milk, or water?"

"Please. The milk."

With her sunglasses off, her eyes were red, and Cole wondered if she had been crying. She caught him looking, and flashed the crooked smile. It was smart and inviting, and could never be made by someone who had just been crying, but there it was. Cole thought, this kid has had plenty of practice hiding herself.

Cole said, "You look familiar."

"I do?"

"Are you an actress?"

"Oh God, no."

She opened the sandwich and made a little squeal that didn't go with the smile.

"This is perfect! I didn't want to be a pain before, but I'm a vegetarian. How did you know?"

"Didn't. I made these for Joe. He's a vegetarian, too."

"*Him?*"

She glanced out at Pike, and Cole thought her smile straightened.

"Red meat makes him aggressive."

She laughed, and Cole found himself liking her. She took a tremendous bite of the sandwich, then another. She watched Pike on the deck as she chewed.

"He doesn't say much."

"He's into telepathy. He can also walk through walls."

She took another bite, though this one was not so large. She went back to staring at Pike again, but her smile was gone and her eyes seemed thoughtful.

"He shot a man right in front of me. I saw the blood."

"A man who was trying to kill you."

"It was so loud. Not like in the movies."

"No. It's loud."

"You can feel it."

"I know."

"They keep finding me."

Cole touched her back.

"Hey—"

Her eyes fixed on Pike.

"Can he get in trouble?"

Cole didn't answer because Pike stepped in from the deck.

"We have a place. Let's go."

She glanced at her sandwich again, then his.

"But you haven't eaten. I haven't finished."

"We'll eat in the car."

Cole followed them out, said his good-byes, and watched them drive away. He did not ask Pike where they were going, and Pike didn't say. He knew Pike would call him when they were safe.

Cole looked at his house, then considered his car. Joe Pike was the only thing that had been in Cole's life longer than the house and the car. They met back when Pike was still riding a black-and-white and Cole was working as an apprentice to old George Feider, Cole still piling up the three thousand hours of experience he needed to be licensed as a private investigator. Pike had referred to George as Cole's T.O.—his training officer. Bud Flynn had been Pike's training officer when Pike was a rookie, and Pike had revered the man.

Cole found himself smiling. A few years later when Cole had the hours and Pike was off the job, George retired, so Cole and Pike pooled their money to buy Feider's business, both of them agreeing Cole's name would be the only name on the door. Pike had no intention of getting a license. He had other businesses by then and only wanted to help Cole part-time, saying without him covering Cole's back, Cole would probably get himself killed. Cole hadn't known whether or not Pike had been joking, but that was part of Pike's charm.

If these people know who I am, they might try to find me through you.

Cole took a deep breath. He drew the air deep, expanding his chest until the pain made his eyes water, then he went back into the house.

They might try to find me through you.

Cole thought, Let'm bring it—I got your back, too, brother.

He went to work.

PIKE CRUISED east on Sunset Boulevard into the pur-
pling sky, driving easy for the first time in twenty hours,
invisible in the anonymous car. When they passed Echo
Lake with its fountain, dim in the twilight, Pike turned
north into the low hills of Echo Park. The houses would
be nicer east of the park, but the twisting residential
streets to the north were narrow and the homes were
clapboard shotguns. Pre-war street lamps were flicker-
ing on when they reached the address.

Pike said, "This is it."

A narrow grey house with a steep roof sat off the
street. A covered front porch guarded the door and a
one-car garage filled the backyard. Pike's real estate
friend had left a key under a potted plant near the door.

Larkin looked warily at the house.

"Who lives here?"

"It's a rental. The owners live in Las Vegas, and
they're between tenants. When you get out, go directly
to the front door."

A sunset breeze out of Chavez Ravine stirred the

warm air. Families were outside on their porches, some listening to the radio and others just talking. Pike heard Vin Scully, calling the game from nearby Dodger Stadium, Dodgers up over the Giants, five to two. Most of the neighbors appeared to be Eastern Europeans. Across the street, five young men who sounded Armenian were standing around a late-model BMW. They laughed together, and one of them spoke loudly, trying to make a point over the laughter.

Larkin didn't move toward the front door. She stared at the house like it was waiting to eat her, then looked at the surrounding houses, then the five men.

Pike said, "It's okay. Let's go."

Pike carried her bags. He could have carried his as well, but didn't. He found the key, then let them into a small living room. A door to their right branched into a bathroom and a front and back bedroom. The little house was fully furnished and the interior was clean and neat, but the furniture was worn and the rooms were small. A single window air conditioner hummed in the living room, left on by Pike's friend to cool the house.

Larkin said, "I've been thinking. No one knows where we are now, right? We have my credit cards. We have my ATM. We can go wherever we want."

Pike dropped her bags.

"It has two bedrooms. Take whichever you want."

Pike continued on through both bedrooms and the bath and kitchen, checking the windows and pulling the shades. Larkin didn't touch her bags or pick a bedroom. She followed him, walking so close that twice she stepped on his heels.

"Just listen. We can take the Gulfstream. My father won't care. We have a fabulous apartment in Sydney. Have you ever been to Oz?"

"You'll be recognized. Someone at the airport, there's Larkin Barkley in her jet."

Pike opened the fridge. Two grocery bags, a case of bottled water, and a six-pack of Corona were waiting.

"My friend left this. Help yourself."

"You're being a prick. Okay, look—we have a house on the rue Georges Cinq a block from the Champs-Elysées. I'll pay our way on a commercial flight. It's not a problem."

"Credit cards leave a trail. Airplanes file flight plans."

Pike headed back into the living room, and Larkin caught up.

"I'll take cash from the ATM. It's really no problem. This place doesn't even have a TV."

The window unit made a heavy *thump* when the compressor kicked on, like someone had stumbled into the wall. The air blowing from the vent roared like a windstorm with a faraway metallic vibration. Pike turned it off. The silence from the dying air conditioner was filled by barking dogs, a motorcycle echoing between the hills, and the laughter of the men across the street.

Larkin looked horrified.

"What are you doing? Why did you turn off the air?"

"I couldn't hear."

"But it's hot. It's going to be an oven in here."

She had crossed her arms, and her fingers had dug into her flesh. Pike knew this wasn't about Paris or Sydney. It was about being scared.

Pike touched her arm.

"I know this isn't what you're used to, but we have what we need. Right here—right now—this is a safe place. We're safe."

"I'm sorry. I didn't mean to be a bitch."

"I'm going to get my things from the car. You okay alone for a few minutes?"

"I miss my dog."

Pike didn't know what to say about that, so he didn't say anything.

Larkin made a tired smile.

"Of course. I'll be fine."

Pike turned off the lamps so he wouldn't be framed in the door, then let himself out. He had left his bags so he could return alone to check his messages. If he needed to call someone, he wanted to speak freely. He climbed into the Lexus, then used his new phone to check the messages left on his old phone. Seven messages were waiting for him. Bud had left three in a row, all pretty much the same—

"Call me, damnit! You can't just disappear with this girl! She's a federal witness, for Chrissakes! They'll have the FBI looking for you!"

Bud had left a fourth message about an hour after the first three. Pike noted Bud was calmer in the fourth message. He wasn't shouting—

"Joe, listen, you have to check in. For all I know those bastards tagged you, and you're both dead. Please don't leave me hanging like this."

Jon Stone had left the fifth message in a quiet and wary voice.

"This is Stone. You got heavy people worried, bro. Don't call me back. Do not call. Stay groovy."

Pike hesitated before deleting Stone's message. Staying groovy had nothing to do with being cool. It was an expression used by small recon units and sniper teams in hostile terrain. They would tell one another to stay groovy when the danger level was so insanely high they popped amphetamines to stay awake and ready to rock twenty-four/seven, because anything less would get them all killed. Stay groovy; take your pill. Stay groovy; safety off, finger on. Stay groovy; welcome to hell. Stone had left a warning within his message, and Pike wondered why.

Pike wanted to call Stone, but assumed Stone told him not to call for good reason. Bud and the feds had probably pushed Stone for information. He wondered if Meesh had done the same.

The sixth message was again from Bud, this time sounding drained.

"Here's what I have so far—the stiffs from Malibu weren't identified. I don't know about Eagle Rock, but I'll find out tomorrow. LAPD and the Sheriff's haven't connected you with the shootings. I spoke with Don Pitman—Pitman's the DOJ agent. He'll do what he can to take care of you with the locals, but he wants to talk to you—he absolutely must talk to you. You gotta call me, man. I don't know what to tell her father. He wants to call the police. Joe, if you're still alive—call."

A dry male voice had left the last message.

"This is Special Agent Don Pitman with the Justice Department. 202-555-6241. I got your number from Bud Flynn. Call me, Mr. Pike."

Mister.

Pike ended the call, then sat listening to the neighborhood. He wondered what Bud meant, saying the stiffs in Malibu weren't identified. Pike had thought the shooters would be identified as soon as they reached the coroner, which would give him a lead to Meesh. Pike had been thinking about Meesh because something Larkin described was bothering him. Her accident had occurred downtown in the middle of nowhere, but Meesh had fled on foot. Larkin told him the Kings had driven away, but Meesh fled on foot. This didn't make sense to Pike, but there was still much he didn't know. He wanted to ask Larkin about it.

Pike unscrewed the interior light so it wouldn't come on, then left the car. It was full-on dark now, and Pike enjoyed the darkness. Darkness, rain, snow, a storm—anything that hid you was good. He circled the house to check the windows, then slipped back onto the porch and let himself in.

Larkin was no longer in the living room, but her bags were gone and he heard her in the kitchen. He took off the long-sleeved shirt, then sat in one of the wing chairs to wait. He couldn't see her, but he knew she was getting a bottle of water. He heard the rattle of the refrigerator as she wrestled a bottle from its plastic wrapping. He heard the door close with a plastic kiss and a zippery crack as she twisted off the cap. Her shadow played on the bright kitchen wall, so he knew she was moving, and he heard the dry slap of bare feet. She came out of the kitchen and was halfway into the living room before she saw him, and startled so abruptly a geyser of water squirted into the air.

"You scared the shit out of me."

"Sorry."

She was gasping the way people do, but she made an embarrassed laugh.

"Jesus, say something next time. I didn't hear you come back."

"Maybe you should put on something."

She had taken off her clothes except for a sheer bra and lime green thong panties. A gold stud glinted in her navel. She straightened to face him full-on, lifting her ribs.

"I got hot. I told you it would be hot without the air. You want a bottle of water?"

Pike said, "Don't do this."

She went to the couch, sat, and put her bare feet up on the coffee table, staring at him between her knees.

"Do what? Are you sure you don't want to go to Paris? It's cooler in Paris."

She stared into his eyes with the crooked smile slashing her face as if she and only she had discovered that everything in the world was about sex and Pike had never seen anything like her before.

Pike said, "Who's Don Pitman?"

Her crooked smile vanished.

"I don't want to talk about this right now."

"I need to know who these people are. He called me."

She closed her eyes. Her feet dropped from the table.

"He's one of the people from the government. It was Pitman and another one—Blanchette. Kevin. Kevin is a lawyer from the Attorney General."

"Are they running the show or do they work for someone else?"

Her shut eyes squeezed tighter, like she was in pain but trying to control it.

"Not now. I cannot talk about this anymore."

"I need to ask some things. I'm going to have to talk to these guys, and Bud, and your father."

"No more. Not now."

She leaned forward to put the bottle on the table, and her breasts showed round and full in her bra in the dim ochre light.

"I have a tattoo on my ass. Did you see it this morning? I wanted you to see it."

Pike stared at her.

"It's a dolphin. I think dolphins are beautiful. You see them racing through the water. They have that wonderful smile. They look so happy, going fast. I want to be a dolphin. I want to be like that."

She came around the table and walked over to Pike and stopped in front of him. Pike shook his head.

"Don't."

She knelt and placed the flat of her hand on his shoulder, covering his tattoo.

"Why did you have arrows? Tell me why. I need to know that about you."

Pike moved just enough to lift her hand away. He took her arms and gently pushed her back.

"Please don't do this again."

She stared at some point between them for a time, then returned to the couch. Pike studied her dark outline, half her face in a murky glow from the kitchen, the other half in shadows. Her eyes glistened in the light from the window.

He said, "It's going to be all right. You're safe."

"I don't know you. I don't know these government people or Meesh or the Kings or anything about laundering money from South America. I only wanted to help. I don't know what I'm doing here. I don't know what happened to my life."

The glisten spread to her cheeks.

"I'm really scared."

Pike knew it was a mistake even as he went to the couch. He put his arm around her, trying to comfort her the way he had comforted people when he was an officer, comforting a mother whose son had been shot, calming a child who had been shaken in a traffic accident. And when he touched her, she snuggled into him, her hand going to his chest, then lower.

Pike whispered, "No."

Larkin ran into the front bedroom, bare feet slapping. The door closed.

Pike sat on the couch in the dark quiet house. He had been awake for thirty-five hours, but he knew if sleep came it would not last more than an hour or two. He took off his sweatshirt, then floated soundlessly through the house, going to each room, listening to the night beyond the windows, then moving on. When he reached Larkin's door, he heard her crying.

A slash of light from the edge of a shade placed a bar on the floor at his feet.

Pike touched the door.

"Larkin."

The crying stopped, so he knew she was listening.

"The arrows. What they mean is, you control who you are by moving forward, never back; you move forward. That's what I do. That's what we're going to do."

Pike waited, but the girl made no sound. Pike felt embarrassed and wished he hadn't tried to explain.

"You know me better now."

Pike turned away and shut every light in the house. He returned to the living room. He stood in the dark, listening, then fell forward and silently caught himself in the push-up position.

He did push-ups. He clicked off one push-up after another, alone with himself, waiting for the night to pass.

Staying groovy.

LIGHT IN WATER

8

THE WINDOWS grew light by five-thirty the following morning, filling the Echo Park house with the brown gloom of a freshwater pond. Pike had already washed and dressed by then. He wore jeans, his sleeveless grey sweatshirt, and the running shoes. He was standing in the living room. From his position, he could see the length of the house from the front door through the kitchen to the back door, and the three doorways branching off the tiny hall to both bedrooms and the bath. He had been standing in this spot for almost one hour.

Throughout the night, Pike had dozed a few minutes at a time on the couch, but had never been fully asleep. Every hour or so he moved through the house, checked the windows, and listened. Houses were living things, as were cattle and forests and ships. When all was well, the noises they made sounded right. Pike listened for rightness. He had entered the girl's room twice and found her snoring softly both times, once on her belly, once on her side, her covers kicked into a heap. Each time, he stood quietly in the darkness, listening to her breathe, then checked the windows before moving on.

Now he stood in the living room.

At five-forty that morning, the girl staggered out of her room and into the bath without seeing him. The bathroom light came on, the door closed, she did her business, the toilet flushed.

Pike never moved.

The door opened as she turned off the light. She shuffled out of the bathroom, carrying one shoulder higher than the other, and in that moment she saw him. Her eyes were puffy slits because she was groggy with sleep.

She said, "Why are you wearing sunglasses in the dark?"

Pike said nothing.

"What are you doing?"

"Standing."

"You're strange."

She shuffled back to her room. The toilet filled. The water stopped. The house was once again silent.

Pike did not move.

At two minutes after six, his new cell phone vibrated. Pike answered when he saw it was Ronnie.

"Yes."

"The alarm at your condo went off twelve minutes ago."

Whenever an alarm was received, the security company would first phone the subscriber to see if everything was all right. False alarms were common. Pike had arranged for his security company to call Ronnie's number if they received an alarm. He had also told them not to notify the police.

Pike said, "What did you tell them?"

"Everything's cool and they should reset the alarm, just like you said. You want me to roll over there?"

"No. I'll take care of it."

Pike thought for a moment.

"Call the security company back. Tell them if they get an alarm at the store, we want a full-on response."

"Got it."

Pike put away the phone, then checked the time. The alarm had probably been tripped when they breached his front door or a window. They were likely still in his home. They would just as likely be gone by the time he arrived unless their plan was to wait, but Pike was okay with it. He had to stay with the girl.

Pike thought about them being in his home. He had figured it was only a matter of time, and now it had come, and he was glad for it. They had gotten his name, found his address, and now were trying to find him. This told him much—someone who knew his name had provided it, and the only people who knew his name were the girl's people, Jon Stone, and Bud Flynn. There was no other way, so someone was selling her out. Pike was right to cut them out of the loop.

Pike hoped they would wait for him at his home, but they would probably move on to his shop, then return to his condo again later. At some point they would learn of his association with Cole, but they would move on his gun shop first. However they handled it would tell him much about the size of their operation and their skills. It was important to know your enemy.

But, for now, the girl was sleeping. The night had

passed. She was still alive. He had done his job, but still had much to do.

Pike let the girl sleep. He phoned Cole to let him know, then stood in the living room, waiting. His heart rate slowed. His breathing slowed. His body and mind were quiet. He could wait like that for days, and had, to make a perfect shot.

9

Elvis Cole

ANOTHER in the long line of classic Pike phone conversations. Like this. Cole, out on his deck sweating through some asanas when the phone rings. Six A.M., who else would it be? Gimps inside. Scores the call.

"Hello?"

Pike says, "Be advised. They just hit my condo."

Click.

No whaddayadoing? No heyhowareya? No whadda-yathinkaboutthat?

Classic.

Cole finished the asanas, showered, then pulled the old .38 George Feider gave him from his gun safe and made a cup of coffee. He brought the gun, coffee, and materials on George King and Alexander Meesh out to his deck. He had spent much of last night pulling things off the Internet. Cole wasn't worried about being stormed by black-shirted hitters, so he used the gun as a paperweight to keep the papers from flying away.

It was a lovely morning, hinting at a brutally hot day.

Cole squinted into the milky haze that filled his canyon, enjoyed the coffee, and noticed a red-tailed hawk circling overhead, searching for field mice and snakes.

Cole said, "What do you think? Is today his day or not?"

A black cat sat nearby on the deck, staring down through the rail into the canyon. The cat didn't answer, which is what you get when you talk to cats.

Cole said, "You're just jealous you can't fly."

The cat blinked as if it was falling asleep, then abruptly licked its penis. Cats are amazing animals.

Cole studied the hawk. The day after Cole came home from the hospital, he went out onto his deck at dawn (just as he had every morning since) and struggled through twelve sun salutations from hatha yoga (just as he had every morning since). He had not done them well that first morning, or completely, but he did what he could, then sat on the edge of his deck to watch the hawk. The hawk returned every day, but Cole never saw it catch anything. Yet every morning it appeared again, circling, searching for something it never found. Cole admired its spirit.

Cole had more of the coffee, then reread the material he'd pulled off the Internet on George King. King was a real estate developer from Orange County who began his career by building a single-family spec house on a shoe-string budget using money borrowed from his wife's parents. It was the classic by-his-bootstraps success story: King sold that first house for a profit, then built three more, and the houses led to a couple of tiny strip malls.

The strip malls led to twenty-, forty-, then one-hundred-sixty-unit apartment houses. The apartments led to a real estate concern that now developed shopping centers, residential tract housing, and high-rise commercial office space throughout California, Arizona, and Nevada. None of the articles hinted at impropriety, illegal activity, or shady business practices. Based on everything Cole read, George King was a solid citizen.

Alexander Meesh was not.

Cole had found nothing about Meesh on the Internet. The last entry in the NCIC report Pike had given him was dated six years ago, and ended with the notice that Meesh had fled the country and was currently believed to be living in Bogotá, Colombia. Absent for six years, Meesh was old news.

Reading the NCIC brief was like reading the *TV Guide* version of a twenty-year criminal career. An expanded version including photographs, fingerprints, and even DNA could be had by special request, but the shorthand version told the tale with a chronological list of crimes, convictions, incarcerations, descriptions, associates, and warrants.

Meesh was a peach. He had been indicted on two counts of first-degree murder, seven counts of conspiracy to commit murder, and sixteen counts of racketeering, all in Colorado. Meesh, who oversaw several hijacking crews, had murdered a truck driver and his wife in Colorado Springs, Colorado. Meesh believed the driver had double-crossed him by laying off a load of flat-screen TVs to a rival hijacking crew. Attempting to recover the flat-screens, Meesh poured hot cooking grease on the driver's wife. Not just once, but repeatedly during a twenty-four-hour torture session. Then he went to work on the driver. Witnesses to the event claimed Meesh wanted the other crews in the area to understand he owned the roads.

Cole reread that part, then studied the hawk. Hawks probably didn't pour boiling grease on other hawks. Cole considered his cat. It was staring down through the slats into the canyon. He wondered if the cat and the hawk were searching for the same thing.

"Hey, buddy."

The cat came over and head-bumped his hand. Petting the cat made it easier to forget about things like deep-fried flesh.

Cole returned to the file. Nothing explained how a homegrown criminal from Denver had become a financial player for a group of South American drug lords, but Cole didn't care. He wanted to find Meesh, and Meesh wasn't in South America. He was in L.A.

All criminal histories listed people with whom the subject was known to associate, including friends, family members, and gang affiliates. Cole had hoped to find a known associate in Los Angeles, but the names, like Meesh's arrests, were all based in Denver. It was possible one of Meesh's friends had moved to L.A. during the intervening six years, but Cole wouldn't know until he checked. The odds were slim, but now he set about listing the names from Colorado. Later, he would see if any of those people had connections in Los Angeles, and work backward to find Meesh.

Cole was making the list when a flick of grey dropped from the sky. Cole glanced up, smiling. He wanted to see what the hawk had caught, but that's when his doorbell rang. His first thought was that Alex Meesh had come to burn him with bacon grease, but Cole was given to wild imaginings. He limped to the front door with his pistol and peered through the peephole.

Two men stared back at him, their faces distorted by the fish-eye lens. They didn't look like bacon-grease killers. The man in front had a golfer's tan and short brown hair. He was wearing a brown sport coat that looked out of place in the L.A. summer, especially at seven A.M. The man behind him was taller and black, wearing a blue seersucker coat and sunglasses.

Cole parked the gun in his waistband behind his back, pulled his T-shirt over it, then opened the door.

The man in front said, "Elvis Cole?"

"He moved to Austria. Can I take a message?"

The man in front held up a black leather badge case showing a federal ID.

"Special Agent Donald Pitman. Department of Justice. We'd like a few words."

They didn't wait for Cole to invite them in.

10

OUTSIDE the walls of the Echo Park house, the neighborhood woke with the slowly rising sun. Finches and sparrows chirped. Sprinklers at the house next door came on, ran for twenty minutes, then automatically stopped. Cars started, then backed out of drives or pulled away from the curb. The brittle shades that covered the windows brightened until the house was filled with a dim golden light. On mornings like this with their silence and peace, Pike sometimes thought he felt the earth turn. He wondered if someone remained at his house.

The girl was still sleeping.

Pike poured ground coffee into a small pot, filled the pot with water, then set it on the range. Pike had been making coffee this way for years. He would bring it to a boil, then pour it through a paper towel or maybe he wouldn't bother with the towel. The coffee would be fine either way. Simple was better.

After a while the coffee boiled. Pike watched it roil for a moment, then turned off the heat and let it settle.

He didn't bother with the towel. He poured some into a Styrofoam cup, then brought it out to the table. He had just taken a seat when his cell phone vibrated again.

Cole said, "Can you talk?"

Pike could see the girl's door from the table. It was closed.

"Yes."

"Two agents from the Department of Justice came by this morning, Donald Pitman and Kevin Blanchette. They brought your gun. It was still in an LAPD evidence bag."

Pike said, "Okay."

"They didn't mention King or Meesh or the girl, or any of that. They didn't ask if I knew what was going on or if I had seen you. They just gave me the gun and told me to tell you they were taking care of it."

"You probably shouldn't call me from your house anymore."

"I walked next door."

"Okay."

"Pitman said if I heard from you I should tell you to call. You want the number?"

"I have it."

"He said the gun was a sign of good faith, but if you didn't call, the good faith would stop."

"I understand."

"You going to call?"

"No."

"Couple more things. Nothing in the record connects Meesh to L.A. or gives us something to work with, so the bodies are our best shot. We get them ID'd we might be able to work backwards to Meesh."

"I'll talk to Bud."

"It's not like I have too much to do. I can call over there."

Pike sipped the coffee, then glanced at Larkin's door.

"Bud's on it. Did you check out the girl?"

Cole hesitated, and Pike read a difference in his tone.

"She hasn't told you about herself?"

"What would she tell me?"

"She's the chick in the magazines."

"She's a model?"

"No, not like that. She's rich. She's famous for being rich. I didn't place her with the short hair, the way people can look different in person. She's always in the tabloids—going wild in clubs, making a big scene, that kind of thing. You've seen her."

"Don't read tabloids."

"Her father inherited an empire. They own hotel chains in Europe, a couple of airlines, oil fields in Canada. She has to be worth five or six billion."

"Huh."

"If she's cool, she's cool, but keep an eye on her. She's the classic L.A. wild child."

Pike glanced at the door.

"She seems all right."

"Just so you know."

Pike had more of the coffee. It had gone cold, but Pike didn't mind. He thought about Pitman and Blanchette showing up at Cole's house with the gun. A show of goodwill. He wondered why two federal agents would do that, but mostly he didn't care. He wanted to find Meesh.

Pike said, "Can you get Bud Flynn's home address?"

"Am I not the World's Greatest Detective?"

"Something I have to do later. I can't take the girl and I don't want to leave her alone. Could you stay with her?"

"Babysit a hot, young, rich chick? I think I can manage."

Pike ended the call, then punched in Bud Flynn's cell number. Flynn answered on the third ring, sounding hoarse and sleepy. Pike wondered if Bud was at a table somewhere, having coffee the way Pike was having coffee, but he decided Bud was in bed. It was only seven-forty. Bud had probably been up pretty late.

Pike said, "You sound sleepy. Did I wake you?"

As he said it, the girl's door opened and Larkin stepped out. She was puffy with sleep, and still wore only the bra and the tiny green thong. She didn't look so wild.

Pike touched his lips with a finger. Shh. Larkin blinked sleepily at him, then went into the bathroom.

Bud said, "You're killing me, Joe. Jesus, where are you?"

"We're good. Why is everyone so upset?"

Pike, having fun.

"You dropped off the world, is why! You're supposed to take care of her, yes, but you can't just disappear. The feds, they're—"

Pike interrupted.

"How many people know I have her?"

"What are you asking? What are you saying, asking that?"

"You, your boys in their nice silk suits, the feds, her

family? Someone hit my home this morning, Bud, so your leak is still leaking. Trust is in short supply."

Larkin came out of the bathroom and into the living room, her bare feet slapping the floor. Pike held up his coffee to show her that coffee was available, then pointed the cup toward the kitchen. She didn't seem self-conscious about her lack of clothes or even aware of it. She went past him into the kitchen.

Bud still had the uncertain voice.

"I understand what you're saying, but we have five bodies to deal with. We have a full-on police investigation, and—"

Pike cut him off again.

"Here's what's going to happen. Larkin and I will meet you. Don't tell her father or those feds or your boys in their silk. Come by yourself, and we'll figure this out. You good with that?"

"Where?"

The girl came out of the kitchen with the pot. She looked confused as she held up the pot, her expression saying what in hell is this? Pike raised a finger, telling her to wait, then checked his watch. It was now thirteen minutes before eight.

"Where are you right now?"

"Home. In Cheviot Hills."

"The subway stop in Universal City at noon. Can you make it at noon?"

"Yes."

"What will you be driving?"

"A tan Explorer."

"Park in the north lot. As far north as you can. Wait in your car until I call."

Pike turned off his phone. Larkin took this as a sign she could speak, so she waved the pot.

"What is this?"

"Coffee."

"It's sludge. There's stuff in it."

Pike finished his cup, then went to the couch and pulled on the long-sleeved shirt.

"Pack your things. We're going to see Bud."

She lowered the pot, staring at him as if she were fully dressed.

"I thought we were safe here."

"We are. But if something happens, we'll want our things."

"What's going to happen?"

"Every time we leave the house we'll take our things. That's the way it is."

"I don't want to ride around all day scrunched in your car. Can't I stay here?"

"Get dressed. We have to hurry."

"But you told him noon. Universal is only twenty minutes away."

"Let's go. We have to hurry."

She stomped back into the kitchen and threw the pot into the sink.

"Your coffee *sucks*!"

"We'll get Starbucks."

She didn't seem so wild, even when she threw things.

11

PIKE didn't bring her to Universal and didn't wait until noon. Cole had Bud's home address before they were out the door.

Cheviot Hills was an upscale neighborhood set on the rolling land south of the Hillcrest Country Club in midtown Los Angeles. Gracious homes with immaculate yards and manicured sidewalks were scattered throughout the area, though the larger homes were closer to the park. The homes farther south and closer to the I-10 freeway were smaller, but still beyond a police officer's salary. Back in the day when Pike rode with Bud, the Flynns had shared a duplex in Atwater Village.

Bud's current home was a small split-level not far from the freeway. A tan Explorer was parked in the drive as if it had been there all night. The house sat at the top of a rise, with a gently sloping drive and a front lawn that struggled against the brutal summer heat. Many of the homes had not been changed since they were built in the thirties, which gave the street a sleepy, small-town feel. A brace of jacaranda trees colored the car and the driveway with purple snow.

Larkin swiveled her head as they drove past the house, alert and excited.

"What are we going to do?"

"You're going to stay in the car. I'm going to talk to him."

"But what if he's not here? What if he left?"

"See the jacaranda flowers on the driveway? They haven't been disturbed."

"What if he wasn't here? What if he lied?"

"Please be quiet."

Pike parked across the mouth of Bud's drive so Larkin would be clearly visible in the car, then got out and went to the front door. Pike stood to one side of the door, positioning himself so he could not be seen from the windows. He called Bud's cell.

Bud said, "Gotta be you, Joe. The incoming call says restricted."

"Look in your driveway."

"Joe?"

"Look outside."

Pike heard movement over the phone, then inside the house. The front door opened. Bud stepped out. He stared at the girl, but didn't yet see Pike. Bud had already dressed for the day, but Pike thought the years had caught up with him in the past thirty-six hours. He looked tired.

Pike said, "Bud."

Bud showed no surprise. He scowled the way he had scowled when Pike was a boot, like he was wondering what he had done to be cursed with this person who was ruining his life.

He said, "What did you think I would do, have Universal surrounded? Have spotter planes up in the sky?"

Pike made a rolling gesture so Larkin would roll down her window.

Pike called out to her.

"Say hi to Bud."

Larkin waved and called back from the car.

"Hi, Bud!"

Pike called out again.

"You want to stay here with him?"

Larkin made a two-thumbs-down gesture and shook her head. Pike turned back to Bud, but Bud was still scowling.

"What do you think you're doing?"

"This is a nice house. You've done all right."

"What in the fuck do you think you're doing? Do you know how much shit I'm in?"

"I'm showing you she's alive and well. You can tell her father and Special Agent Pitman she's fine. You can say she doesn't want to come back because she likes staying alive."

Bud grew irritated.

"Now waitaminute, goddamnit—this isn't only about the girl. You dropped five bodies in two days. You think, what, Pitman can tell LAPD, hey, it's all right, our civilian killed those dudes to protect our witness, and Northeast Homicide will let it go? You have to help straighten this out."

Pike didn't care if they let it go or not. He wondered why Bud hadn't mentioned that Pitman had returned his gun. Then he wondered whether or not Bud knew, and, if not, why Pitman hadn't told him.

"What does Pitman want?"

"You, the feds, a couple of assistant chiefs from Parker and the Sheriff's, that's what we're talking about. You and Larkin answer their questions, Pitman says the locals will go away."

"Won't happen."

"Pitman says if you don't come in he'll issue a warrant for kidnapping."

The corner of Pike's mouth twitched, and Bud reddened.

"I know it's bullshit, but you're out here running around and nobody knows what's happening. The feds believe they can protect her. They think the problem is me, and that's what they're telling her father. He's this close to firing me."

"So tell me, Bud—is she safer with you now or me?"

"I turned over my personal records to the DOJ. I gave them my guys—their cell records, hotels and expenses, everything. Her father, he gave Pitman an open door on his lawyer, his staff, their e-mails and phones—all of it. We'll plug the leak."

"Who's checking Pitman?"

Bud blinked as if he was facing a dry wind, and finally shook his head.

"I can't keep her safe. I can't even cover for you. I know that was part of the deal, but now I don't know."

"My way, the leak doesn't matter."

Bud finally looked at him. His eyes were hard stones hidden by flesh weakened with age.

"Joe. What are you doing?"

"I'm looking for Meesh."

"You aren't just looking. I don't want to be involved

with anything like this. You want my help, but I don't even want to know."

"I only have two leads back to Meesh—the men in the morgue and the Kings. If the Kings were in business with him, then they probably knew where he was staying and how to reach him. Maybe I can find him through them."

"They're still missing."

"The feds must have something. Can you help with that?"

"Pitman has their home and office under twenty-four-hour surveillance. He has their phones tapped. He even has someone watching their yacht. If those people fart, the feds will be on them. If you try to get close to anything they own, the feds will be on you, too."

"Then the men I killed are my last door back to him. What do you know?"

Bud darkened, but glanced at the girl and wet his lips. "I gotta get my keys. Inside in the entry. That okay?" Pike nodded.

Bud stepped into his house, but only long enough to fish his keys from a blue bowl inside the door. Pike followed him out to his car. Bud opened the Explorer and Pike saw the same cordovan briefcase he had seen in the desert. Bud took out three pictures. They were the security stills taken when the Barkleys' home was invaded. Pike had seen them up in the desert, too.

Bud handed them to Pike, and tapped the top picture.

"This man was one of the original home invaders. You shot him in Malibu. He's the only one of the five you shot who was also one of the home invaders."

"What's his name?"

"I don't know. But this man—"

Bud shuffled the pictures to point out a man with prominent cheekbones and a scarred lip.

"—he's the freak who beat the housekeeper. You recognize either of these other guys from Malibu or Eagle Rock?"

"Who are they?"

"Don't know. We haven't been able to identify any of the five people you put in the morgue. The Live Scan kicked back zero. No IDs were found on the bodies, and they weren't in the system. You can keep these pictures, you want."

Pike stared at the pictures, thinking it didn't make sense that none of the five had been identified. The type of man you could hire to do murder almost always had a criminal record. The Live Scan system digitized fingerprints, then instantly compared them with computerized records stored by the California Department of Justice and the NCIC files, and those files were exhaustive. If a person had ever been arrested anywhere in the country or served in the military, their fingerprints were in the file.

Pike said, "That doesn't sound right."

"No, it does not, but all five of these guys were clean."

"No IDs or wallets?"

"Not one damn thing of a personal nature. You arrested a lot of people, Joe. You remember many shitbirds smart enough to clean up before they did crime?"

Pike shook his head.

"Me neither. So here we are."

Bud slammed his trunk, then stared at the girl.

"I guess I should apologize, getting you involved in this mess, but I won't. You could just give her back to Pitman. It's your choice, playing it this way."

Bud studied Larkin for a moment longer, and Pike wondered what he was thinking. Then Bud turned, and with the new angle of light, Pike thought he looked as hard as ever.

Bud said, "I'm trusting you won't let this little girl down."

Pike watched Bud walk away, then returned to the Lexus and immediately drove away.

Larkin said, "He seems like a nice man."

"He was a good officer."

"That's what he told my dad about you, that you were a good policeman. What he said was, you were the best young officer he ever worked with."

Pike didn't answer. He was thinking about the five nameless killers, cleaned up for crime with no criminal records. Pike thought he might still use them to find Meesh, and he believed he knew how.

DEPLOYMENT PERIOD ONE
RAMPART DIVISION ROLL CALL
EVENING WATCH, 1448 HOURS

His dark blue uniform was crisp and fresh, with creases as straight as ruled lines. His stainless steel and copper badge caught light like a mirror, and the black leather of his holster and shoes gleamed as they had in the Marine Corps. Military-issue sunglasses hung from his pocket in the approved position. Pike's kit, gear, and appearance were in order and by-the-book perfect, which was the way Pike liked it.

Pike, Charlie Grissom, and Paul "P-bag" Hernandez were seated in the front row in the roll call room of the Rampart Division Police Station. This being their first official day on the job after having graduated from the Los Angeles Police Academy, they wore badges and carried loaded weapons for the first time. Today, they would begin their careers as probationary police officers, known within the Los Angeles Police Department as boots.

Pike and the other boots sat erect with their eyes on Sergeant Kelly Levendorf, who was the evening watch commander. Slouching, slumping, or leaning on the table was not permitted. Being boots, they were required to sit in the first row, face forward, and were not allowed to look at the veteran officers who filled the room behind them. They were not allowed to join in the banter during roll call, or react or respond to the veterans, no matter how many spitballs came their way. They had not yet earned that right. Though they had graduated from the academy, they would spend the next year becoming "street certified" by experienced senior officers known as P-IIIs—Pee Threes—who would be their teachers, their protectors, and their Gods.

Two things would happen at this first roll call. They would meet their P-IIIs, which Pike was looking forward to, and they would introduce themselves to the veterans, which Pike dreaded. Pike wasn't much for talking, and talked about himself least of all.

Levendorf made car assignments, then rolled through everything from suspected criminal activity and suspects known or believed to be in the area, to officer birthdays and upcoming retirement parties. He read most of his announcements from a thick, three-ring binder. When he finished he closed the book and looked up at the shift.

"Okay, we have some new officers aboard, so we'll let'm introduce themselves. Officer Grissom, you have one minute, one second."

Pike thought, Here it comes.

At the academy, each recruit was given one minute plus one second to introduce himself. The recruit was expected to be brief and on point—just as he or she was expected to be when dealing with superiors, radio dispatchers, and the public.

Grissom surged to his feet, all gung ho enthusiasm, and turned to face the crowd. He was a short, chunky kid with delicate blond hair, who always seemed anxious to please.

"My name is Charlie Grissom. I graduated from San Diego State with a degree in history. My dad was an officer in San Diego, which is where I was born. I like to surf, fish, and scuba dive. I'm always looking for dive buddies, so look me up if you're interested. I'm not married, but I've been dating the same girl for about a year. Being a police officer is all I've ever wanted. My dad wanted me to go on the San Diego PD, but I wanted to be with the best—so I'm here."

This brought a roar of approval from the shift, but as it died a ragged voice behind Pike cut through the din.

"He kisses ass real good."

Pike saw Grissom flush from the corner of his eye as Grissom took his seat.

Levendorf said, "Officer Hernandez—one minute, one second."

Hernandez glanced over at Pike as he stood, and Pike made an imperceptible nod of encouragement. Pike and Hernandez had been roomies at the academy.

Hernandez turned to face them.

"My name is Paul Hernandez. My grandfather, my dad, and two uncles were all LAPD—I'm third generation—"

The shift cheered and clapped until Levendorf told them to knock it off, then ordered Hernandez to continue.

"I had two years at Cal State Northridge playing baseball before I got hurt. I love baseball, and I bleed Dodger blue. I'm married. We're expecting our first this June. I became an officer because I look up to officers, what with my family and all. That's the way I was raised. It runs in the blood."

The shift cheered again as Hernandez returned to his seat.

Levendorf quieted the crowd, then looked at Pike.

"Officer Pike—one minute, one second."

Everyone said pretty much the same things—they talked about their education and their families, but Pike hadn't gone to college and wouldn't talk about his family. He couldn't see that it mattered or why it was anyone else's business, anyway. Pike figured all that mattered was what a man did in the moment at hand, and whether or not he did right.

Pike stood and turned. This was the first time he had seen the officers assembled behind him. They were all colors and ages. Many were smiling and loose; others looked stern; and a lot of them looked bored. Pike noted those officers with two stripes on their sleeves. Civilians always confused these for corporal stripes, but these were the P-IIIs. One of them would be his training officer.

"My name is Joe Pike. I'm not married. I pulled two combat tours in the Marines—"

The shift broke into wild applause and cheers, with many of the officers shouting "Semper fi." LAPD had a high percentage of Marine Corps veterans.

Levendorf waved them quiet and nodded at Pike to continue.

"I want to be a police officer because the motto says to protect and to serve. That's what I want to do."

Pike took his seat to scattered applause, but someone in the back laughed.

"Got us a regular Clint Eastwood. A man of few words."

Pike saw Levendorf frowning.

Levendorf said, "We call this part of the program 'one minute, one second,' Officer Pike—so I figure you got about forty seconds to go. Perhaps you'd offer a bit more, self-illumination-wise; say, about your family and hobbies?"

Pike stood again, and once more faced the crowd.

"I qualified as a scout/sniper and served in Force Recon, mostly on long-range reconnaissance teams, hunter/killer teams, and priority target missions. I'm black belt qualified in tae kwon do, kung fu, wing chun, judo, and ubawazi. I like to run and work out. I like to read."

Pike stopped. The shift stared at him, but Pike didn't

know whether or not to sit down so he stared back. No one applauded.

Finally, an older black P-III with salt-and-pepper hair said, "Thank God he likes to read—I thought we had us a sissy."

The shift broke into laughter.

Levendorf ended the roll call, and everyone herded toward the exits except for Pike and the other new guys. They stayed behind to meet their P-IIIs.

Three senior officers bucked the departing crowd to make their way forward. The burly black officer who made the crack about Pike being a reader went to Grissom. The second P-III was an Asian officer with a face as edged as a diamond. He offered his hand to Hernandez. Pike watched the third P-III. He was shorter than Pike, with close brown hair, a rusty tan, and a thin, no--nonsense mouth. Pike guessed he was in his late thirties, but he might have been older. He had three hash marks on the lower part of his sleeve, signifying at least fifteen years on the job.

He came directly to Pike and put out his hand.

"Good to meet you, Officer Pike. I'm Bud Flynn."

"Sir."

"I'll be your training officer for your first two deployment periods. After that, if you're still around, you'll swap T.O.'s with the other boots, but you're mine for the first two months."

"Yes, sir."

"You can call me Officer Flynn or sir until I say otherwise, and I will call you Officer Pike, Pike, or boot. We clear on that?"

"Yes, sir."

"Got your gear?"

"Yes, sir. Right here."

"Grab it and let's go."

Pike hooked the gear bag over his shoulder and followed Flynn out to the parking lot. The mid-afternoon sun was hot and the air was hazy from the smog bank that heated the city. Flynn led Pike to a dinged and battered Caprice that had probably racked up over two hundred thousand hard miles. When they reached the car, Flynn pointed at it.

"This is our shop. Its name is two-adam-forty-four, which will also be your name after I teach you to use the radio. What do you think of our shop, Officer Pike?"

"It's fine."

"It is a piece of shit. It has so much wrong with it that it would be down-checked on any other police force in America. But this is Los Angeles, where our cheap-ass city council won't give us the money to hire enough men, or buy and maintain the proper equipment. But do you know what the good news is, Officer Pike?"

"No, sir."

"The good news is that we are Los Angeles police officers. Which means we will use this piece of shit anyway, and still provide the finest police service available in any major American city."

Pike was liking Flynn. He liked Flynn's manner, and Flynn's pride in the department, and Flynn's obvious pride in his profession.

Flynn put his gear on the ground at the back of the car, then faced Pike with his hands on his hips.

"First we're going to inspect the vehicle, then load our gear, but before we get going I want to make sure we're on the same page."

Flynn seemed to want a response, so Pike nodded.

"I respect your service, but I don't give a rat's ass about it. Half this police force was in the Marines and the other half is tired of hearing about it. This is a city in the United States of America. It isn't a war zone."

"Yes, sir. I understand."

"That piss you off, me saying that?"

"No, sir."

Flynn studied Pike as if he suspected Pike was lying.

"Well, if you are, you hide it well, which is good. Because out here, you will not show your true feelings to anyone. Whatever you feel about the lowlifes, degenerates, and citizens we deal with—be they victim or criminal—you will keep your personal opinions to yourself. From this point on, you are Officer Pike, and Officer Pike works for the people of this city no matter who and what they are. We clear?"

"Yes, sir."

Flynn popped the trunk. It was tattered and empty. He pointed inside.

"This is the trunk. I'm driving, so my gear will go on the driver's side. You're the passenger, so your gear goes on the passenger's side. This is the way we do it on the Los Angeles Police Department."

"Yes, sir."

"Stow your gear, but don't stop listening."

Pike stowed his gear as Flynn went on.

"The academy taught you statutes and procedure,

but I am going to teach you the two most important lessons you receive. The first is this: You will see people at their creative, industrious worst—and I am going to teach you how to read them. You are going to learn how to tell a lie from the truth even when everyone is lying, and how to figure out what's right even when everyone is wrong. From this, you will learn how to dispense justice in a fair and evenhanded way, which is what the people of our city deserve. Clear?"

"Yes, sir."

"Any questions?"

"What's the other thing?"

"What other thing?"

"The first lesson is how to read people. What's the second?"

Flynn's eyebrows arched as if he was about to dispense the wisdom of the ages.

"You will learn how not to hate them. You'll see some sorry bastards out here, Officer Pike, but people aren't so bad. I'm going to teach you how not to lose sight of that, because if you do you'll end up hating them and that's the first step toward hating yourself. We can't have that, can we?"

"No, sir."

Flynn inspected the trunk to make sure Pike had stowed his gear correctly, grunted an approval, then closed it. He turned back to Pike again, seemed to be thinking, and Pike wondered if Flynn was trying to read him.

Flynn said, "Now I have a question. When you said why you became an officer, you quoted the LAPD motto, to protect and to serve. Which is it?"

"Some people can't protect themselves. They need help."

"And that would be you, Officer Pike, with all that karate and stuff?"

Pike nodded.

"You like to fight?"

"I don't like it or not like it. If I have to, I can."

Flynn nodded, but the way he sucked at his lips told Pike he was still being read.

Flynn said, "Our job isn't to get in fights, Officer Pike. We don't always have a choice, but you get in enough fights, you'll get your ass kicked for sure. You ever had your ass kicked?"

"Yes, sir."

Pike would not mention his father.

Flynn still sucked at his lips, reading him.

"We get in a fight, we've failed. We pull the trigger, it means we've failed. Do you believe that, Officer Pike?"

"No, sir."

"I do. What do you think it means?"

"We had no other way."

Flynn grunted, but this time Pike couldn't tell if his grunt was approving or not.

"So why is it you want to protect people, Officer Pike? You get your ass kicked so much you're overcompensating?"

Pike knew Flynn was testing him. Flynn was probing and reading Pike's reactions, so Pike met Flynn's gaze with empty blue eyes.

"I don't like bullies."

"Making you the guy who kicks the bully's ass."

"Yes."

"Just so long as we stay within the rule of law."

Flynn considered him for another moment, then his calm eyes crinkled gently at the corners.

"Me being your training officer, I read your file, son. I think you have what it takes to make a fine police officer."

Pike nodded.

"You don't say much, do you?"

"No, sir."

"Good. I'll do enough talking for both of us. Now get in the car. Let's go protect people."

Their first hour together was light on protecting people. Each basic radio car normally patrolled a specific area within the division, but Flynn started off by giving Pike a tour of the entire division. During this time, Flynn reviewed radio procedures, let Pike practice exchanges with the dispatchers, and pointed out well-known dirtbag gathering points.

Easing into their second hour, Flynn let Pike write two traffic citations.

After the second citation, which was to an elderly woman who was angry and resentful at having been tagged for running a red light, Flynn painted Pike with a large smile.

"Well, how do you like the job so far?"

"A little slow."

"You did fine with that lady. Didn't punch her out or anything."

"Maybe next time."

Flynn laughed, then told the dispatchers to begin pitching them calls. Over the next two hours, Pike took a stolen car report from a sobbing teenage girl (the car belonged to her brother, who was going to kill her for getting his car stolen), interviewed a pet shop owner who had made a public drunkenness complaint (a drunk had entered her store, let the dogs and cats out of their cages, then left), took a shoplifting report from the manager of a convenience store (the shoplifter was long gone), took a report from a man who had returned home from work to find his house burglarized (the burglar was long gone), took a stolen bicycle report (no suspects), took a stolen motorcycle report (also no suspects), and checked out a report from a woman who believed her elderly neighbor was dead in an upstairs apartment (the elderly neighbor had gone to her daughter's cabin at Big Bear Lake).

At every criminal call they answered, the suspect or perpetrator was long gone or never present, though Pike dutifully and under Flynn's direction logged the complainant's statement, filled out the necessary form, and performed all communications.

They were proceeding east on Beverly Boulevard when the dispatcher said, "Two-adam-forty-four, domestic disturbance at 2721 Harell, woman reported crying for help. You up for that?"

Pike wanted it, but said nothing. It was up to Flynn. Flynn glanced over and seemed to read the need. He picked up the mike.

"Two-adam-forty-four inbound."

"Roger, stand by."

Domestic calls were the worst. Pike had heard it again and again at the academy, and Flynn had already mentioned it in the few hours they had been together. When you rolled on a domestic call, you were rolling *into the jagged eye of an emotional hurricane. In those moments, the police were often seen as saviors or avengers, and were always the last resort.*

Flynn said, "Evening watch is prime time for domestics. We'll probably get three or four tonight, and more on a Friday. By Friday, they've been working up to it all week."

Pike didn't say anything. He knew about domestic violence firsthand. His father had never waited until Friday. Any night would do.

Flynn said, "When we get there, I'll do the talking. You watch how I handle them, and learn. But keep your eyes open. You never know what's what when you answer one of these things. You might be watching the man, and the woman will shoot you in the back. The woman might be some scared-looking dishrag, but once we get her old man cooled out, she might turn into a monster. I saw that once. We got the cuffs on this guy, and that's when his old lady felt safe. She chopped off his foot with a meat cleaver."

Pike said, "Okay."

Pike wasn't worried. He figured clearing a domestic disturbance call couldn't be much different than clearing houses in a combat zone—you watched everything, you kept your back to a wall, and you assumed everyone wanted to kill you. Then you would be fine.

They rolled to a small apartment building south of Temple near the center of Rampart. Motionless palms towered overhead, catching the shimmer of dying light to make the building more colorful than it was. The dispatcher had filled them in: Call was placed by one Mrs. Esther Villalobos, complaining that male and female

neighbors had been arguing all afternoon and had esca-
lated into what Mrs. Villalobos described as loud crash-
ing, whereupon the female neighbor, identified by Mrs.
Villalobos as a young Caucasian female named Candace
Stanik, shouted "Stop it!" several times, then screamed
for help. Mrs. Villalobos had stated that an unemployed
Caucasian male she knew only as Dave sometimes lived
at the residence. The dispatcher reported no history of
officers being dispatched to this address.

Pike and Flynn would learn more later, but these
were their only available facts when they arrived at the
scene.

They double-parked their patrol car, then stepped
into the street. Pike scanned his surroundings automatically as he exited the car—vehicles, the deepening shadows between the buildings, the surrounding roofs—a
gulp of space and color he sensed as much as saw. Clear.
Good.

Flynn said, "You ready?"

"Yes, sir."

"Let's go see what's what."

Pike followed Flynn toward Candace Stanik's apartment.

Mrs. Villalobos lived in the rear unit on the ground
floor. Candace Stanik lived in the ground unit next door.
Pike and Flynn would only contact Mrs. Villalobos in the
event they could not gain access to Stanik's unit or if no
one was home.

Flynn stopped outside Stanik's door, motioning Pike
to remain silent. The windows were lit. Pike heard no
voices, but hacking sobs were distinct. Flynn looked at
Pike and raised his eyebrows, the look asking if Pike

heard it. Pike nodded. He thought Flynn looked green in the strange evening light.

Flynn pointed to the side of the door and whispered.

"Stand here out of the way. When I go in, you come in right behind me, but take your cue from me. Maybe the guy's already gone. Maybe they've made up and are in there all lovey-dovey. Understand?"

Pike nodded.

"Don't draw your gun unless you see me draw mine. We don't want to escalate the situation. We want to cool it. Understand?"

Pike nodded again.

Flynn rapped at the door three times and announced them.

"Police officer."

He rapped again.

"Please open the door."

The crying stopped and Pike heard movement. Then a young woman spoke from the other side of the door.

"I'm okay. I don't need anything."

Flynn rapped again.

"Open the door, miss. We can't leave until we see you."

Flynn raised his hand to knock as the door opened, and Candace Stanik peered through a thin crack. Even with the narrow view, Pike saw that her nose was broken and her right eye was purple with the mottled skin tight over a swelling lump. The eye would be closed in another few minutes. Pike had had plenty of eyes like that. Mostly as a kid. Mostly from his father.

Flynn placed his hand on the door.

"Step away, hon. Let me open the door and take a look."

"He's gone. He went to his girlfriend."

Flynn's voice was gentle but firm. Pike admired the way Flynn could direct so much emotion by his voice.

"Miss Stanik? That your name, Candace Stanik?"

Her voice was soft, but thin and strained. Pike wasn't listening to her; he listened past her, searching for other occupants. A crisp medicinal smell of ether came from her apartment, telling him that someone had been freebasing.

"Yes. He went—"

"Let us in now, hon. We can't leave until we come in, so just let us in."

Flynn pushed gently on the door until she backed away. Pike shadowed inside, then quickly stepped to the side so they weren't bunched together. Together, they would make a single large target; apart, two targets more difficult to kill. Pike kept his back to the wall.

Stepping into the apartment was like entering a furnace. Pike began sweating. They were in a cramped living room. As Flynn approached the girl, Pike noted an entry closet to the left and, across the living room, a tiny kitchen and dining area. A short hall branched off the dining area. The apartment appeared neat and squared away except the coffee table was turned on its side and the floor was spattered with blood. Candace Stanik was pregnant. Pike guessed seven or eight months, though he knew little about women or pregnancy. Her T-shirt was streaked with blood over the mound of her belly, and more blood spattered her legs and bare feet. Pike noted a thin kitchen towel bundled with ice that she had probably been using on her eye. Her lips were split in two places and her nose was broken, and she held her belly as if she was cramping.

Flynn spoke softly over his shoulder to Pike.

"Paramedics and additional units."

Pike keyed his rover, sending a request for paramedics and additional units to the dispatcher. Pike saw Flynn reach to touch the girl and the girl jerk her arm away as her voice rose—

"I want you to get him! You have to go get him. He went to his fucking slut girlfriend—"

The girl was growing more agitated and Flynn was working to calm her, lowering his voice, sharing his calm.

"Let's take care of that baby first, all right, hon? Nothing's more important than your baby."

Flynn had her arm again, and this time she let him, but her face contorted.

"He's going to get away—"

"Shh. He won't get away."

Flynn was everything he had to be—a strong, comforting father figure. You would be safe if you trusted him. He would take care of you if you let him. Flynn slipped his arm around her shoulders, an arm that would protect her and make all the pain go away, murmuring—

"You have to sit down first, hon. Let's get some ice on that nose. I'm going to take care of you."

Flynn motioned at Pike. They had been inside less than one minute.

"I'm okay here. You good with getting the back?"

Pike nodded.

"Be careful."

Pike moved past with no great feeling of apprehension. He glanced in the kitchen, then stepped into the hall. The bathroom door was open, showing a sink mottled with built-up soap film, a tiny tub, and a toilet. Pike turned to the bedroom. The door was half open and the light was on. Pike remembered Flynn's caution about drawing his weapon, but he drew it anyway, then pushed the door wider. The bedroom was a minefield of shopping bags, dirty clothes, and boxes. The double bed was dingy with rumpled grey sheets. A closet door hung open on the far side of the bed. Two windows were framed in the wall, but they were closed like all the others.

Pike listened, but the girl was at it again, telling Flynn to go get the bastard, saying he and his bitch were going to Vegas.

Pike wanted to get back to the living room, but kept his eyes on the closet. He moved quickly and silently the way he had in the woods as a boy, hiding from his father. Silence was everything. Speed was life. He dropped to a knee, then jerked the tumbled sheets up and glanced under the bed. Nothing. He looked back to the closet.

Pike didn't believe anyone would be in the closet, but he had to check. The girl was louder and even more insistent, and Pike wanted to give Flynn a hand.

The closet door was open about six inches. The bedroom was lit but inside the closet was dark and impenetrable. Pike stood as far to the side as possible, then jerked open the door, letting light flood the dark space behind. Nothing.

They had been in the apartment for less than two minutes.

In the moment Pike saw the closet was empty, a loud crash came from the living room, riding on top of the thuds of men moving hard as a voice grunted—

"Kill'm."

Pike moved fast across the bed, into the hall, then into the doorway. The closet door off the entry had been thrown open. Candace Stanik's boyfriend, who would later be identified as one David Lee Elish, had one arm hooked around Flynn's neck and was holding Flynn's gun arm to prevent Flynn from drawing his weapon. A second man, who would later be identified as Kurt Fabrocini, a parolee who had been released from custody earlier that day, was stabbing Flynn repeatedly in the chest with a Buck hunting knife. Candace Stanik was curled on the floor. Later, it would be learned that both Elish and Fabrocini had enough alcohol and crack cocaine in their systems to numb an elephant.

Over and over, Elish was grunting, "Kill'm."

Pike brought his 9mm up without hesitation and shot Fabrocini in the head. Pike would have shot Elish, too, but the angle was bad. Pike was moving before Fabrocini's body hit the floor.

Pike drove hard directly into Flynn, knocking both men to the floor. Pike knew exactly what he had to do and how. He kept driving, digging hard with his legs. He shoved past Flynn and hit Elish hard in the face with his pistol. Elish, trying to rise, had eyes that were wild and frenzied. Pike hit him a second time, and then Elish grew still. Pike turned him over, pinned him to the floor with a knee, and twisted Elish's arms behind his back for the handcuffs.

Only after Elish and the knife were secure did Pike turn back to Flynn, scared the man was bleeding to death.

Pike said, "Officer Flynn—"

Flynn looked up, fingers laced through the tears in

his shirt, his eyes wide and glistening, and his face white.

"Fucking vest. Fucking vest stopped the knife."

Pike thought Flynn was laughing, but then he saw the tears.

Three hours later, they were released to leave. A shooting team had come out, along with the evening shift commander, two Rampart captains, and two use-of-force detectives from Parker Center. Pike and Flynn had been separated for questioning, but now they were back in their car.

Flynn was behind the wheel. He had started the engine, but hadn't taken it out of park. Pike knew Flynn was shaken, but he figured it was up to Flynn whether or not he wanted to talk about it. After all, Pike was only a boot.

Flynn finally looked over, moving his head as if it weighed a thousand pounds.

"You okay?"

"Yes, sir."

Flynn fell silent again, but now he seemed to be considering Pike in a way that left Pike feeling uncomfortable.

"Listen, I want to go over what happened in there— you saved me. Thank you for that."

"You don't have to thank me."

"I know, but there it is. I want you to know I appreciate what you did. You saw those two guys on me, you saw the knife, you made a fast call. I'm not saying you did anything wrong. I just want you to think about what you did. Sometimes we have to kill people, but our job out here isn't to kill people."

"Yes, sir. I know that."

"What happened in there was my fault, not clearing that closet. I saw that damned door."

"We were clearing the apartment when it happened. No one's fault."

"You're a boot. Your first day on the job, and you sure as hell saved my butt."

Flynn was still watching him, but his eyes had narrowed as if he was trying to make out something vague and far away, and Pike wondered what.

Flynn suddenly reached out and covered Pike's hand.

"You're calm as a stone. Me, I'm shaking like a leaf—"

Pike felt it in Bud Flynn's hand—a faint humming like bees trying to escape a hive.

Bud suddenly pulled back his hand as if he had read Pike's thoughts and was embarrassed. Officer-involved shootings were rare, but gunfights had been part of Pike's life since he left home, and home, in those rare moments when he thought about it, had been worse— his father's rage; fists and belts and steel-toed work boots falling like rain in a strangely painless way; his mother, screaming; Pike, screaming. Combat was nothing. Pike remembered a kind of intellectual acceptance that he had to kill other men so they couldn't kill him. Like when he finally grew big enough to choke out his father. Once his father feared him, his father stopped beating him and his mother. Simple. Pike's only concerns now were in following the rules of the Los Angeles Police Department. He had. He had made a clean shoot. Bud was alive. Pike was alive. Simple.

Pike touched Bud's hand. He wanted to help.

Pike said, "We're okay."

Bud wiped at his face, but his eyes still fluttered, and returned to Pike again and again.

"I'm looking at you, and it's like nothing happened. You just killed a man, and there's nothing in your eyes."

Pike felt embarrassed and drew back.

Flynn suddenly seemed embarrassed, too, and ashamed of himself, as if he realized he was talking nonsense. He forced out a laugh.

"You ready to go? We got a hellacious amount of paperwork. That's the worst part about shooting someone, you have all these damned forms."

Pike took out his sunglasses and put them on, covering his eyes.

Flynn laughed again, louder, showing even more strain.

"It's pitch-black. You going to wear those things at night?"

"Yes."

"Well, whatever. That business with you calling me Officer Flynn and me calling you Officer Pike? We're past that. My name is Bud."

Pike nodded, but Bud was still trembling and the phony smile made him look pained.

Pike wished none of it had happened. He wished they had not taken the call, and their day hadn't ended this way. He felt sick, thinking he had disappointed his training officer. He vowed to try harder. He wanted to be a good and right man, and he wanted to serve and protect.

12

PIKE was driving hard toward Glendale and the LAPD's Scientific Investigation Division when his cell phone buzzed. He glanced at the number and saw it was Ronnie.

"Go."

"They hit your store fourteen minutes ago. Those boys are willing to work in broad daylight. They want you, m'man."

Larkin, beside him, said, "Who is it?"

Pike held up his finger, telling her to wait.

"Did the security guys roll?"

"Code three, lights and sirens, and they called in LAPD. Denny and I are rolling over right now. You wanted a full-on response, you got a full-on response."

"File a report with the police. If we have any physical damage, have an insurance adjuster come out. If anything needs to be repaired, call out the repairmen today."

"I get it. You want noise."

"Loud."

Pike put down the phone, and Larkin punched him in the arm.

"I hate how you just ignore me. I asked you a question, you just show me your finger."

She showed Pike a finger, but it wasn't her index finger.

Pike said, "We're going to see someone in Glendale, then we're going to meet Elvis where you had your accident—"

"Why can't we just go back to the house?"

"Someone is trying to kill you."

"Why can't we just hide?"

"Someone might find you."

"You have an answer for everything."

"Yes."

She punched him in the arm again, but this time Pike ignored her. He watched her out of the corner of his eye as she slumped back in the seat, sullen.

Pike was glad for the silence. They climbed up through the Sepulveda Pass, then down into the San Fernando Valley. The valley was always much hotter, and Pike could feel the increasing heat even with the air-conditioning. He watched the outside air temperature rise on the dashboard thermometer. From Cheviot Hills to Van Nuys, they gained fifteen degrees.

Larkin was quiet for exactly nine minutes.

Then she said, "Would you like to watch me masturbate?"

Pike didn't look at her or respond, though he wondered why she would ask such a thing. She had probably wanted to shock him. Shocking statements probably worked with some people, but Pike wasn't one of them. Shock was relative.

"I could do it right here in the car. While you're driving. Would you like that?"

She slid her hands down over her belly to where her legs met. When she spoke, her voice was a whisper.

"I'll ask your friend. I bet he'd like to watch."

Pike glanced at her, then continued driving.

"Day I got to Central Africa, I watched a woman. Her family had been murdered that morning, just two hours before we rolled in. She cut the fingers off her left hand, one by one, one each for her husband and her four children. She started with the thumb."

Pike glanced over again.

"That was how she mourned."

Larkin folded her hands in her lap. She stared at him, then turned to the window. The silence was good.

They drove through the valley heat.

13

John Chen's Secret Mission

DESPERATION bred innovation, and John Chen was a desperate man. That same desperation also bred lies, deception, and masterful acting, all of which John had employed with convincing brilliance because—well, face it—he was the smartest senior criminalist employed by LAPD's Scientific Investigation Division. In the past few years, John had broken more cases (necessary for career advancement [read that: money]), amassed more face time on the local news (mandatory for hitting on chicks [read that: At six-two, one twenty-seven, and with an Adam's apple the size of a goiter, he needed all the help he could get]), and garnered more merit pay raises (essential for leasing a Porsche [read that: This isn't a gearshift, baby, I'm just happy to see you]) than any other rat in the lab. And how had he been rewarded for putting SID on the map and ascending to criminalist stardom?

More work.

A larger caseload.

Less time to enjoy the fruits of his labors.

Namely, poontang.

John Chen was all about the 'tang. He was the first to admit it, and did, often, to anyone who would listen, including the young women of his acquaintance, which probably explained why he couldn't get a date. He was a man obsessed when it came to the 'tang; hungry to make up the poontang shortfall which had been his lifelong burden; convinced, as he was, that every single straight male in California had enjoyed a veritable all-you-can-eat smorgasbord of the stuff since puberty. Except him.

But now was the payoff.

John Chen had scored a girlfriend. Well, okay, she wasn't *really* his girlfriend. He knew that; he wasn't kidding himself. Ronda Milbank was a married secretary with two kids from Highland Park who liked to drink. Every couple of weeks she told her husband she was going to a movie with the girls, but what she really did was hit a few bars hoping somebody would buy her a drink. John Chen had delivered the goods. *Hey, princess, what are you drinking?* Gimlets. She liked the sugar.

Well, he hadn't really said that; he had been too scared. But he sat next to her, and after a while Ronda spoke to him. A couple of weeks later, he saw her again at the same bar. That was last night. He bought her a drink, and then another, and then—after having three or four drinks himself—he asked if maybe he could, you know, kinda see her sometime. And Ronda said, sure, tomorrow between eleven and noon—my husband will be at work and my kids will be at school.

SCORE!!!!

But then came the problem. As Jack Webb said: This is the city—Los Angeles. Four hundred sixty-five square miles; millions of civilians; untold criminals, all of whom were out doing crime; nine thousand of the world's finest police officers, all of whom were out busting said miscreants; *hundreds* of crime scenes, more every day, more every *hour* of every day; an unending tsunami of crime scenes and evidence; each and every item of which had to be preserved, documented, recorded, tested, and analyzed by LAPD's understaffed, underfunded, overworked, but world-class—

Scientific Investigation Division.

So John knew the answer even without asking. I mean, *what*? "Oh, sure, John, you need a 'tang break midway through the morning, be my guest." Yeah, like *that* could outlast a snowball in hell.

Here's how John Chen orchestrated his departure: That morning, he secured a small bit of dental enamel from a comparison kit, then waited for the height of the mid-morning coffee break when lab techs, scientists, or criminalists (who were all too overworked to leave their workstations) wolfed down muffins and Cheetos between sperm samples and bloodstains. At exactly fifteen minutes after ten, John made a point of walking past his supervisor just as he took a bite of his Ralphs Market raspberry-swirl muffin, and screamed—

"AHHHHHH!!!"

John jumped sideways, grabbing his jaw as he spun in a circle, not stopping until he saw that everyone in the crime lab was looking.

Then he opened his hand to show the enamel, and shouted—

"SONOFABITCH!!! I BROKE MY TOOTH! I GOTTA SEE MY DENTIST!"

Harriet eyeballed the enamel.

"It doesn't look very big. Maybe you just chipped it."

"JESUS CHRIST, HARRIET! IT'S KILLING ME. THE NERVE IS EXPOSED!"

Harriet said, "Here. Let me see."

John covered his mouth, backing away.

"I NEED ICE! I NEED ASPIRIN! I GOTTA SEE MY DENTIST!"

John noted that Harriet had already frowned at the clock. She would let him die rather than fall further behind their caseload.

"John, please. I've broken teeth. The pain will fade. In a few minutes you won't even feel it."

You see how she was?

"It's a broken tooth, Harriet—shattered, ruined! I gotta see a dentist."

"Why don't you call first? Maybe he can't see you until later."

"He's my cousin! Look, the sooner I get there, the sooner I'll be back. I'll call him on the way. If I leave right now, I'll probably be back by one-thirty or so."

Having cleared out before the husband and kids showed up.

Harriet scowled at the clock again, but finally relented.

"All right, but don't take your personal car. Take a van. I might send you straight to a crime scene from the dentist."

Chen thinking, fat fucking chance.

He grabbed a cup of ice to make his story look bet-

ter, then snatched his keys and evidence kit and ran for
the exit. He stopped at the door long enough to make
sure no one was following him, then tossed the ice. No
way was he gonna tool up to Ronda's house in a clunky
SID van. He washed the Boxster before work so that
Black Forest 'tang-magnet *gleamed*! He intended to roll
up to Ronda's in style!

Chen had just reached the first line of parked cars
when he saw Harriet watching from the door. Sonofa-
BITCH—

The vans were parked together on that same row, so
John veered toward them. He stopped at the first van,
grabbed his jaw as if the pain was excruciating, then
waved at Harriet. She didn't wave back. He made his way
down the line of vans, watching her from the corner of his
eye. That bitch was anchored in place. He found the van
he normally used, ran behind it to hide, then counted to
one hundred. When he peered out, Harriet was finally
gone, and John Chen punched the air. All his hard work,
sacrifice, and local news face time was about to pay off.
The burden of his geekiness was about to be lifted. John
Chen—Master Criminalist—was going to get laid.

Chen turned to run for his car when—

—someone who hadn't been there a moment ago
blocked his path.

Chen startled so bad he screamed again, but this
time he meant it—

"AHHH!"

—and lurched backwards, falling, until hands as
hard as vise grips caught him and held.

Joe Pike quietly said, "Take it easy, John. You'll hurt
yourself."

Chen hated it when Pike did that—appearing from nowhere as if the freaky psycho had stepped through a hole in the smog. Only an asshole did stuff like that, sneaking up and scaring people, and Chen had been afraid of Pike since they first met. Chen had taken one look at the guy and known Pike was one of those vicious, double-Y chromosome, beer-commercial slope-brows who loved showing up other people. True, Pike had also given him the tips that led to Chen's first breakthrough case and the acquisition of the 'tangmobile, but Pike still made him nervous.

Chen said, "You scared the shit out of me. Where'd you come from?"

Pike tipped his head toward a green Lexus parked in the next row.

Chen immediately stood taller. A smokin' hot babe with spiky black hair and the nastiest lips Chen ever saw was in the front seat. She gave him a little wave, and Chen damn near popped in his pants. That bitch totally vibed SEX FREAK.

Chen said, "Man, that chick is hot. Does she put out?"

"I need a favor, John."

Chen remembered Ronda and his one-hour window of opportunity. He started to edge away.

"Sure, yeah, but I gotta get going. I have an appointment—"

"It can't wait."

Chen froze in his tracks, certain that Pike would beat him to death if he took another step. The best Chen could muster was a meek little squeak.

"But—"

Pike said, "Big case, John. You could make the papers again."

Ronda vanished like a popping bubble, and suddenly Chen didn't feel so tiny. Pike and his partner, Cole, had come through before, and John had the car to show for it. Another headline case, and he might even be able to quit working for the city. Spear a gig with a private lab and earn some lifestyle cash. Might even bag the Holy Grail of anyone involved in L.A. law enforcement: He might land a job as the technical advisor for a TV series! Move up to a Carrera.

He studied the girl again.

"I know I've seen that girl. She do porno?"

Pike fingered John's chin away from the girl so they were eye-to-eye. Prick.

Pike said, "You know about the two men who were shot in Malibu?"

"That's the Sheriff's. Their lab handles all that."

"The three men who were killed in Eagle Rock?"

Chen wondered where Pike was going with this.

"Yeah, sure. We got that one, but it isn't mine. What do you want?"

"The identities of the dead men."

Chen was relieved, and almost at once thought about Ronda again. He thought Pike might want something difficult.

"No worries. I'll call the coroner investigator this afternoon. He'll know."

"No, John, he won't. Live Scan came back empty. None of the five were in the system."

"So the detectives probably recovered—"

"No identifying information was found on the bodies."

Chen saw his miraculous breakthrough evaporating. "Then what can I do?"

"Run their guns, John. Run the casings."

Chen knew what Pike was asking and didn't like it. The police and the criminalists covering both crime scenes would have recovered any weapons and spent shell casings found with the bodies. Those weapons would have serial numbers and identifying characteristics that might or might not lead back to their owners, but running the guns was almost impossible. SID employed only two firearms analysis specialists, and the backlog of guns waiting to be analyzed numbered in the thousands. The workload was so horrendous that trials often began before the results were in. Judges actually issued court orders demanding that wait-listed guns be jumped ahead in the line.

The elation Chen felt dimmed.

"I dunno, dude, that backlog is brutal."

"You came through before."

"Yeah, but running a gun doesn't mean you'll come up with a name. Most guns like this were stolen or bought off the street."

"One more thing—"

Pike gave him a date.

"An automobile accident occurred that night. LAPD towed the vehicle the next day, a silver Mercedes owned by a man named George King. They kept it for twenty-four hours, during which they examined the vehicle. I want to know what they found."

Chen thought back but couldn't remember the night or the car or anyone mentioning the car.

"Was a crime committed in the vehicle?"

"It was involved in a traffic accident."

"They had some of our guys examine a traffic collision?"

"I want to know what they found. Call Elvis when you know. I won't be around."

Chen eyed the girl again and figured he knew exactly where Pike would be.

Chen said, "What's in this for me?"

"The bullets from the Malibu bodies will match the bullets from Eagle Rock. Same shooter, John. L.A. and the Sheriff's have not yet made the connection. Neither has the press."

John Chen stared.

"Are you sure?"

Pike's mouth twitched.

Chen's heart began pounding. John had not worked the Eagle Rock killings, but he had been in the lab when the evidence arrived. The criminalist who worked Eagle Rock had not mentioned a connection between the two shootings. With the bullets in two different labs, unless the police had some other connecting evidence, it might take months or even years to connect the two shootings. They might *never* be connected—until and unless a superstar criminalist made a miraculous breakthrough.

Chen said, "What about the gun? Is the weapon one of the guns we have?"

"You might dig around about that, too. Compare the number of weapons logged into evidence with the weapons you have. See if the numbers add up."

John Chen's heart was pounding so hard his ears hurt. Pike was implying some sort of conspiracy and possibly a cover-up. Forget the local news losers—if Chen played his cards right, he might end up on the national news. Maybe even *60 Minutes*! All thoughts of Ronda were gone.

Pike drifted away toward the Lexus.

"Check it out, John. Call Elvis."

Pike slipped into the car like he was made of hot butter, then drove away. Chen stared after them, watching the girl, certain she would go down on the lucky bastard before they reached the exit.

Chen turned back to the lab, scowling. After the way he carried on about seeing a dentist, Harriet would wonder why he never left the parking lot. But then Chen realized she had already given him an out—she had told him the pain would pass, and he would tell her it had. Everyone liked being told they were right, and he would also earn points by selflessly returning to work so they wouldn't fall further behind!

John Chen was not the world's smartest criminalist for nothing.

John ran back to the lab, and immediately went to work.

Ronda would get over it.

14

LOSING TIME was like losing blood, and Pike felt the seconds draining away. Pike knew the girl was uneasy about returning to her neighborhood. This was where her nightmare began. The accident. The Kings. Alexander Meesh. But this was exactly why she had to return. Animals left trails where they passed, and so did men. Since Meesh and the Kings had been at this place, they might have left a trail. Pike intended to drop off the girl with Cole, then head for home. The man or men who entered his home had left a trail, too, and Pike already knew where to find it.

The drive south from Glendale was tedious with the heavy afternoon traffic, and ugly with the power cables and train yards that bordered the river. It was a dirty, grey part of Los Angeles that never seemed clean, even after the rains, and when they finally crossed back to the west side, the area in which Larkin lived wasn't much better. The streets were lined with warehouses waiting to be brought up to earthquake standards or razed, and other buildings housing storage units or sweatshops where minimum-wage immigrants built cabinetry and decorative metalwork. Everything about the area was industrial.

Cole was waiting on the block where the accident occurred, only three blocks from the girl's building. His yellow Corvette was parked on the opposite side of the street, but Cole was standing in a nearby doorway, out of the sun.

When Larkin saw him, she said, "What's he doing here?"

"Working. He came down earlier to establish the scene at the time of the accident."

"I don't think it's safe. What if they're waiting for me?"

"Elvis would wave us away."

"How does *he* know?"

Pike didn't bother answering. He was already missing the silence.

The curbs were lined with cars, but Pike found a spot to park half a block past the alley. Cole waited for an eighteen-wheel van to pass, then crossed the street to join them. Cole was wearing olive green cargo shorts, a floral short-sleeved shirt, and a faded Dodgers cap. Pike thought he was moving a little more easily today.

Cole grinned at the girl.

"Nice neighborhood. Reminds me of Fallujah."

"Nice clothes. Reminds me of a twelve-year-old."

Cole turned the grin toward Pike.

"I love it when she talks that way."

They were at the exact spot where the girl plowed into the Mercedes. A thin alley opened onto the street. It was a dirty fissure between two dingy warehouses.

Dozens of shirtless men and chunky women wearing straw hats milled around outside the alley, ordering up orange sodas and bottles of water from a catering van at the curb. Pike scanned the rooflines and windows, then turned back to Cole. He wanted to roll on, but he also wanted Cole's report.

Pike said, "Okay."

"Nada. I talked to every business for two blocks in each direction. Everything closes at six o'clock, and none of these people carry a night watchman except for a shipping company down there—"

Cole tipped his head toward the block behind them.

"See the fence with the concertina wire? They use a night guy, but he didn't see anything. Says he didn't even know an accident happened until the feds came around."

Pike raised his eyebrows at that, and Cole nodded.

"Yeah. Your feds have been grinding this thing. I asked about security cams, too, thinking we might luck into a street angle off one of these parking lots, but that was another goose egg. Couple of inside cameras, but nobody runs a camera showing the street."

The girl said, "You just knocked on their doors and asked?"

"Sure. That's what investigators do."

"Dressed like *that*?"

"Amazing, isn't it?"

Pike said, "Did you get the accident report?"

"Yeah—"

Cole pulled folded papers from his cargo shorts and used them to point at the street.

"The accident occurred here at the mouth of the

alley. Ms. Barkley was proceeding up the street toward us—"

Cole pointed in the opposite direction.

"—heading for home, which is three blocks farther down."

Cole glanced at Larkin—

"Nice building, by the way. Nicely done."

—then opened the papers to show a sketch drawn by the accident investigator on the night of the accident. A rectangle showed the position of Larkin's car, along with lines illustrating the relevant skid marks, and measurements. Pike had drawn several such sketches during his boot year as a patrol officer. One set of skids was labeled ASTON MARTIN. A shorter set was labeled UNKNOWN.

Larkin moved closer to see.

"What is this?"

"I had a friend sneak me a copy of the accident report. I wanted to see what happened."

"I told you what happened."

"I know, but I wanted to see the report. Accident like this, the officers list witnesses."

Pike said, "They find someone?"

"That would be way too easy. No one was found at the scene except Ms. Barkley."

Cole turned back toward the alley and went on with his report.

"The alley continues through to the next street. The building here on the right is abandoned. Doors on the front, back, and sides are chained, and you can tell from the dust and rust they haven't been opened in years. The other building here is set up as a factory. They make ceramic knickknacks and souvenirs. Considering that one building is empty and the other is filled with replicas of the Hollywood Bowl, it's a pretty good bet the Kings weren't down here for a sex party."

Larkin said, "I told you. They were backing out."

Cole raised his eyebrows at her.

"Yeah, but why here and why then? We know why you were here. You were going home. Why were they here?"

The girl said, "I don't know."

"That was rhetorical."

Pike studied the position of the cars in the sketch, and pictured the girl's Aston Martin sideways in the street. She had slammed into the Mercedes on the driver's side behind the rear wheel as it backed into the street. The force of the impact kicked the Mercedes a quarter turn counterclockwise, and her car had spun to a rest, pointing toward the Mercedes, one headlight smashed but the other illuminating the scene. The police sketch matched everything the girl had described. She had gotten out of her car to help, then returned to her car for her phone. The Kings drove away. Meesh left the scene on foot.

Pike said, "Which way did Meesh go?"

The girl stepped between them as if something was waiting for her and pointed up the street.

"That way. He ran up the middle of the street. The Mercedes went the other way."

Cole stepped into the street for a better look.

"Did you see him turn off?"

"I wasn't looking."

"That time of night, all these cars would be gone, and it's pretty well lit. Maybe he ducked into a building."

"I don't know. I had 911 on the phone. The Mercedes was gone. I was writing their license number on my arm and talking to the 911."

Cole shrugged at Pike.

"There's nothing down here, man. I walked eight blocks in each direction, all the way to the bridges. Two blocks east is the river, but I covered those streets, too, then three blocks to the west. The people I talked to say this area is abandoned, that time of night. There aren't any gas stations—I couldn't even find a pay phone. It's nothing but commercial space and construction sites except for three or four loft conversions like Larkin's. I'll talk to them."

Pike grunted, ready to let Cole get on with it. Pike wanted to keep moving, but something Cole said was bothering him.

. . . That time of night, all these cars would be gone, and it's pretty well lit . . .

Pike looked back at the crowd of workers and the catering van, then at the cars lining both sides of the street. He opened the accident report again and studied the skid marks.

"Was the Mercedes backing out when you hit it or was it stopped?"

The girl shook her head.

"I don't know."

Cole frowned at her because now he was thinking about it, too.

"You told the police they backed out."

"I don't know what I told the police. I can't even remember talking to them. Why does it matter?"

Cole said, "If they were parked, then what were they

doing? Were they looking at something or someone in the alley? Had they just gotten into the car or were they getting out? You see how one thing leads to another?"

Pike glanced back at the street and realized what was bothering him. It didn't have anything to do with why or why not Meesh and the Kings were here.

He said, "With the street empty, your sight line was clear. You hit them, which means they were in front of you. Seems like you would have seen them."

Larkin widened her stance, revealing a tension in her shoulders.

"I'm not lying."

The skid marks bore out her version of the accident, but Pike wondered why she hadn't been able to avoid the collision. He thought she had probably been drunk or high, so he flipped to that page in the report. Nope. The tests had come back clean.

"Not saying that. Just trying to figure it out."

"Well, it sounds like you're accusing me. I can't help I didn't see them. Maybe they backed out really fast. Maybe I was looking at the radio. How much longer are we going to stay here? I'm scared and I don't like it."

Pike glanced at Cole and Cole shrugged.

"I have everything I need from here to go forward. I can take her back."

Larkin squinted at Cole, still tense with irritation.

"Was there something here I missed?"

Pike said, "He's taking you back to the house. He'll stay with you until I get back."

Pike started back to the Lexus, but the girl followed him.

"And when was all this decided?"

Pike didn't answer. He didn't see why it was necessary.

"You can't come with me. You'll be safer at the house."

"I don't want to stay with him. He'll rape me as soon as you're gone."

Cole said, "In your dreams."

She ignored him, staying with Pike.

"Listen to me, you—you're being paid to protect me. You're working for *me*. My father won't like you dumping me off with the B-team."

Cole spread his arms.

"B-team?"

Pike got into the Lexus, but Larkin stepped inside the door so he couldn't close it. Her face seemed as brittle as a ceramic mask, and Pike suddenly remembered how she had looked up in the desert when she was unloading on her father. Only now she didn't seem so much angry as betrayed.

Pike gentled his voice.

"I'm sorry if I should have discussed it with you. I didn't think it would be an issue."

She stood in the door, breathing.

"You can't come with me, Larkin. I'll see you this evening."

Pike tugged at the door, nudging her. Time was still passing. It ran up his back with cleated boots, and here was this girl, blocking the door. Pike made his voice harder.

"Step away from the car."

She didn't move.

His voice hardened more.

"Step away."

Cole said, "You want me to knock her out?"

The girl stepped back, uttering a final word as Pike pulled the door.

"Asshole."

Pike drove away without looking back, heading for Culver City.

15

ONCE PIKE was alone, he felt the way you might feel when you float in a pool on a windless day, the sun hot on your skin, the sky overhead clean. He did not fear what he would find or think much about it. The men who set off his alarm would either be waiting for him or not, and you had to take such things as they came.

Twenty-five minutes later, Pike stopped under a sycamore tree on a residential street six blocks from his condo. Two girls and a boy scorched past on bikes. Three houses away, two older boys traded fastballs. A white dog bounced between them, barking when the ball flew overhead.

Pike got out of the car, took off the long-sleeved shirt, then went to the trunk. He looked through the things Ronnie had left. He drank half a bottle of Arrowhead water, then collected his SOG fighting knife, a pair of Zeiss binoculars, the little .25-caliber Beretta, and a box of hollowpoints for the .45. He wouldn't need anything else.

Pike got back into his car, then drove to a Mobil station located on the other side of the wall outside his complex. He parked behind the station next to the wall. Pike bought gas there often and knew the staff, so they didn't mind. Before he left his car, he fitted the .25 to his right ankle and the SOG to his left. He made sure the Kimber was loaded, then clipped it behind his back.

Pike went to the office and waved at the man behind the counter.

"I have to leave my car here for a while. That okay?"

"Whatever, bro. Long as you want."

Pike moved quickly. He dropped into the condo grounds behind a flat building that faced an enormous communal swimming pool. A lush curtain of banana trees, birds-of-paradise, and canna plants hid a sound wall baffling the pool equipment, and continued around the pool and walkways. Pike slipped behind the greenery and made his way across the grounds.

People were still out and about, but Pike moved easily, twice covering almost two hundred yards to avoid an opening thirty feet wide. Pike didn't mind. He enjoyed the freedom of not being seen.

Pike worked his way from pod to pod, around three parking areas, and finally to his condo. He did not approach his door, or try to enter. He took a position behind the rice paper plants at the corner of his building, and settled down to watch. It was a good spot with a clean view of the parking lot and the buildings that faced his own. If they were waiting, they would be inside his condo or positioned with a view of his door. It wouldn't make sense for them to be anywhere else.

Pike studied the cars in the parking lot, and the curtains on the far windows, and the wall of plants that was exactly like the wall of plants in which he was hidden. Pike never moved, and for the first time that day did not feel the passing of time. He simply *was*; safe in his green world, watching. He watched until he knew the shadows between the branches and how the lowering light dappled through the leaves, and which residents were home across the way and which were not. Two hours later, Pike was finally satisfied no one was hiding, but he still didn't move. If someone was waiting for him, they were inside his home.

Pike watched the world grow golden, then burnish to a deep copper, then deepen with purple into a murky haze. Cars came and left. People banged through their gates, some wearing flip-flops on their way to the pool. Pike watched until it was full-on dark and his world behind the green was black, and then he finally moved, rising with the slowness of melting ice. He crept along the side of his condo, checking each window as he reached it, and found that the second window had been jimmied. Raising the window had tripped Pike's alarm.

Pike peered inside but saw only shadows. Nothing moved, and no sounds came from within. He removed the screen in slow motion, then slowly raised the window and lifted himself inside.

The room was dark, but the doorway opening into his living room was bright. Pike had left on the lamp. He drew the Kimber and crept into the living room, moving with absolute silence. No one sat on his couch or on the Eames chair in which Pike read. The only movement came from the fountain in the corner—a bowl with water burbling quietly over stones. Pike listened beyond the water, straining to feel the sense of the space, but the only sounds were the water and the whisper of the air conditioner.

Pike found no one. They had tried to be careful so Pike wouldn't know, but an address book was missing from the kitchen, and the phone in his bedroom was in a place Pike never left it. The clothes in his closet were not in their usual positions.

Pike returned to the living room. His television sat in an entertainment center opposite the fountain, along with a CD player, a TiVo, and other electronics. A security camera Pike had installed himself fed into a hard drive stacked among the equipment. Pike turned on his television, then watched the recording. Single-frame captures taken in his living room had been made at eight-second intervals, so the pictures appeared as a jerky slide show. A man with a pistol entered from the same room through which Pike had entered. He wasn't wearing a mask or gloves or face-black; just a dark T-shirt and jeans and running shoes. His hair was longish, and straight, and dark. He was Anglo or Latino, but Pike couldn't tell which. The pictures showed his path in sharp jumps—first as he entered, then across the room, then at the stairs. A man could cover a lot of ground in eight seconds. Then the man was at the front door, and now a second man entered. This man was smaller than the first man, and wore a dark shirt with the tail out over jeans. His hair was also longish and dark, but his skin was darker, and Pike decided this man was Latino.

In the next picture, the first man had returned to the kitchen, and the second man was kneeling at the door. A small black case was on the floor, and the second man seemed to be holding the doorknob with both hands. The pictures progressed, and Pike realized the second man was making keys. The first man returned from searching the house as the keymaker tested the keys.

Pike froze the picture. It was the best view yet of the first man, showing a three-quarter shot of his face. Pike took out the pictures Bud had given him, and compared them. The keymaker wasn't among them, but the first man was one of the three men who invaded Larkin's home. He wasn't the man who beat the housekeeper, but he was present.

Pike backed up the images until he found the best angle on the keymaker, pressed a button, and a laser printer in the entertainment center hummed. Pike tucked the new pictures away.

The remaining security captures showed the two men leaving.

Pike turned off the television. He stood in his empty home, listening to the fountain. It was the good sound of a stream in the deep woods, natural and comforting.

Pike powered up his cell phone and called Ronnie. Ronnie said, "Yo."

"I need you and Dennis on the house. Two men, twenties to thirties, dark hair straight and on the long side, five-eight to five-ten. The shorter guy is probably Latino."

"They at your place now?"

"No, but they'll be back. They made keys."

"Ah. You want'm field dressed?"

"Just let me know."

Pike reset the alarms, reset the surveillance camera, then went to his fridge. He opened two bottles of Corona, poured the beer down the sink, then placed the empty bottles on the counter. The counter had been clean when the men were here, but now the bottles stood out like tall ships on the horizon. When the men returned, they would see that Pike had been home. They would tell themselves if he came home once, he would come home again, and they might decide to wait.

Pike wanted them to wait.

16

Elvis Cole

LARKIN CONNER BARKLEY wouldn't talk to him. Cole asked about the property owners and tenants near her loft, but he might as well have spoken in a foreign language. Her lips pulled into a pensive bud, and she stared down the street as if Pike's car had been a shimmering mirage.

"I can't believe he left me like this. He *dismissed* me."

Cole said, "The nerve of him. That cad."

"Fuck you."

"That's the second time you've hinted at sex, but I still have to refuse."

Larkin crossed the street without waiting for him and went directly to Cole's car. Some people didn't appreciate humor.

Cole decided to give her some space, so they drove back in silence. He couldn't blame her for being tired of answering questions and talking about the same things over and over, and he didn't want to get down on her for showing the strain. He still had questions, but the answers would keep until later.

On the way back to Echo Park, he stopped at a small grocery store in Thai Town, figuring the odds were better she wouldn't be recognized at a small ethnic market. He expected her to give him an argument when he asked her to come in with him, but she didn't. She seemed calmer by then. She quietly inspected the strange labels and odd packages while he filled two bags with food, milk, a kid's drawing pad, a plastic ruler, and two bottles of plum wine. The only time she spoke was when she saw the wine.

"I don't drink."

"You can watch me. You want anything special? Fruit? Some kind of dessert?"

"I don't want anything."

She said nothing else. Her slack expression returned, and Cole felt even worse for her. Back in the car, he dug around in the glove box for his iPod and dropped it in her lap.

"You know how it works?"

"He won't let me have it."

"He'll let you have this one."

Larkin held it, but made no attempt to listen.

When they got back to the house, she took a bath. She didn't tell him she was going to take a bath or anything else; she disappeared into the bathroom and soon the water was running. Cole put away the groceries, then brought the pad and his notes to the table. His notes completely filled the backs of each page of the accident report, and described in detail every building and business in Larkin Barkley's neighborhood. Cole set to work drawing a map, building it block by block, one block per page. He divided each block into boxes to represent buildings and labeled each building with its address. He listed the names of the businesses as well as their phone numbers and any other notes he had made.

He was finishing the first map when he grew worried. The water had stopped. It had stopped running a long time ago, but Larkin was still in the bathroom.

Cole went to the door and knocked.

"You okay?"

She didn't answer.

Cole tried the knob, but the door was locked. He knocked again. Harder.

"Larkin?"

"I'm soaking."

At least she wasn't killing herself.

Cole returned to the table and went back to work. The tub glugged as it drained, and water ran again, but he let her soak. If she wanted to look like a prune, that was up to her. After a while, she emerged from the bathroom wrapped in a towel, went into her bedroom, and closed the door. Cole completed his map of her street, then set to work charting the surrounding streets. He was convinced that Meesh and the Kings had been in the area for a purpose. They had been going to or coming from a target destination, and that target was likely one of the buildings or businesses on his map. Cole was also convinced the feds believed the same; twelve of the sixteen people Cole interviewed had also been questioned by agents of the U.S. Department of Justice. Pitman, Blanchette, and at least two other agents had questioned them about the accident, the Kings, and Meesh.

Cole thought nothing of it until he went through his notes to build a timeline of events. Then he discovered a discrepancy.

Cole worked steadily for almost an hour before Larkin came out of the bedroom. She came out wearing fresh five-hundred-dollar jeans, a tight black Ramones T-shirt, and the iPod. She looked fresh and clean without makeup or jewelry, and her feet were bare. She stretched out on the couch with her feet hanging over the arm, closed her eyes, and rocked to the iPod, her right foot moving with the beat.

Cole said, "Hey."

Her eyes opened and she looked at him.

Cole said, "The feds didn't know Meesh was Meesh until you identified him?"

"No."

"That's what they told you?"

"Yeah. They got all excited when we finally had his name."

Cole returned to his timeline, but didn't really work after that. The twelve people who had been questioned by the feds had all been questioned the day after the accident. The very next day. All twelve stated the feds had shown them pictures of two men, and all twelve had described the same two pictures. It was as if Pitman knew or suspected Meesh was the missing man even before he met with the girl, and had lied about what he knew.

Twenty minutes later, Cole saw movement and glanced up. Larkin rolled off the couch, went to the win-

dow, and peered out at the street. The day was dimming, and soon they would have to pull the shades.

Cole said, "If you're getting hungry I'll make dinner.
I just want to finish this."

She didn't hear him. She was looking up the street,
then shifted position to look in the opposite direction.

Cole wadded up a piece of paper and bounced it off
her back. When she turned, Cole touched his ear, telling
her to take off the headset.

She said, "Did you say something?"

"If you're hungry I'll make dinner."

"Shouldn't we wait for him?"

Him.

"He might be late."

"I'm okay."

She went back to the couch and resumed her position, only now her foot didn't move. Cole went on with
his work.

"Was he really in Africa?"

Cole glanced up. She was still stretched out on the
couch with her feet up, but now she was looking at him.
Cole was surprised Pike told her about Africa. Pike
never mentioned those days, and had rarely spoken of
them even back when he was making the trips. Way it
had been, Pike would say something like, I'll be gone for
a while. Cole would say okay, and a few days later Pike
would vanish. Couple of weeks after that, Pike would
call, say something like, Everything okay? Cole would
say, Sure, everything's fine, and Pike would say, I'm back
if you need me.

Larkin misread Cole's silence and made a cynical
laugh.

"I thought so. I knew he was making it up."

Cole tamped the pages together and settled back. He had done a lot of work on the map and now had more questions than answers.

"What did he tell you?"

"He watched a woman cut off her own fingers. What a gross thing to say. Like I'm supposed to be impressed by that. What a gross and disgusting thing, trying to scare me."

"You changed your mind about dinner? I'm pretty much finished here."

"No."

She wrapped her arms across her breasts and stared at the ceiling.

"Is he married?"

"No."

"Ever?"

"You crushing on Joe? I think Larkin is crushing on Joe."

"I asked him, but he didn't answer. He does that. I'll say something and I know he hears, but he ignores me. I don't like being ignored. It's rude."

"Yes, it is."

"Then why does he do it?"

"I asked him once, but he ignored me."

Larkin didn't find it funny.

"So he's the one who won't talk, and you're the one who makes a joke out of everything."

"Maybe Joe doesn't answer you because he figures the answers are none of your business."

"What about the courtesy of polite conversation? Here I am stuck with a man who won't talk. He never laughs. He won't smile. He has absolutely no expression on his face."

"Jeez, with me he's a laugh riot. I can't shut the guy up."

"You're not funny. You're one of those people who thinks he's funny but isn't. I'm bored, and he gets us this place with no television."

"Yeah. Having no television is hell."

"Of course you'd say something like that. You're his friend."

Cole laughed.

"You're probably used to people trying to impress you—they're trying to be funny or get your attention or make you like them. Don't confuse that with being interesting. It isn't. Pike is one of the most interesting men you'll meet. He just doesn't want to entertain you, so he doesn't."

"It's still boring."

"Try reading. Beautiful rich chicks can read, can't they?"

The corners of her mouth made the curl.

"You talk a lot. Does that mean you're trying to entertain me?"

"It means I'm trying to entertain myself. You're kinda dull."

Larkin rolled off the couch and went back to the window.

"Shouldn't he be back by now?"

"It's still early."

She returned to the couch, but this time she pulled her feet up and crossed her legs. Cole could see she didn't want to let it go. She was frowning at him as if he was keeping something from her.

"Well, is it true? Was he in Africa?"

"He's been to Africa many times. He's been all over the world."

"Why would he do that?"

"Joe didn't cut off her fingers."

"I mean being a mercenary. I understand being drafted and all, but I think it's sick, getting paid to play soldier."

"Joe wasn't playing. He was a professional."

"I think it's disgusting. Anyone who enjoys that kind of thing is insane."

"I guess that depends on what you do and why you do it."

"You're just making excuses for him. You're probably just as sick as him."

Cole loved her certainty so much he smiled.

"That story he told you about the woman, did he tell you why he was there?"

"Of course not."

"You still want to know?"

She stared at him as if it was a trick question, but when she finally nodded he told her. He told her the one story. He could have told more.

"A group called the Lord's Resistance Army was running around Central Africa, mostly in Uganda. They kidnapped girls. What they would do was, they'd blow into a village out in the middle of nowhere, shoot up everything with machine guns, loot the place, and grab the teenage girls. Not one or two, but all of them. They've kidnapped hundreds of girls. They take them as slaves, rape them, do whatever. It's the Third World, Larkin. It's not like here. Most of the planet isn't like here. You understand?"

She managed to nod, but Cole sensed she didn't understand, and couldn't. They didn't have police; they had warlords. They didn't have Republicans and Democrats; they had tribes. In Rwanda, one tribe would target another and hack a million people to death in less than three months. How could an American understand something like that?

"The people in those villages, they're farmers, maybe have a few cattle, but sometimes these villages get together and pool their money. They figured they needed professionals to stop the kidnappings, so Joe made the trip. Joe and his guys—I think he had five guys with him that time—they arrived in the afternoon. The morning of the day they arrived, a raiding party shot up another village and stole more girls. That woman's husband and her sons were murdered that morning. That's the first thing Joe saw when they rolled in that day, this poor woman mutilating herself."

Larkin stared at him as if she was waiting for more, but when Cole only stared back she wet her lips.

"What did he do?"

Cole knew, but decided to keep it simple.

"Joe did his job. The raids stopped."

Larkin glanced toward the front windows, but it was darker now, and the light in the room made it impossible to see out.

Cole said, "I'm getting hungry. You want dinner?"

Cole wanted to go into the kitchen. He wanted to have

a glass of the wine and cook, but the girl stared at the windows, wetting her lips.

"He did that a lot?"

"He's been all over the world."

"Why?"

"Why would he hire out?"

She nodded.

"He's an idealist."

She finally looked back at him.

"I still think it's creepy. He wouldn't do that kind of thing if he didn't enjoy it."

"No, probably not. But he probably doesn't enjoy it the way you mean. C'mon, let's make dinner."

She turned back to the windows.

"I'm going to wait."

Cole went to the kitchen, but didn't begin their dinner. He thought about Pitman. Pitman had told Larkin and her family a version of events that no longer fit with the facts, and probably never had. Cole had caught Pitman in a lie, and now he wondered if Pitman had lied about anything else.

17

John Chen

THE FIREARMS analysis unit was called the gun room. You went in there, all you saw were guns. The walls were lined with cabinets filled with hundreds of guns from the floor to the ceiling. Pistols sprouted from the inner walls of the cabinets like fruit from a dangerous tree; row after row of pistols, impaled on rods in their barrels, one gun next to another, stored that way because so many guns had been backlogged the analysts had no room to store them any other way; each gun with a tag hanging from the trigger guard to identify its make, model, and case number; each gun confiscated, used or believed to have been used in a crime. It was a harvest of bitter fruit.

John Chen eyeballed the hall outside the gun room, cursing his rotten, born-to-be-screwed luck as he made sure no one was coming. Chen hated hanging around so late in the day, but the firearms analysts were so overworked and ever-more-falling-behind that the slave-driving bitch Harriet Munson was constantly on their ass, which meant she was constantly in the gun room, which meant Chen had to wait until Harriet had gone home, which was later than anyone else on the day shift because even Harriet was overworked and behind. And to make matters worse—and matters were always growing worse, which seemed to be John's inescapable lot in life—Pike was probably working himself into a killer rage at this very moment because he hadn't heard from Chen about the guns. Chen's stomach grew queasy as he imagined it. Pike was a monster, a cold-blooded killer, and would probably snap Chen's neck like a pencil—

—which would be Harriet Munson's fault, too. That bitch.

That morning, Chen thought for sure he would be able to get what Pike needed ASAP and be well on his way to a 'tangmobile upgrade—but no. As soon as Pike left, Chen had ripped back into the lab with his story of heroically returning to work. He had planned on badgering one of the firearms analysts into jumping the Eagle Rock evidence to the head of the analysis line, but John never had the chance. There he was, describing his courageous recovery from the broken tooth—and what did that bitch, Harriet, do? She ordered him out to a crime scene—right then, right there, right away; do not pass Go or even stop to take a piss. A domestic knife murder in Pacoima, for Christ's sake. And THEN, as if that wasn't enough, she sent him on to a body in Atwater, one of those homeless dudes who lived on an island in the L.A. River, found with his skull caved in like a casaba melon, almost certainly having been beaned by another homeless dude over pussy or dope or territory. Now, was THAT any way to reward a guy who overcame a broken tooth to return to work? Chen didn't get back to the lab until almost six, only to find Harriet haunting the gun room like the Ghost of Christmas Future. Pike was certain to be impatient with the delay and no doubt would be growing angrier and angrier—at John.

Chen lived in an absolute agony of nerves until Harriet left and his chance to corner the firearms analyst appeared. Now, all he had to do was convince her to let him have the Eagle Rock evidence, and he could finally get Pike off his back.

Chen had come prepared.

The duty analyst that day was a tall, thin woman with close-set eyes and yellow teeth named Christine La-Molla. Chen was convinced she was a lesbian.

John crept down the hall, made sure no one was coming, then pressed the buzzer. Being filled with guns, the gun room was kept locked. He heard the lock click, pushed open the door, and entered.

LaMolla turned from her computer and peered at the coffee, smile-less. Lesbians never smiled.

Chen held out the cup. He had raced out to the nearest Starbucks and bought their largest mocha. Even lesbians liked chocolate.

Chen gave her his toothiest smile.

"For you."

"I didn't ask for this."

Chen tried to smile enough for both of them.

"I know you work late. I thought you might need it."

LaMolla glanced at the cup again as if she thought it was laced with acid. John had once asked her out, but she turned him down flat. Lesbian.

Now she eyeballed Chen with equal suspicion. She still hadn't touched the coffee.

"What do you want, John?"

"You know the shootings we had in Eagle Rock? I need to see the guns."

Mr. Nonchalant. Mr. Just Another Day at the Office.

Her eyes narrowed even more.

"You didn't cover the Eagle Rock case."

"Nah, but something came up in one of my old Inglewood cases. I think they might be connected."

LaMolla peered at him even harder, then took the coffee. She smelled it, but didn't taste, then went to the door. She locked it, then leaned with her back to the door, blocking his exit.

John got an unexpected, more-than-a-little-hopeful notion that maybe she wasn't a lesbian after all; that maybe his luck in all things was about to forever change, and he smiled even wider—

—but then she dropped the mocha into a trash can.

She said, "What the fuck is going on?"

Chen didn't know what to say, and wasn't even sure what she meant.

"What do you mean, what's going on?"

"Eagle Rock."

Her beady eyes made her look like a bird of prey. Chen was confused. He tried to cover it by looking, well, confused.

"Yeah, Eagle Rock. I gotta see the guns, Chris. No biggie."

She studied him, and Chen felt himself squirm. He knew if she kept it up much longer his nervous twitch would fire up like a chain saw. He shrugged, and did his best to look innocent.

"Hey, all I wanna do is see the guns. What's going on?"

"That's what I want to know."

"Whattaya mean, you wanna know? Jesus Christ, you gonna let me see the guns or not?"

She slowly shook her head.

"The feds took them."

Chen blinked.

"The feds?"

"Mmm. The three semi's and the wheel gun bagged in Eagle Rock. Here's what's really weird. They took the wheel gun last night—a .357 Colt Python. But then they came back this afternoon for the semi's."

Chen saw his chances for a Carrera upgrade circling the drain. Visions of his lost opportunity with Ronda flashed like lightning at the edge of his horizon. But mostly he imagined Joe Pike beating his ass. Pike wasn't a man you let down. Pike would get even.

Chen blurted, "But that was LAPD evidence! The feds can't just take our stuff. That's *our* stuff!"

"They can when Parker tells us to let them have it."

"Parker Center gave them permission?"

LaMolla slowly nodded, still watching him with tiny eyes.

"All I know is, Harriet got the call, and she wouldn't tell me anything about it, John. She said the sixth floor says let'm have what they want—"

The sixth floor of Parker Center was the power floor—the realm of the Assistant Chiefs.

"—so we did. They took the guns."

John was frantic. His mind was racing for some angle or explanation that might appease Joe Pike when a desperate idea came to him.

"What about the shell casings? Did they take the casings?"

Spent casings would have been gathered at the scene, and like the guns, they could be compared and analyzed.

But Christine was shaking her head, her eyes boring into him now as if searching him.

"They took everything. Even the casings."

Chen wondered why she was looking at him that way, and then he felt a last dismal shred of hope.

"Chris—you didn't, you know, keep one of the casings, did you?"

She slowly sighed.

"I kept two, but they went through the evidence list. They checked off every item we recovered, so I had to give them up. But you know what was really weird?"

Chen shook his head.

"They wouldn't sign an evidence receipt."

Any time evidence was transferred or moved between departments or agencies, a receipt and an acceptance of possession had to be signed. It was standard operating procedure. This ensured that the chain of evidence remained intact. This prevented evidence tampering. This prevented evidence from being lost. Or stolen.

Chen said, "But they *had* to."

LaMolla simply stared at him.

"No, John, they didn't. And now here you come, wanting those same guns. And the casings. What's going on?"

"I don't know."

LaMolla, who clearly didn't believe him, said, "Mmm."

Pike had hinted at some kind of conspiracy, but Chen figured he was talking about a couple of crooked cops. Now it looked like the feds and Parker Center were involved, and no one seemed to know why, or what they were doing, even though they were doing things that no legitimate police agency would do. The chain of evidence was sacrosanct, and now the evidence was gone.

John Chen grew afraid; afraid in a way to which his earlier, overwrought, overly melodramatic fear could not compare.

No Carrera was worth this. No job in TV as a technical advisor, or even the smokin' hot 'tang that would follow.

John Chen suddenly felt trapped; caught in a claustrophobic nightmare between a homicidal maniac (Pike), the federal government (rife with known assassins), and the shadowy powers within Parker Center (still hiding the truth about the Black Dahlia killer), none of whom could be trusted, and any of which might snuff his life and career without hesitation. Chen's hands trembled. The tic beneath his left eye sputtered like a fire raging to life as he saw his future unfolding: LaMolla telling Harriet he had asked about the guns, Harriet ratting to

Parker Center; Chen suddenly at the center of an investigation. Or worse.

Chen tried to speak, but his mouth was too dry. He worked up some spit.

"You're not—listen, Chris, you're not going to tell—well, I mean, Harriet doesn't need to—"

LaMolla, still considering him with her calm, predatory eyes, uncrossed her arms and spread her hands wide like Moses parting the waters.

"This is the gun room. This room is mine. These guns are mine. The evidence here? This is *my* evidence. I don't like someone taking it. I don't like *you* knowing something about it that I don't."

She lowered her arms and stepped away from the door.

"Get out of here, John. Don't come back without something to tell me."

Chen stepped quickly past her and fled down the hall. He ran directly to his car, jumped in, and locked the doors. He started the engine but sat with his hands clenched in his lap, shaking and terrified. Danger was everywhere, just like when he was the tall geeky kid other kids picked on. Destruction might come from any direction. Just like when he was a child—just walking, man; maybe going to his locker or crossing the parking lot, and someone would bean him with a clod of dirt. Hit him just like that, out of nowhere, bang, right in the head, and he never even saw it coming. But it always came. Always.

Chen fished his cell phone from his pocket. The shaking made it difficult to scroll through the numbers, but Pike had told him to call Elvis Cole when he had something. Pike would almost certainly blame Chen because the guns were missing. He might even think that Chen was making everything up, and fly into a murderous rage, but Cole was Pike's friend. Chen had the vague hope that Cole could convince Pike not to kill him. It was Chen's only chance. His last best hope. Everyone knew Joe Pike was a monster.

18

IN THE quiet of the later night, a violet glow from Dodger Stadium capped the ridges as Pike eased up to the Echo Park house. The air was warmer than the evening before, but the same five men still clustered at the car beneath the streetlight, and families still sat on their porches, listening to Vin Scully call a game that many of them knew nothing about only a few years before. Cole's Sting Ray was missing, but Cole would have left it on an adjoining street. The house was a dim cutout against the blacker night, lit only by the street lamp and the ochre rectangles that were its windows.

Pike parked in the drive and crossed the yard to the porch. The five men glanced over, but not in a threatening way.

The porch, hidden by its overhang from the street lamp, was a cave. Cole opened the door as Pike reached it, and stepped out onto the porch. In that moment when the door opened, Pike smelled mint and curry, and wondered why Cole had come out.

Cole spoke low, hiding his voice from the men.

"How'd it go?"

Pike described the two men who searched his home, and unfolded their pictures. Cole cracked open the door wide enough to light the pictures, then closed it again. This time when the door opened, Pike glimpsed the girl, standing in the kitchen at the far end of the house. She was wearing an iPod. Pike had made her get rid of her iPod in the desert.

Pike said, "Where'd she get the iPod?"

"It's mine. I made Thai, you want something to eat. That's what we had."

Pike put away the pictures. The Thai sounded good. But then Cole moved farther from the door and lowered his voice even more.

"I got a call from John Chen this evening. You talk to him?"

"This morning."

Cole glanced at the door, as if he suspected the girl had her ear to the crack.

"The feds confiscated everything from Eagle Rock. The guns, the casings, all of it."

"Pitman?"

"All Chen knew was the feds."

"John run the guns before they were taken?"

"They moved in too fast. Here's what's really wild— they took the stuff without paper. Said Parker called down and told them to let it go, no questions asked."

Pike raised his eyebrows.

"No questions."

"Those D-3s at Homicide Special wouldn't roll over just because Pitman's a fed, not with five unidentified stiffs on the plate. Someone must have—no pun intended—put a gun to their heads."

Pike agreed. Pitman had used a lot of muscle for evidence that might not lead anywhere. It made more sense to let LAPD run the guns. If nothing came up, the guns didn't matter. If LAPD found something, Pitman could have used it. Confiscating the guns had only drawn LAPD's attention to an investigation Pitman wanted to keep secret.

Pike said, "He's scared."

"Yeah. Only reason to take those guns is he doesn't want LAPD anywhere around this. That, or he's hiding more than this case he's building against the Kings."

"Like what?"

"I don't know. But I know he's a liar."

Pike tried to read Cole's face. Even with the darkness and deep shadows, he could see Cole was troubled.

"Funny that Pitman gave back my gun."

"He was trying to buy you. Also, your gun can't hurt him. Your gun can only hurt you. He probably had your gun test-fired so he can match your bullets to the bodies if he needs the leverage."

"Leverage for what?"

Cole glanced at the door again, then stepped even closer.

"He hasn't been straight with the girl or her family. Remember what they told her? They didn't know Meesh was the missing man until she identified him?"

Pike nodded. That was the way both Bud and the girl had told it.

Cole said, "The day they first saw her—that morning before they talked to her—they had already worked her street, and they weren't only asking about the Kings. They were asking about Meesh. They didn't use his name, but they already knew or suspected Meesh was in the car."

Pike glanced at the men under the street lamp. He listened to their serious voices, and realized Cole had come outside so they could talk about this without the girl hearing.

"How do you know that?"

"I heard it from half a dozen people today. Agents from the Department of Justice, they said. One black, one white, showing pictures of two men. I had them describe the pictures, and I'm pretty sure one was King, and the other was Meesh."

"Pitman and Blanchette did this before they met her?"

"Before. I wasn't sure about the timeline until I sat down with my notes this evening. Now I'm sure. They knew Meesh was with King, and they knew his identity before she identified him."

Pike wondered why Pitman and Blanchette had misled the girl. She was clearly important to them, but if Pitman and Blanchette already knew Meesh was with King, maybe she hadn't been their only witness. Maybe their other witness had been killed. Pike didn't like it, but none of this affected his mission. Find Meesh. Eliminate the threat. Protect the girl. He could deal with Pitman and Blanchette later.

Pike tipped his head toward the door.

"Does she know?"

"I figure she's scared enough without being scared of the cops. Not until we know why Pitman lied."

"Good. Let's go back to her neighborhood tomorrow. I was hoping we'd pick up Meesh's trail, but maybe Pitman's trail is more important."

"She's not going to like it. She wasn't happy when you left."

Pike turned toward the house, wondering if the girl was still in the kitchen. He wondered what she was listening to on Cole's iPod.

Cole said, "You told her about Africa."

Pike glanced back at Cole, and now Cole was smiling.

"You tell someone about Africa, talk about zebras and lions. Don't tell them about women cutting off their fingers."

Pike didn't want to mention the girl's offer to masturbate. Not because mentioning it would embarrass him, but because he was embarrassed for the girl.

Pike said, "That food smells pretty good. That curry?"

Cole smiled wider, and they went into the house. The girl was stretched out on the couch with the headset fixed to her ears. Her eyes were closed, but she looked up when they entered.

Pike said, "How's it going?"

She didn't sit up, and she didn't speak to him. She raised a hand in a kind of a wave, then closed her eyes again and went back to the music. Her foot bounced with the beat. Pike figured she was still pissed off.

Cole left a few minutes later, and Pike went into the kitchen. Cole had made vegetable curry rice. Pike stood in the kitchen, eating from the pot. He ate it cold. When he finished eating, he filled a paper cup with the plum wine, drank it, then drank a bottle of water. He was drinking the water when the girl came to the door.

She said, "I'm going to bed."

Pike nodded. He wanted to say something, but he was still wondering why Pitman had put the girl in this position. Meesh was a murderer, but his prosecution would be handled at the state level by the courts in Colorado. For Pitman, Meesh was nothing more than a way to bag the Kings. The Kings were his target, but his case against them was for money laundering. Paper. He had put this girl's life in jeopardy for paper, and he had somehow gotten LAPD to go along. Pitman had a lot of juice for a mid-level fed running a money case. Pike wondered if Bud knew.

The girl turned away without another word, went into her bedroom, and closed the door.

Pike finished the water, then went to the bathroom. He shaved, brushed his teeth, then flossed with great care. After the flossing, he showered. He brought the clothes he wore that day into the shower with him, and washed them with hand soap in the running water. He wrung them out as best he could, hung them, then dressed in fresh clothes. He washed his sunglasses, put them on, then looked at himself in the mirror. His hair was getting long. Almost an inch on top, and now touching his ears. Pike liked it short. He would have to cut it soon.

The house was quiet in a way that made the emptiness seem larger. Pike checked the windows and doors, then shut the lights and took his place in the chair. He sat there for a while, in the dark, then went to the couch.

Pike put his pistol on the floor in easy reach, then stretched out and closed his eyes. The couch was still warm from her, and the impression left by her body was soft.

Larkin Barkley

Jethro Tull woke her. She emerged from her dream as the lion disappeared into the dry grass, and pulled the headset from her ears, thinking no wonder everyone in the sixties was stoned all the time, their bands singing about disease. But then, still more asleep than awake, she glimpsed the lion again, its scarred head pushing through the grass, its muzzle stained with blood, the heavy muscles in its shoulders bunching in the last foggy moments of her dream before it dissolved.

Larkin lay in the darkness, waking, then awake as she realized she had to pee.

The house was dark, so she figured he was sleeping or just standing somewhere in that creepy way, so she went directly into the bathroom. She closed the door before she turned on the light. His clothes were hanging from the shower rod, but she didn't think anything of it. She peed, then drank water from the tap, using her hand as a cup. When she finished, she turned out the light, opened the door, and that's when she heard him.

Soft, frantic grunts and a jerky, cloth-on-cloth swoosh came from the living room. She hesitated, listening as her eyes adjusted, then crept into the living room.

He was asleep on the couch. His body was clenched; his arms rigid at his sides as he jerked and trembled.

Even in the poor light, she saw the sweat on his face as his head snapped from side to side and the grunts hissed past his teeth.

He was dreaming, she thought. Ohmigod. He was having a nightmare.

She wondered if she should wake him. She couldn't remember if you were supposed to wake people who were having a nightmare or not. Maybe waking him would be bad.

Larkin moved closer, trying to decide what to do. His legs lurched as if he was running, but in that paralyzed way when you're trapped in a dream. His hands flexed like claws, then shook and fluttered, and his eyes rolled wildly beneath the lids. Larkin thought, Man, this must be one monster of a nightmare. He looked like he was fighting for his life.

Then he spoke. She couldn't make it out, but between the grunts and moans, she was sure he had spoken.

Dah . . .

It sounded like dah. Dah or duh.

She strained closer to try to make out what he was saying, but all she heard were mumbles and slurs.

Then, little by little, he calmed. The lurching slowed. His hands relaxed. His head stopped jerking.

Larkin was very close then, over him, when he mumbled again.

Duh . . . dah . . .

It sounded like *daddy*.

Larkin waited to hear it again, but he fell quiet, and she thought she was probably wrong. People mumbled nonsense when they dreamed. A man like him might have nightmares, but not about his daddy. It was difficult to imagine a man like him ever having been a child.

She watched him. He was calm by then, and his breathing was even, but his expression seemed pained. No, she thought, not pained. He was afraid. It had been a nightmare. Even men like him were afraid in their nightmares.

She wanted to touch him. She wanted to reach out the way you always want to reach through the bars at a zoo to touch the big animals.

Larkin stood with him for a moment longer, then crept back to her room.

DAY THREE

GUN MONEY

19

THE NEXT morning, Pike was cleaning his pistol at the dining table when the girl came out of her room. Pike had been up for three hours. It was ten minutes after eight.

The girl had the puffy, bleached-out look she had every morning, but today she wasn't naked. She wore an oversize T-shirt draped to her thighs. She wrinkled her nose.

"Ugh. I can smell that all the way in my room. You get high breathing that stuff?"

Pike had broken down the pistol into its components. The barrel, bushing, recoil spring plug, recoil spring and its guide, slide stop, slide, frame, and magazine were laid out on a paper bag Cole brought from the Thai market. Pike was swabbing the barrel with powder solvent, which had the strong odor of overripe peaches. The girl didn't like it. She complained about it the first night they were together when Pike cleaned his gun, and had complained every time since. Pike cleaned his guns every day.

He said, "There's coffee."

Pike's phone was on the table. He was waiting for Cole so they could meet at the girl's loft. Pike had also decided to call Bud. He was going to tell Bud about Pitman, and thought Bud might be able to find out what Pitman had done with the guns. Bud still had connections in the department. Even at Parker Center.

The girl said, "You were dreaming last night. You had a nightmare."

"Don't remember."

"It was bad. I didn't know if I should wake you."

"That's okay."

Pike never remembered his dreams. When he woke from them, he could never go back to sleep.

He said, "I want to make sure I have something straight. Let's go back to the beginning—"

She rolled her eyes and crossed her arms.

"Not again. I hate the beginning. The middle and wherever we are now aren't so great, either."

"How many days after your accident was it when Pitman and Blanchette came to see you?"

"Three days."

"Not the day after, not the second day?"

"Didn't we go through this?"

"There's a lot to keep straight."

"You know what it takes to find a clear spot on my father's calendar? And his attorney? People can't just drop over to our house. You don't just *see* us. You have to make an appointment. It was the third day."

Pike finished swabbing the barrel and picked up the frame. The solvent in the barrel would loosen debris while Pike worked on the other parts.

"Uh-huh. So they came over and they wanted to know about King's passenger?"

"Yeah. About the accident, and what happened, and all. They wanted to know who was in the car with the Kings. Because of their investigation."

"They didn't know it was Meesh?"

"They only knew what was in the accident report. They wanted to identify the other man. Jesus, I haven't even had my coffee yet."

"I'm going back to your neighborhood to see some people Elvis found. Then I'm going to see Bud."

The girl didn't say anything. She stood quietly for a moment as if she was thinking, then went into the kitchen.

Pike finished cleaning the frame. He saturated the swab with fresh solvent, then went to work on the slide, working the solvent into every groove and cut in the metal, and liberally over the breech face.

The girl returned with a cup of coffee. She sat at the table across from him without saying anything. When Pike glanced up, he saw she was watching him. She looked serious.

Pike said, "Want to help?"

"I hate guns."

Pike wiped the excess solvent from the slide, then returned to the barrel. He ran a brass wire brush from the business end out through the chamber, then into the chamber and out through the business end. He followed it with a clean cotton swab dipped in more solvent.

The girl said, "We have to talk."

"Okay."

"I didn't like the way you left me yesterday. If you

had told me what you were doing, it would have been fine, but you didn't tell me. You don't even talk to me. Okay, I know you're not a talker. I get that. Elvis says you barely talk to *him*. Okay. But I'm an adult. These people are trying to kill *me*. I don't need a babysitter, and I don't like being treated like a child. This is a trust issue. We have a trust issue, is what I'm saying, and we have to deal with this. Here we are in this crappy little house, and it is either safe here or it isn't. If you don't think it's safe, let's go somewhere else. I suggested Paris, but no, you want to stay in Echo Park. Fine. We've been here two days and they haven't found me, so I guess it's safe. Okay, good, thank you. But I don't like it here, and I also don't like spending all day in the car just because you think I'm stupid. I resent it. I don't know how those people kept finding me, but it wasn't me. I don't want to go see Bud, and I don't want to sit in the car while you and Elvis talk to people. It's boring, and I'm tired of it. I would rather stay here, and I can stay here by myself."

Pike put down the barrel. He looked at her.

"Yes."

"Yes, I can stay here?"

"I said I was going to see Bud. I didn't say we. I'm sorry about yesterday. I should have been more considerate."

The girl's mouth opened, but she didn't say anything. She sipped the coffee, holding the cup with both hands.

Pike slipped the barrel into the slide, dropped the recoil spring guide into place beneath the barrel, then fed the recoil spring onto the guide. He reassembled the gun in seconds. Pike could take the gun apart or put it together blindfolded, in the dark, dead on his feet from lack of sleep, and with gunfire raging around him. Putting the gun together was easy. Talking to the girl was difficult.

The girl finally spoke.

"Okay. Thanks. That's cool."

Pike said, "Cool."

His cell vibrated, making a loud buzz on the table. Pike read the screen, thinking it would be Cole, but it wasn't.

Pike placed the phone to his ear.

Ronnie said, "You have company."

The girl was watching him, but Pike showed nothing. They were hunting hard for him, just as he was hunting for them. And as he would return to the girl's home for their trail, they had no choice but to return to his condo. You went where the animals lived.

Pike said, "How many?"

"One guy this time. I don't know if he's one you told me about, but he could be. Under six, I'd say; hair's kinda long and dark."

"Where is he?"

"Inside. He just let himself in, walked right in like he owned the place. You want me to introduce myself?"

Pike watched the girl watching him. If she knew what he intended to do, she would be worried or ask questions, and Pike had used up his talking allowance.

"No, I'll come over and have a word. I'm on my way. If he leaves, you have my phone."

"Yup."

Pike put down the phone, pushed the magazine into the gun, then jacked the slide and set the safety. If Pike could ever know bliss, it filled him now, but he showed nothing. He had them. He had a line that might bring him to Meesh, and then he would clear the field. All these bastards trying to kill this girl, this one girl, all of them ganged against her, and he would clear the field, but not for justice. It would be punishment. Punishment was justice.

He said, "So. What are you going to do while I'm gone?"

"Who was that?"

"Ronnie. He found someone who might be able to help, so I'm going to meet them. You're going to be okay?"

"Uh-huh."

Pike stood, pocketed the phone, then holstered the Kimber and clipped it to his waist. He pulled on the long-sleeved shirt to cover his tattoos and the gun.

"You want me to pick up something?"

"Maybe some fruit."

"What kind?"

"Strawberries. Maybe bananas."

"I'll be a while. You sure you're okay?"

She was still staring. Pike hoped she was having second thoughts about staying alone and had changed her mind.

She said, "How long will you be?"

"Most of the day, maybe. I can have Elvis come over."

"No, that's okay."

"Sure?"

"Yeah."

"Okay, then. I'll see you later."

Pike was disappointed, but he showed nothing. He had mixed feelings about leaving her, but he had convinced himself there was more to protecting her than just keeping her alive. He didn't want her to feel abandoned again. If she needed to feel trusted, then he would trust her. It was a decision he would regret.

20

PIKE WORKED his way south to the Santa Monica Freeway in the sluggish morning traffic. He didn't hurry. If the man in his condo left, Ronnie would follow. Pike filled Cole in from the car. Cole asked if Pike wanted help, but Pike declined, saying Cole's time would be better spent on Pitman as they had planned. Pike still wanted to talk with Bud, but everything might change in the next few hours, so Pike decided to wait. He told Cole about the girl.

Cole said, "You want me to watch her?"

"Not watch her, but I'd like you to stop by."

"She wouldn't know I was watching her."

"I understand, but no. She doesn't want that. Maybe you could stop by. I don't know how long I'm going to be with this. Just stop by. Don't stay."

"I'll swing by later. I'll drop off some food."

"Strawberries."

"What?"

"She wants strawberries. Maybe bananas."

"Sure. Whatever."

"See she's all right, then let me know."

"Joe. You worried?"

"Just doing my job."

"Right."

"If she wants you to stay, you can stay."

Cole laughed, so Pike hung up.

Pike hadn't heard from Ronnie again by the time he left the freeway, so he called.

Pike said, "I'm five out. Is he still in my house?"

"Nope. He only stayed inside a few minutes. Now he's hiding in the bushes. Bet the sonofabitch went in to take a dump."

"Only one guy?"

"Yep."

"Where?"

"You know the two dumpsters at the back of your parking lot? He's under the bushes behind the dumpsters, looking out between them so he can see your front door. Been there about twenty minutes now."

"What's he driving?"

"No idea. He approached on foot along the main drive, so he's probably parked out by the main gate, but I'm only guessing. Somebody might've dropped him off."

Pike thought it through as he turned toward his complex. Since the man had taken a position by Pike's condo, Pike could drive through the main gate and park on the grounds. This would allow Pike easy access to his car, which could be important.

Pike said, "What's he wearing?"

"A short-sleeved green shirt with the tail out. The shirt has these little stripes. And jeans."

"Can you leave your position without being seen?"

"No problem."

"Call you when I'm in."

Pike drove through the main gate, but turned away from his condo to a parking lot behind a group of adjoining pods. He left the Lexus without bothering to hide, and made his way forward. Pike knew exactly where the man was and what the man was able to see, so Pike wasn't concerned. When he reached the last of the adjoining pods, he stepped behind a large plumeria and once more disappeared into a world of green. Pike moved along the wall to the end of the building, then turned the corner. The parking lot where he normally parked and the dumpsters were directly in front of him. He studied the thick wall of oleander bushes behind the dumpsters. The man would have a narrow field of view between the dumpsters, but he had picked a good place to hide. Pike couldn't see him through the heavy lace of leaves. Pike changed his location twice before he found an angle he liked. He still didn't see the man, but thought the angle would work. Pike watched the oleanders for almost twenty minutes, and then a bar of light moved behind the leaves.

Pike called Ronnie, cupping his hand over the phone.

"Got him. Thank Dennis for me. You, too."

"We going to take him?"

Ronnie lived for this stuff, but Pike didn't want him around for the rest of it. If Pike needed him, Pike would have asked him, but better for Ronnie if Ronnie was gone.

"Good-bye, Ron."

Pike put away his phone. He didn't see Ronnie leave, but didn't expect to. Pike sat on the hard soil without moving and watched the play of light and color in the changing face of the oleanders that was not one face, but many—the outer leaves a pale grey-green patchwork bleached by the sun; the seams in the patches showing darker leaves beneath, while still smaller cuts and dimples revealed the linear shape of branches; light over dark over darker, the inner darkness finally dappled by pinpoints of light; until finally, as Pike watched, a shadow moved within the shadows, revealing a glimpse of green that did not fit with the surrounding greens; first one bit of shadow, and then another shade of green, until Pike saw a pattern within the pattern and the man within the leaves. A branch swayed, telling Pike the man was antsy and bored. Moments later, a different branch shivered. The man probably resented having to sit in the bush, and was unwilling to sacrifice his comfort to remain motionless. Pike read his lack of discipline as weakness. Pike could kill him now, or take him, but innocent people lived in these homes, so Pike waited.

Forty minutes before the man left his hide, Pike knew it was coming. The man shifted and fidgeted with increasing frequency, and made the bush tremble. His lack of discipline was appalling.

Three hours and twelve minutes after Pike took his position, the man rose to a crouch, peered out from between the branches to make sure no one was looking, then duck-walked out from behind the dumpsters. He brushed himself off, crossed the parking lot, then turned toward the main gate. He took a cell phone from his pocket as he walked, but Pike couldn't tell if he was making a call or receiving one. Maybe he hadn't quit; maybe someone had told him to leave.

Pike slipped from his cover and hurried back to his car. He drove fast through the rear gate, then circled the complex, pushing hard toward the front entrance. He pulled to the curb two blocks from the main gate just as the man in the green shirt stepped through a pedestrian gate built into the wall. You needed a passkey to enter, but you didn't need anything to leave.

The man was now wearing sunglasses, but Pike could see he wasn't one of the men he had seen before. He was dark, with hard shoulders and a lean face, and almost certainly Latino. When he moved, his shirt pulled in a way that showed a gun in the waist of his pants. He stopped at a dusty brown Toyota Corolla. A moment later, the Corolla pulled away.

Pike made the Corolla for an early '90s model. It was dark brown in color with mismatched wheels and rusty acne on the trunk. Pike copied the plate number. He stayed between three and four cars behind, only tightening up when the Corolla beat him through an intersection and traffic began to slow.

They climbed onto the I-10 at Centinela and dropped off the freeway at Fairfax. The Corolla stopped for gas, then continued north up through the city at the same unhurried pace. When they reached Santa Monica Boulevard, the Corolla turned west, skirting the bottom of West Hollywood, then Hollywood, then into a dingy area of Triple-X video stores, strip malls, and free clinics. The Corolla turned into the parking lot of a two-story motel called the Tropical Shores Motor Hotel. A sign shaped like a palm tree grew from its roof, with arrows pointing down the trunk to a vacancy sign. The palm tree and the arrows were outlined in neon, but the tubes were broken and faded, and probably had been for years. A small sign in the office window read HOURLY RATES AVAILABLE.

Pike jerked into a red zone, then trotted back to the drive. The motel was shaped like an L, with an open staircase where the legs of the L joined. The motor court was empty except for the Corolla, two other cars, and a green Schwinn bicycle chained to a metal post. Individual air conditioners jutted from the rooms like tumors, but most of the air conditioners were silent.

Pike reached the office as the man in the green shirt got out of the Corolla. Pike tried to see if anyone was in the office, but the window was opaque with grime. The office door faced the parking lot, but the door was closed and an air conditioner hummed loudly.

The man in the green shirt didn't bother locking his car. He went to a soft-drink machine against the wall, bought a soda, then walked to a ground-floor room. He stood at the door with his back to the parking lot as he searched for his key.

Pike approached the man from behind. He shifted left or right just enough to stay in the man's blind spot, moving so quickly that he was outside the office one moment and across the lot in the next, watching the key go in the lock, seeing the door open—

Pike hooked his left arm under the man's chin, and lifted. He closed his arm on the man's throat and squeezed as hard as he could, shoving the man into the room as he brought out the Kimber, using the man as a shield.

Pike expected more men, but the room was empty. A single room and a bath.

Pike toed the door closed, still holding the man. The drapes were open, so Pike could see no one was in the parking lot and no one had stirred from the office.

The man kicked and thrashed, but Pike held him up and off balance with a knee. The man punched backwards, clawed at Pike's arm, and made a gurgling sound. He was a strong man in very good shape. His nails cut into Pike's skin.

Pike slipped his free arm across the back of the man's neck and pushed the man's throat into the crook of his elbow. Pike squeezed and pushed and held it.

The thrashing slowed.

The man stopped kicking.

His body went limp.

21

THE CHOKE hold cut off blood to a man's brain, putting him to sleep like a laptop when its battery is low. It was an effective way to subdue a person, though sometimes that person did not wake up. Pike sat on the edge of the bed, waiting for the man to wake.

The man did not sleep for long. His eyelids fluttered and his head came up. He had the vague expression of a boxer with a mild concussion, but he stiffened when he realized he could not move. Pike had duct-taped the man to a chair. His ankles, thighs, trunk, and arms were bound.

Pike was directly in front of the man, only inches away. He was holding an old Browning 9mm pistol. The man had been carrying the Browning, a cell phone, keys to the car and the room, twelve dollars and sixty cents, a pack of Marlboros, a butane lighter, and a Seiko watch. The man had not been carrying a wallet, credit cards, or any form of identification.

Pike watched the man's eyes, which were worried but confident. He had a wide, angular face, with small scars laced into his eyebrows and across the bridge of his nose.

Pike said, "You know who I am?"

The man glanced at the door, maybe thinking someone would be there to save him.

Pike repeated himself.

"Do you know who I am?"

The man answered in Spanish.

"Fuck you."

The Browning flicked out and rocked his head. Pike moved so quickly the man did not know what was happening until his cheek split and blood dripped to his shirt. Pike had not wanted to knock him out.

When the man's eyes regained focus, Pike reached out with his left hand. This time he moved slowly, as if he were going to caress the man's cheek. He dug his thumb into the nerve where the jaw hinged with the zygomatic arch. The man tried to twist away, but he was taped to the chair. Pike held the pressure for a long time.

When Pike let go, the man gulped air as if he had been under water. He worked his jaw, giving Pike the eyes you gave someone when you were telling him you would kill him.

Pike's expression never changed.

Pike said, "I'm going to do that again."

Pike tucked the Browning into his pocket, then went to the window. The room was small and dingy, with two double beds facing a built-in dresser and desk, and a ragged club chair by the window. Pike had pulled the drapes, but they were the sheer kind through which you could see. A man with a bulging belly was outside the office, smoking, and the office door was open, probably so he could listen for the phone. Pike had already searched the Corolla, and now he searched the room.

The dresser and desk drawers were empty, but Pike found four travel bags heaped in the closet: two canvas duffels, a blue nylon gym bag sporting the Nike swoosh, and a black backpack. Each of the four bags contained men's clothing, cigarettes, and toiletry items. Pike found an envelope in the backpack containing twenty-six hundred dollars. Tucked in beside the envelope, he found a page from a spiral notebook with handwritten notes and numbers, and a photograph of Larkin Conner Barkley. It hadn't been clipped from a magazine, but was an actual print, tight on her face, showing her smile.

Hidden among the clothes in each bag were U.S. passports and round-trip airline tickets between Quito, Ecuador, and Los Angeles. The passports showed four men, one of whom was in the chair. The name on the passport was Rulón Martínez, but Pike doubted it was real.

Pike recognized two of the men in the other passports, but not the third. Two were among the crew that invaded the Barkleys' home. One was the man with the scarred lip who had beaten the Barkleys' housekeeper. The passport showed his name as Jésus Leone. The other was Walter Bloch. Pike found that odd. A German name. The remaining man, who Pike had never seen, was Ramón Alteiri. The passports claimed all four men were residents of Los Angeles and United States citizens. Pike studied the passports. If they were fakes, they were good fakes. The black backpack with the picture of Larkin belonged to the man with the scar.

Pike shook the clothes and toiletries out of the backpack and put in the passports, the tickets, the Browning, and the other things he wanted to keep, but not the picture of Larkin.

Pike returned to the bed with the picture and held it so the man could see. Pike didn't say anything; he just made the man look. Then he put it away.

"I can speak Spanish, but English would be better. That good with you?"

The man made a nasty grin like he didn't give a shit one way or the other.

"You better run, muddafokka. You don' know what you messin' with."

Pike dug his index finger into the soft tissue beneath the man's collarbone where twenty-six individual nerves joined into the brachial plexus. The supraclavicular nerve, which carried information into the spinal cord, ran close to the skin at that point, following a groove in the bone. When Pike crushed the nerve bundle hard into the bone, the entire brachial plexus fired a pain signal not unlike that from a root canal without novocaine.

The man made a high-pitched buzzing moan. He tried to tear free of the tape and throw over the chair, but Pike pinned his foot with a toe. Veins jumped in the man's neck like writhing snakes, and tears streamed over his face, streaking the blood on his cheek. He begged Pike to stop, going back to the Spanish, but Pike didn't stop.

When Pike finally released the pressure, he knew the pain would burn on with the ferocity of ant poison, so he touched another spot, this one in the man's neck, which reduced the pain. The man sagged, and his face paled to the color of meat left in water.

Pike said, "This is dim mak. That's Chinese. It means death touch."

Dim mak was the dark side of acupuncture; in one, pressure points used to heal; in the other, to damage.

Pike said, "I want Alex Meesh."

"I don' know."

Pike raised his finger. The man jerked back so violently the chair rocked, but Pike kept him in place with the toe.

"I don' know what you want! I don' know!"

"Alex Meesh."

"I don' know!"

"You don't know Alex Meesh?"

The man shook his head so violently blood flew from his cheek.

"No no no! I don' know!"

The man seemed too scared to be lying, but Pike wanted to see. He held up the man's passport.

"What's your real name?"

The man answered without hesitation.

"Jorge Petrada."

"Why were you watching my house?"

"For de girl."

He didn't even blink, saying it. Pike decided he was telling the truth. Jorge didn't know Alex Meesh.

"Did Meesh tell you to find her?"

"I don' know dis Meesh, I dunno."

"Who told you to find her?"

"Luis. Luis say."

"Who's Luis?"

Jorge glanced at the passports, so Pike held up the man with the scarred lip. The one with the picture.

"Si. Luis."

"Luis is your boss?"

"Si."

Luis didn't look like a boss. Bosses didn't attempt kidnappings in Beverly Hills or get into gunfights. Bosses told other people to take all the chances.

Pike checked his watch, then went back to the window—time was passing, and one or more of the other men would likely return soon. The manager was still smoking, but now he was on a cell, laughing about something. Pike went back to the bed.

"How did you know where to find the girl?"

"Luis. He say your address."

"How did you know our location in Eagle Rock and Malibu?"

"I dunno thees Eagle Rock. I dunno."

"You tried to kill her in Eagle Rock and Malibu. You tried up north in the Bay. Who told you where to find her?"

"No no no. I just got here, man. I been here only two days. I don' know nutheen' about dat."

Pike took the airline tickets from the bag and checked the flight dates. Jorge was telling the truth again. He had flown in with Alteiri only two days ago. Bloch arrived twelve days ago. Luis had been here for sixteen days. Luis would be the man with information.

Pike was returning the tickets to the bag when his cell phone vibrated. It was Cole. Pike stared at Jorge as he answered the call.

"Yes?"

Cole said, "Just left her. She's doing fine."

"Good."

"I dropped off some food and magazines, stuff like that. I brought a coffeemaker so she doesn't have to drink that stuff you make."

"She wanted strawberries. Strawberries and bananas."

"Yeah."

"Okay."

"What's wrong? Everything good on your end?"

"Good."

"Okay. You need anything, call."

Pike closed his phone. He was staring at Jorge, and Jorge was scared.

Pike said, "Who is Donald Pitman?"

"I dunno."

"Have you heard that name?"

"No. I dunno know who dat is."

"Bud Flynn?"

"No."

"Who does Luis work for?"

The man looked surprised that Pike didn't know, and straightened against the tape. He seemed to grow stronger for the first time since he wet his pants.

"Esteban Barone. We all of us work for Barone. This is why you have made a mistake, my friend. You will know fear if you know Barone."

"What is he? A gangster? A businessman? You understand what I'm asking?"

"You know dis word, cartel?"

"Si."

A coarse smile split the man's face, as if he took pride in being part of this thing.

"Barone, he have many soldiers. How many you have?"

Pike took the pictures of the five dead men from his pocket. He held them up one by one, watching the man's face darken.

Pike said, "I'm evening the odds."

The man muttered something in Spanish, but Pike did not understand.

Pike went to the window again. The manager was gone, but the office door was still open. Pike wanted the door closed. He planned to drive away in the Corolla with Jorge, but for now he returned to the bed.

"How many of you are left?"

The man spit.

This time Pike did not move slowly. He dug his thumb into a dim mak point between the man's ribs, beneath his pectoral muscle.

"*Siete!*"

Pike released the pressure.

"Four of you sleep here. Where do the other three sleep?"

"I don' know nutheen' about dat."

Pike dug his finger into the dim mak point again, and this time the man shrieked. Pike dug harder and held it until the man sobbed. Then he released the pressure.

"Where do they sleep?"

"I don' know where dey stay. Carlos, he put us here from de LAX. He don' say where dey are. He bring us to Luis, an' Luis say dis where we stay. I not even see dem!"

Pike sat back. Carlos. A new player had entered the game.

"Who's Carlos?"

"Norte Americano. He meet us at de airport. He bring us here an' take care of us."

"What's his last name?"

The man glanced at the window, and Pike looked with him. The thin, airy drape showed the roofline and the sun glinting off the cars, but nothing else.

"All I know, Carlos. He give us things. De phone, de guns."

"All right. Where are the others right now?"

"I don' know. I have my job, dey have dere's."

The man wet his lips. He was growing more nervous and glanced at the window again. Pike wondered if he had seen something.

"They coming back now, Jorge?"

"No. No, dey not comin' back."

Pike drew his pistol as he watched the window.

Jorge said, "Tonight dey come. Dey come tonight."

A shadow crossed the drapes, then three fast explosions shattered the glass. The drapes billowed in like a sail catching air, but Pike was already on the floor; the door crashed open, Luis with a gun, shooting even as Pike fired back, his shots punching Luis into the wall. Then the room was silent. Luis slid down the wall, leaving a red smear.

Pike stayed on the floor, but no more men appeared. He glanced at Jorge, but Jorge's head now sagged, and most of his forehead was missing. Pike went to the door, irritated that he had failed to control the situation. Luis had probably heard Jorge shrieking or was tipped off by the drapes, but either way the man who was likely his best source of information was dead. Now, the overweight man had come out of his office and a housekeeper stood at the far end of the motel. Pike pulled Luis out of the way and closed the shattered door.

Pike holstered his gun, then went through Luis's pockets. He found a cell phone, keys, twenty-four dollars, and a torn scrap of newspaper with a phone number in the margin. Pike put all of it into the backpack, then went back to the drapes. The overweight man had returned to his office. He would be calling the police. The housekeeper was inside with him, peeking out the open door.

Pike hurried into the bathroom. It was a cramped space right out of the fifties, with cheesy tile, crumbly grout, and a small opaque window over the tub. The housekeeper had left two glasses wrapped in plastic on the lavatory. Pike took them to the bodies. He removed a glass from its plastic, folded Jorge's fingers onto the glass, then placed the glass back in its wrapper. He did the same with Luis, and that's when he saw the watch. Luis was wearing a platinum Patek Philippe that was as out of place on this man as a diamond on a pile of dung. Pike took off the watch and turned it over. The back of the watch was engraved: *For my lovely George.*

Pike put the watch and the glasses into the backpack, wiped the surfaces he had touched, and trotted into the bathroom as he heard the approaching sirens. Pike broke the bathroom window with his pistol, hoisted himself through, and dropped into an alley. He hooked the backpack over his shoulder and trotted around the side of the building. He slowed when he reached the street, and walked past the motel office as the first patrol car arrived. People on both sides of the street were hiding behind cars and in doorways as if they might be shot, and others ran into stores. Pike watched like everyone else for a moment, then continued to his car. He drove away as the second police car arrived.

It occurred to him then as it had in the past that policemen were people who ran toward danger. Everyone else ran away.

22

PIKE PULLED into a shopping center near the base of Griffith Park. A high-pitched whine hummed in his ears from the gunshots, and his shoulders ached. Later that night when the girl was sleeping, he would put himself in a peaceful green forest. Jorge and Luis would fade like spirits between the trees, but now the shooting lived in him and kept him on edge. It was a good edge. It helped him stay groovy.

The motel manager would describe him as a man wearing sunglasses, a brown shirt, and jeans. Anonymous. He had been careful to leave no prints. Nothing about the bodies or crime scene would point to Eagle Rock or Malibu or himself, until—and if—the bullets were matched, and that would take weeks. The police would have no reason to make the connection, and Pitman would have no reason to take notice. Jorge and Luis would be two more unidentified bodies in the City of Angels; an open homicide with questions but no answers, likely a drug buy gone bad.

Pike reloaded his pistol, then looked through the things he had taken. He went through the papers and maps first, searching for something immediately useful like Meesh's name or the name of a hotel, but found nothing. He would go over these things more closely with Cole, so for now he put them away.

He gave a cursory glance to the watch and the guns, but hesitated with the girl's picture. He imagined Luis showing it to the others; telling them, This is the one. He saw Meesh giving the picture to Luis; saying, We're gonna kill her. Pike stared at the picture, thinking, No, you won't.

Pike brushed over the other things because he wanted the phones. The phones might give him a direct and immediate connection to Alexander Meesh.

The two cell phones were identical and not unlike the phone Pike now used—bought anonymously with cash and front-loaded with prepaid calling time. Pike studied Jorge's phone first, then used the menu to bring up Jorge's number and calling history. Jorge had made only three calls, and all were to the same number. Pike guessed it was probably Luis's number—the new guys got into town, Luis would give them his number, tell them, Here, this is how you reach me. Pike pressed the send button on Jorge's phone to redial the number. Luis's phone rang. Pike turned off Jorge's phone and returned it to the backpack.

Luis had made many calls. Pike scrolled through a lengthy list that included at least a dozen calls to Ecuador. Each entry showed the number called, the date, and the time of the call. Later, he and Cole would copy the numbers, but now Pike was more interested in the recent calls.

Luis made his final call only four minutes before he died. Luis would have been at the motel, and had likely called for help or to inform the others. Pike scrolled back through the call history and found Luis had called this same number five or six times every day. No other number had been called as often.

Pike wondered if it was Meesh.

Maybe Luis had heard him with Jorge and called Meesh to see how Meesh wanted him to play it.

Pike pressed the send button to redial the number. The phone at the other end rang four times. The person at that end would see the number and think Luis was calling. Calling back to report what happened in the room.

A man answered on the fifth ring.

"Did you get the sonofabitch?"

The man had a deep, resonant voice, but did not sound like a gangster from Denver or Ecuador. His voice was cultured, and held a trace of something Pike thought might be French.

"Hello? Did we get cut off? Can you hear me?"

Pike said, "Alex Meesh."

"Wrong number."

The man hung up.

Pike pressed the send button again.

This time the man answered on the first ring. "Luis?"

"Luis and Jorge are dead."

The line was silent. This time when the man spoke, his voice was wary.

"Who is this?"

"The sonofabitch."

The man hesitated again.

"What do you want?"

"You."

Pike turned off the phone.

23

John Chen

JOHN CHEN was terrified after Pike called. He was so scared he thought he might toss his cookies; Pike on the phone, not even waiting for an answer, just growling out the threat—

"Meet me outside in an hour."

Yeah. Right.

First thing Chen did was run to the bathroom. He was convinced Pike was going to kill him. Pike probably blamed him for losing the guns, and would probably beat him to death in full view of everyone.

Chen paced in the bathroom for over an hour, sweating buckets, getting on and off the pot, trying to figure out what to do. He considered asking the security guards to follow him to his car, but decided the only chance he had of talking his way out of it was by pretending everything was cool. Make like he could get back the guns. Make up a believable lie.

Chen crept out of the bathroom, made his way to the

lobby, and peered through the glass doors into the parking lot. He saw his 'tangmobile easily enough, but he did not see Pike, or Pike's red Cherokee, or the green Lexus Pike used to shag the hottie. Chen stepped outside, glanced back inside at the waiting area, then scanned the parking lot again.

Still no Pike.

Chen wasn't sure what to do. Maybe Pike had already come and gone. Maybe Pike had not yet arrived, and Chen could still get away!

Chen sprinted for the 'tangmobile. He hadn't planned to run; he just *ran*. He flat-out hauled ass, wheezing and puffing after only fifty feet, but stoked on adrenaline. Chen jabbed his remote 'cause he had it made—he was home free, MOTHERFUCKER!!—and was throwing open that beautiful German-built door when—

—Pike spoke behind him.

"John."

"*Ahh!*"

Chen jumped sideways, but Pike once again caught him and held the door.

"Get in."

Pike was carrying a black backpack. Chen was certain it contained a gun.

Chen latched onto the door like a cat clinging to a sofa, the nervous tic under his eye popping in spasms.

Chen said, "Please don't kill me."

Pike pointed inside.

"Don't be stupid. Get in."

Pike pushed him in, then went around to the passenger side. Chen couldn't take his eyes off the backpack.

"I know how this works. You're going to take me

someplace deserted. You're going to shoot me in the head—"

Pike said, "Breathe."

Chen couldn't stop talking. The words rushed out with no more thought than his decision to run.

"The feds took the guns. I would have run them, honest to God. I didn't have anything to do with—"

One moment Chen was talking; the next, Pike's hand clamped his mouth like a vise.

Pike said, "You're my friend, John. You don't have to be afraid. Can I let go now?"

Chen nodded. His friend?

Pike let go. He opened the backpack, then held it out. Chen thought it might be a trick guys like Pike were always playing on guys like him; you look in the bag and a snake jumps out.

Chen slowly peeked into the bag, ready to jump, but it wasn't a snake.

"What is this?"

"Guns the feds don't know about and two sets of fingerprints."

Chen peered into the bag but touched nothing. He saw two small glasses in plastic sleeves, and what appeared to be two 9mm pistols, both pocked with rust and beat to hell. He knew right away from their shabby condition they were street guns; guns that had been stolen many years earlier, then traded for dope or sold, then sold or traded again, passing from scumbag to scumbag. He also saw three spent shell casings.

"Where did you get this stuff?"

"The feds who confiscated the guns—did you get their names?"

Pike had ignored his question.

"Pitman. Pitman and something else."

"Blanchette?"

"I don't know. Harriet didn't remember."

Chen glanced back at the shell casings. Their once-gleaming brass was scorched, and the backpack smelled of burnt gunpowder. Chen began to feel afraid again, but not afraid Pike would beat him to death; afraid of something deeper. Chen found Pike watching him. John saw himself reflected in Pike's dark glasses as if they were reflecting pools. In a weird way he would later wonder about, Chen grew calm. Here was Pike, calm there in the water, and his calmness spread to Chen.

John settled back.

"Are there more bodies to go with these guns?"

"Two."

"Are they connected with Eagle Rock and Malibu?"

"Yes. LAPD is on the scene now. Shots were fired, so they'll know guns are missing, but they won't know who has them. Bullets will be recovered, and those bullets will match one of these guns—the Taurus—but not the other."

Chen nodded, taking it in. If his shift hadn't ended when it did, he might have rolled out to the crime.

"If the feds knew we had these guns, would they take them?"

"Yes, but they won't know. Only you and I know, John. You're going to have to make a choice."

Chen didn't understand.

"Choice about what?"

"Seven men are dead. The Department of Justice is involved. Here we are with these guns. Least case, you could be looking at obstructing a federal investigation. Worst case, accessory to homicide."

Chen still didn't understand.

"What are you saying?"

"Tell me you want no part, I'll walk away."

Chen was stunned. He was *flabbergasted*.

"Wait. Waitaminute. You're giving me a choice?"

"Of course, it's your choice. What did you think?"

Chen stared at Pike and wondered how Pike could be so calm. His impassive face; his even voice. He studied Pike, and once more saw himself in Pike's glasses, two faces in one. In that moment, Chen remembered a meditation pool he once saw at a Buddhist monastery, its surface flat, featureless, and perfect. Chen was six years old. His uncle brought him to the monastery, and Chen had been fascinated by the pool. The mirrored surface was absolutely smooth; no leaf, no mote of dust or insect marred it; no breeze stirred its face. The pool was so like a mirror that Chen could not see beneath the surface, and believed it was no more than a few inches deep. His uncle turned away, and Chen decided to jump. It was a hot day in the San Gabriel Valley, and Chen was only six. He wanted to splash in the cool water and run to the other side. Only an inch or two deep. As empty as glass. Chen readied himself to leap, but in that moment the surface roiled and a monster reached for him, scaled in glistening armor. Red, black, and orange plates, shimmering and horrible; it broke the surface with frightening power and then it was gone. A koi, his uncle later told him, when Chen stopped crying; but the lesson was not lost on John Chen, even at six years old. A calm surface could hide great turmoil.

Chen said, "What's going on?"

"I'm trying to find out. I think the feds confiscated your evidence to hide something. If they knew about these guns, they would confiscate them, too."

"This is tied in with Eagle Rock and Malibu?"

"Yes."

Chen stared down at the guns again.

"The firearms analysts are specialists, man. What they do, it isn't just science—it's an art. She's already gone home."

"First thing tomorrow."

"I can't just walk in, here's two guns. I need a case number."

"Use the Eagle Rock number."

"She knows the feds took those guns. *She's* the one who told me."

"Tell her you got them back. Make up something, John. It's important."

Chen knew it was important. Everything Pike and Cole brought to him had been important.

He looked into the backpack again.

"What are the glasses, the fingerprints? Or you want me to print the guns?"

"The men who used these guns will end up with the coroner, but the coroner won't be able to identify them. You will."

Chen shook his head.

"I can lift the prints and run them, but it's all the same database. Live Scan is Live Scan. If the coroner didn't pull a hit, neither will I."

"These people aren't in the database. They came from Ecuador."

Chen glanced at the glasses again. A standard NCIC/Live Scan search was not a worldwide search. An international search required a special request, and even then you pretty much had to request each search by country. No single worldwide database existed, so if you didn't know where to look, you were shit out of luck.

Pike said, "Can you do that, John?"

"This is something big, isn't it?"

"Yes. Big, and getting bigger."

Chen chewed at his upper lip as he thought through what he would have to do, both for the guns and the prints. He was pretty sure he could get LaMolla to run the guns; she was still bat-shit furious with the feds for taking her toys, and doubly furious that neither Harriet nor Parker would tell her why. LaMolla would run the guns just to fuck them over.

Chen said, "I can do this. I'll take care of it."

Pike got out and walked away.

Chen stared after him, thinking Pike wasn't so bad when you got to know him. Not so scary, even though, well, you know, he was scary.

You're my friend, John.

Chen lifted out the glasses. He held them up, one by one, and saw the clean definition of fingerprint smudges even through the plastic wrappers. Chen smiled. The coroner had five unidentified stiffs, and now he would have two more. Everyone would be scratching their heads, wondering who in hell these guys were, but they wouldn't know—

—until John Chen told them.

Chen smiled even wider.

The guns would keep until tomorrow, but now was

the best time for the glasses. The lab crew was reduced, Harriet was gone, and no one would ask what he was doing. Chen stuffed the guns under his seat, locked his car, and hurried inside with the glasses.

Chen wanted to identify these guys, not only for himself and what he would get from it, but for Pike. He did not want to let down his friend Joe Pike.

24

PIKE STOPPED for takeout from an Indian restaurant
in Silver Lake even though Cole dropped off food earlier that day. He bought a spinach and cheese dish
called saag paneer, vegetable jalfrezi, and garlic naan,
thinking the girl would like them, and a quart of a
sweet yogurt drink called lassi. The lassi was rich like a
milk shake, and flavored with mango. Pike enjoyed
smelling the strong spices—the garlic and garam
masala; the coriander and cardamom. They reminded
him of the rocky villages and jungle basins where he
had first eaten these things. Pike was starving. A
queasy hunger had grown in him as the stress burned
from his system.

The sun was long down by the time Pike arrived at
their house and turned into the drive. Everything looked
fine. The door was closed and the shades glowed from
the light within the house. In the abrupt silence when
he turned off the car, his ears still whined, though less
now than before. Pike was not going to tell the girl about
Luis and Jorge, but he would tell her he had made

progress, and thought that might make her feel better about things.

Pike locked the car, went to the door, and let himself in. He remembered how his silent appearances frightened her, so this time he announced himself. He knocked twice, then opened the door.

"It's me."

Pike felt the silence as he stepped inside. Cole's iPod was on the coffee table beside an open bottle of water. Her magazines were on the floor. The house was bright with light, but Pike heard nothing. He concentrated, listening past the whine, thinking she might be playing with him because she hated the way he always surprised her, but he knew it was wrong. The silence of an empty house is like no other silence.

Pike lowered the bag of food to the floor. He drew the Kimber and held it down along his leg.

"Larkin?"

Pike moved, and was at her bedroom. He moved again, checking the second bedroom, the bath, and the kitchen. Larkin was not in the house. The rooms and their things were in order and in place, and showed no sign of a struggle. The windows were intact. The back door was locked, but he opened it, checked the backyard, then moved back through the house. The doors had not been jimmied or broken.

Pike looked for a note. No note.

Her purse and other bags were still in her bedroom. If she ran away she had not taken them.

Pike let himself out the front door and stood in the darkness on the tiny porch. He listened, feeling the neighborhood—the streetlight above its pool of silver, the open houses with golden windows, the movement of the neighbors on their porches and within their homes. Life was normal. Men with guns had not come here. No one had carried a struggling girl out to a car or heard a woman screaming. Larkin had likely walked away.

Pike stepped off the porch and went to the street, trying to decide which way she would go, and why. She had credit cards and some cash, but no phone with which to call her friends or a car. Pike decided she had probably walked down to Sunset Boulevard to find a phone, but then a woman on the porch across the street laughed. They were an older couple, and had been on their porch every night, listening to the Dodgers. Tonight their radio played music, but Pike could hear their voices clearly.

He stepped between the cars through the pool of silver light.

He said, "Excuse me."

Their porch was lit only by the light coming from within their house. The red tips of their cigarettes floated in the dark like fireflies.

The man drew on his cigarette, and the coal flared. He lowered the volume on the radio.

He said, "Good evening."

He spoke in a formal manner with a Russian accent. Pike said, "I'm from across the street."

The woman waved her cigarette.

"We know this. We see you and the young lady."

"Did you see the young lady today?"

Neither of them answered. They sat in cheap aluminum lawn chairs, shadowed in the dim light. The old man drew on his cigarette again.

Pike said, "I think she went for a walk. Did you see which way she went?"

The old man grunted, but with a spin that gave it meaning.

Pike said, "What?"

The woman said, "This is your wife?"

Pike read the weight in her question and took sex off the table.

"My sister."

The old man said, "Ah."

Something played on the woman's face that suggested she didn't believe him, and she seemed to be thinking about how to answer. She finally decided and waved her cigarette toward the street.

"She go with the boys."

The old man said, "Armenians."

The woman nodded, as if that said it all.

"She talk with them, the way they stand there all the time, them and their car, and she go with them."

Pike said, "When was this?"

"Not so long. We had just come out with the tea."

An hour ago. No more than an hour.

Pike said, "The Armenians. Where do they live?"

The woman jabbed her cigarette to the side.

"Next door, there. They are all cousins, they say, cousins and brothers. Armenians all say they are cousins, but you never know."

The old man said, "Armenians."

The house the old woman pointed to was dark, and the BMW was not on the street. She seemed to read Pike's thoughts.

"No one is home there. They all drive away."

"You hear them say where they were going?"

The woman tipped her chair back and craned her head toward the open window.

"Rolo! Rolo, come here!"

A boy wearing a Lakers jersey pushed through the screen door. He was tall and skinny, and Pike figured him for fourteen or fifteen.

"Yes, Gramma?"

"The Armenians, what is that place where they go?"

"I don't know."

The old man seemed irritated and flipped his hand in a little wave, saying stop kidding around.

"The Armenians. That club where you must never go."

The old woman cocked a brow at Pike.

"He knows. He talks with those Armenian boys. The young one. They have this club."

Rolo looked embarrassed, but described what sounded like a dance club not far away in Los Feliz. Rolo didn't remember the name, but described it well enough—an older building north of Sunset that had been freshly whitewashed and had a single word on its side. Rolo didn't remember the word, but thought it was something with a "Y."

Pike found the building twenty minutes later, just north of Sunset where it was wedged between an Armenian bookstore and a Vietnamese-French bakery. The sign across the top of the building read CLUB YERE-VAN. Beneath it, a red leather door was wedged open. Three heavy men stood on the sidewalk outside the door, talking and smoking, two in short-sleeved dress shirts and one in a gleaming leather jacket. A smaller sign above the door read PARKING IN REAR.

Pike turned at the corner. An alley behind the storefronts led to a parking lot, where a parking valet in a tiny kiosk guarded the entrance. It was still early, but already the lot was filling, with one valet waiting at the kiosk while another parked a car. A small group of people was gathered at the club's back door.

Pike didn't waste time with the parking lot or attempt to find the BMW. She would be here or she wouldn't, and if she wasn't he would move fast to continue his search. Pike pulled over behind the Vietnamese bakery and got out of his car. The valet at the kiosk saw him and hurried across the alley, waving his hands.

"You cannot park there. Parking there is not allowed."

Pike ignored him and pushed through the crowd. The whine was back, and louder than ever, but Pike didn't notice. He shoved past young women with brown cigarettes and smiling men whose eyes never left the women. He stepped into a long narrow hall where more people lined the walls, shouting at each other over a booming hip-hop dance mix that still could not drown out the whine. He shoved open the men's room door, looked, then shoved open the women's room. The people around him laughed or stared, but Pike moved on without paying attention.

The hall turned, then turned again. More and more people were packed in the hall as Pike neared its end, and the music grew louder with a throbbing bass beat, only now the beat was underscored by the crowd. The people were chanting, their palms overhead, pushing with the beat as they raised the roof, chanting—

GO baybee, GO baybee, GO baybee, GO—!

Pike threaded between the sweating bodies that spilled into the main room, and saw her. Larkin was up on the bar, peeled to her bra, playing the crowd like a stripper as she rocked her ass with the chant. She made a slow turn, running her hands from her hair to her crotch as she squatted toward the bar, making the nasty smile, and all Pike saw was the dolphin, jumping free over her hips, screaming to be recognized.

The girl saw him as he reached the bar, and stopped dancing as abruptly as if she were a child caught being naughty. She straightened and stared down at him, looking guilty and scared. Pike stopped at her feet, and in that moment they were the only two people not raising the roof.

Pike shouted over the pounding bass.

"Get down."

She didn't move. Her face was sad in a way he found confusing. He didn't tell her a second time. He wasn't sure she had heard him.

Larkin did not resist when he pulled her off the bar.

Pike turned away with the girl, and the crowd did not know what to make of it, some laughing, others booing; but then the two oldest cousins and a thick man with a large belly fronted him, the oldest cousin stepping close to block Pike's way as the thick man grabbed Pike's arm. Pike caught the man's thumb even as it touched him, peeling away his hand, rolling the hand like water turned by a rock, snapping the man face-first into the floor like a wave exploding on shore.

The people around them pulled back.

Pike had not looked away from the oldest cousin, and did not look away now.

The crowd surrounding them edged farther away. No one moved. Finally, when Pike felt they understood, he led the girl out of that place.

25

THE PEOPLE crowding the hall and the back door had not seen her dancing or what happened at the bar, but Pike pulled her directly to the car. She got in without a word. He backed out of the alley fast, then jammed it for Sunset, all the while deciding what to do about the cousins, and whether or not they should go back to the house. Pike was angry, but anger would only get in the way. His job was to keep her alive. He didn't speak until they were two blocks away.

"Did you tell them who you are?"

"No."

"What did you tell them?"

"Mona."

"What?"

"My name. They had to call me something. I told them Mona."

Pike kept watch in the mirror, checking to see if they were being followed.

"Did anyone recognize you?"

"I don't—how would I know?"

"The way someone looked at you. Someone might have said something."

"No."

"The questions they asked. A comment."

"Just dancing. They asked if I dance. They asked what movies I like. Stuff."

They were four blocks away when Pike pulled to the curb outside a liquor store. He cupped her jaw in his hand and tipped her face toward the oncoming headlights.

"Are you drunk?"

"I told you I don't drink. I'm sober a year."

"High?"

"A year."

He studied the play of light in her eyes and decided she was telling the truth. He let go, but she grabbed his hand and kept it to her face. He tugged but she held tight, and he didn't want to hurt her.

She said, "Take off those stupid glasses. Do you know how creepy this is, you with the glasses? Nobody wears sunglasses at night. Let me see. You looked at my eyes, let me see yours."

She had wanted to see his eyes up in the desert when they met. She had been all attitude then, but now she was angry and frightened.

Pike said, "They're just eyes."

He opened her fingers and took back his hand. Gently, so he would not hurt her. Not like with the man at the bar.

"What you did could get us both killed. Do you want to die? Is that what you're doing?"

"That's stupid—"

"Tell me what you want to do. You want to go home, I'll take you home. You want to live, I will end this."

"I didn't—"

Pike clamped both her hands in his.

"I will sell my life dear, but not for a suicide. I will not waste my life."

She stared for a moment as if she was confused.

"I'm not asking you to—"

Pike gripped her hands harder and cut her off again.

"If you want to go home, let's go. If you want to die, go home, *then* die, because I will not allow it."

Maybe he squeezed too hard. His hands were gristle and bone and calloused, and he was strong. Her chin dimpled and her eyes filled with tears.

"All I was doing was driving my car!"

Pike slapped the steering wheel.

"This wheel, it doesn't care. The air we're breathing, doesn't care. Suck it up—"

"You're an asshole!"

"Do you want to live or go dancing? I can have you home in twenty minutes."

"You don't know what it's like being me!"

"You don't know what it's like being me."

Headlights and taillights played on her, moving the way light plays in water; yellow and green and blue lights on the shops and signs around them painted her with a confusion of moving color. She didn't speak, and didn't seem able to speak.

Pike softened his voice.

"Tell me you want to live."

"I want to live."

"Say it again."

"I want to *live!*"

Pike let go of her hands, but she still didn't move. He straightened behind the wheel.

"We're not so different."

The girl burst out laughing.

"Ohmigod! Oh my God—*dude!* Maybe *you're* high!"

Pike put the car in gear, but kept his foot on the brake. Their sameness seemed obvious.

"You want to be seen; me, I want to be invisible. It's all the same."

The girl stared at him, then straightened herself the way he had straightened himself.

She said, "An idealist."

Pike didn't know what she was saying, so he shook his head.

She said, "Your friend. Elvis. He said you're an idealist."

Pike pulled out into traffic.

"He thinks he's funny."

She started to say something but fell silent the way people are silent when they think. They drove back to the house in that silence, but once, just the once, she reached out and squeezed his arm, and once, just the once, he patted her hand.

26

LATER, when the rhythm of her breathing suggested the girl had fallen asleep there on the couch, Pike turned off the final lamp, and the room and the house went dark. He would go out later, and wanted no light when he opened the door.

Pike sat quietly, watching her. They had eaten the Indian food, though not much of it; speaking little, her mostly, making fun of the music on Cole's iPod, and now, still wearing the headphones, she had fallen asleep.

The girl seemed even younger in sleep, and smaller, as if part of her had vanished into the couch. With her asleep, Pike believed he was seeing her Original Person. Pike believed each person created himself or herself; you built yourself from the inside out, with the tensions and will of the inside person holding the outside person together. The outside person was the face you showed the world; it was your mask, your camouflage, your message, and, perhaps, your means. It existed only so long as the inside person held it together, and when the inside person could no longer hold the mask together, the outside person dissolved and you would see the original person. Pike had observed that sleep could sometimes loosen the hold. Booze, dope, and extreme emotions could all loosen the hold; the weaker the grasp, the more easily loosened. Then you saw the person within the person. Pike often pondered these things. The trick was to reach a place where the inside person and the outside person were the same. The closer someone got to this place, the stronger they would become. Pike believed that Cole was such a person, his inside and outside very close to being one and the same. Pike admired him for it. Pike also pondered whether Cole had accomplished this through design and effort, or was one with himself because oneness was his natural state. Either way, Pike considered this a feat of enormous import and studied Cole to learn more. Pike's inside person had built a fortress. The fortress had served, but Pike hoped for more. A fortress was a lonely place in which to live.

Pike decided Larkin's original person was a child, which might be good but might be bad. A child could not hold for long. A child would weaken with the strain of holding the outer person together, and something would give. The child would be crushed and torn into something else, which might be good or might not, but either way the original person would change. Some philosophies believed that change was good, but Pike wasn't so sure. That belief had always struck him as self-serving; change often seemed inevitable, so if it was inevitable, we might as well put a good spin on it.

After a few minutes, Pike moved to the dining table, broke down his pistol exactly as he had that morning, and set about cleaning it for the second time that day.

He had no intention of sleeping. He still had to decide whether or not they would abandon the house, and much would depend on the Armenians. Pike was waiting for them.

Pike had no trouble working in the dark. He swabbed the parts with powder solvent, but was careful not to use much because he didn't want the smell to wake her. He wanted the girl to be asleep when the cousins returned.

Pike was brushing the barrel when he heard them. He went to the front window and saw the five cousins getting out of their BMW.

Pike slipped through the front door and down off the porch. The oldest cousin got out from behind the wheel. They didn't see him until he reached the sidewalk, and then the youngest, who was on the far side of the car, said something, and they turned as Pike stepped into the street.

It was quiet, this late, there in the peaceful neighborhood. The porches were empty. The old people and the families were sleeping. Cars were parked and streets were empty except for Pike and the five cousins, there in the cone of blue light.

Pike stopped a few feet away, looking at each of them until he settled on the oldest, the one who had tried to front him in the bar.

Pike said, "I figure she didn't tell you we're married. I figure you didn't know, which is why you took her out. I figure now that you know, we won't have this problem again."

The oldest cousin raised his palms, showing Pike he regretted the misunderstanding.

"No problems, my friend. She said you just shared the house, that's all. Roommates. She said you were roommates."

The younger one nodded along.

"Hey, we were just chillin' out here, dude. She came out and started talkin' with us."

The youngest had become so Americanized he spoke hip-hop with an Armenian accent.

Pike nodded.

"I understand. So we don't have a problem between us."

"No, man, we are cool."

Pike read their expressions and body language, not to see if they were cool, but to see if they had recognized her. If they or someone they knew at the club had recognized her, they would have been talking about it the rest of the evening. Pike decided they neither knew nor suspected. Larkin was just another out-of-her-mind chick to these guys, another girl gone wild. He decided they were safe.

Pike said, "Mona has done this before and it's caused problems. There's a man, he's been stalking her. We moved, but we know he's trying to find her. If you guys see anyone, will you let me know?"

The oldest said, "Of course, man. No problem."

Pike put out his hand, and the oldest shook.

The second oldest, who had been staring with a kind of awe, finally spoke.

"What was that you did at the club? What do you call that, what you did?"

The youngest laughed.

"He opened a can of whup ass, fool!"

Two of the cousins laughed, but not the oldest, who told them it was late and they should go inside.

The oldest cousin waited until the others were gone, then turned back to Pike with sympathy in his eyes.

He said, "I am sorry you suffer this, my friend. You must love her very much."

Pike left the oldest cousin there in the blue light and returned to the house. Larkin was still sleeping. He brought the spread from her bedroom, covered her, then went to the kitchen for a bottle of water. He drank it. He took the carton of leftover jalfrezi from the fridge, but did not eat much. Pike resumed cleaning the pistol. He enjoyed the certainty of the steel in his hands—the hard and definite shapes, the predictable way the assembled weapon would function, the comfort of its simplicity. He didn't have to think when he worked with his hands.

Pike watched the sleeping girl while he waited for the following day.

STARING AT
THE SUN

27

PIKE SLEPT only a few minutes that night, falling into listless naps between meditations that left him more anxious than rested. The hunt was picking up speed, and now Pike wanted to push harder. The harder he pushed, the faster Meesh would have to react, and the more demands he would make on his men. His men would grow resentful and Meesh would get angry, and Pike would push faster and harder. This was called stressing the enemy, and when Meesh felt enough stress, he would realize he was no longer the hunter. He would accept that he was the prey. This was called breaking the enemy. Then Meesh would make a mistake.

At sunrise, Pike went into the bathroom so he wouldn't disturb the girl. He phoned Cole and told him about the motel. Pike knew Cole was irritated by the tone of his voice.

"Were you made at the scene?"

"No."

"Are you *sure*?"

Pike didn't answer, and finally Cole sighed.

"Okay, maybe not. The cops haven't kicked down my door. Give me time for a shower, then I'll head over."

When Pike left the bathroom, the girl was up. This was the earliest she had been up since he met her. She glanced away as if she was still embarrassed about the night before.

She said, "You make coffee?"

"Didn't want to wake you."

"I'll do it."

She started for the kitchen, but he stopped her.

"I have some things here. Come look."

Last night he had not told her about the motel, but now he took her to the table, where he had the passports and papers waiting for Cole. He held up Luis's passport, open to the picture. She studied it for a moment, then shook her head.

"Jésus Leone. Who is he?"

"One of the men who invaded your home. The one who beat your housekeeper. His real name was Luis. I don't know his last name."

Pike showed her the other passports one by one, but she recognized none of the men. She barely glanced at their pictures.

"Where did you get these?"

Pike ignored the question.

"Have you heard the name Barone?"

"No."

"How about someone named Carlos?"

She shook her head, then picked up Luis's passport again. She studied the picture, but Pike knew she wasn't thinking about Luis.

"Does it bother you when, you know, you—?"

"No."

"It doesn't?"

"No."

She dropped the passport back with the others.

"Good."

When Cole arrived, he brought a small television. Pike had not asked for it and neither had the girl, but Cole brought a thirteen-inch Sony.

"It was just sitting in the guest room," he said. "I'm not even sure it works."

Pike doubted Cole would have gone to the trouble of lugging it out to his car without checking to see if it worked, but he didn't say anything. They had no cable, but the set came with rabbit-ear antennas. They put it on a table in the living room, turned it on, and the little set worked fine. They couldn't get any of the cable channels, but it showed the local L.A. stations with a clear, sharp picture.

Larkin thanked Cole for the television, but with no great enthusiasm. She had been subdued all morning; not distant, just quiet. She had made a shy smile at Cole when he arrived, and watched silently as they set up the TV, and once it was going she parked herself on the couch with a cup of coffee. She stared at one of the local morning shows, but whenever Pike glanced over, she didn't seem to be paying attention. Like she was thinking about other things.

When the girl was squared up with the TV, Pike showed Cole the passports. Cole angled their pages to catch the light.

"These are good fakes. Excellent fakes. A dozen of these guys came up?"

"What the man said. Now there are five."

Cole put the passports aside.

"Unless they call reinforcements."

Pike showed Cole the maps, the airline tickets and the spiral notebook page he took from Luis. The ratty page had been folded and refolded dozens of times, and probably crushed into Luis's pockets dozens more. Indecipherable handwritten notes covered the front and back of the page at all angles, with no sentence more than a few words long. Before the girl woke, Pike had spent almost twenty minutes trying to read it, and failed. Luis had probably taken notes while he was driving, likely with a phone wedged under his ear and one hand on the wheel. Pike guessed they were names and directions. The numbers were clearly phone numbers.

Cole frowned at the page.

"Guess they don't teach penmanship in thug school."

Cole glanced at the plane tickets and maps, stacked them with the spiral notebook page, then examined the watch. His eyebrows went up when he read the inscription.

"George as in George King?"

"It's a sixty-thousand-dollar watch."

"I can run the serial numbers."

Cole put the watch on the maps, then turned to the phones. Pike had made a list of the outgoing and incoming numbers in each phone's call history. He had labeled the phones JORGE and LUIS. Jorge had made only six calls, all to Luis's number. Luis had made forty-seven calls to nineteen different numbers. Cole glanced at Pike's list, then the two phones.

"Which is which?"

Pike touched one phone, then the other.

"Jorge. Luis."

Cole turned on the phones, then studied their buttons.

"Too bad we don't know the passwords. We could hear the messages. If they have messages."

"Leave them on. Maybe someone will call."

"Maybe you calling that guy wasn't the world's greatest idea. He'll probably dump the phone and buy another. He's probably already thrown it away."

"They would have known we had the phones when they found Luis and Jorge. I wanted to stress him."

Cole glanced at the girl to make sure she wasn't listening, and lowered his voice.

"You've killed seven of his people. He's slugging Maalox."

"Now it's personal. Better this way."

"What if he figures it's so personal he goes back to Colombia?"

"I'll go after him."

Cole glanced at her again.

"But you don't think the guy you spoke with was Meesh?"

"There was the accent. It was slight, but I could hear it. French, maybe. Or French with Spanish. Yesterday I thought he couldn't be Meesh, but now I'm not sure."

"Why?"

"How does a thug from Denver sound? His file didn't mention an accent, but those briefs leave out a lot."

Cole skimmed the numbers again.

"Okay, even if they dump their phones, I might be

able to do something with this. These nineteen numbers mean he called nineteen phones, and those phones called other phones. Not all of these phones are going to be throwaways. I'll talk to my friend at the phone company. Maybe she can get call records from the other service providers. Sooner or later we'll hit real phones listed to people with real names."

Pike caught the girl watching him. The morning show hosts were talking about a paternity suit filed against a movie star, but she hadn't been paying attention.

Pike said, "How're you doing?"

"I'm real good."

She turned back to the television.

Cole had returned to the airline tickets and was making notes of his own. Neither the maps, nor the tickets, nor the little scraps of paper contained a breakthrough clue, something like a hotel receipt signed by Alexander Meesh, but Pike had not expected anything so direct. Cole would have to run the numbers just like Chen was running the guns. Sooner or later something would pay off and Pike would be closer to Meesh. Pike was patient with the process. The chase was about gaining a single step. Then you gained another. Pretty soon you had the guy in your crosshairs. It was all about gaining the one single step.

Pike left Cole to check the front windows. The cousins' Beemer remained in its spot, and the street and the houses were normal. No new cars had appeared, and no strangers lurked in the bushes. Nothing seemed out of place.

Even though it was still early, Pike felt the day warming and saw what the heat would bring. A light haze hung in a fading sky. By noon, the air would be rich with hydrocarbons and ozone, and would eat at their skin like invisible bugs.

He turned from the window. The girl was staring at the television, but had been watching him again. He caught the motion as her eyes went back to the screen.

He said, "We'll turn on the AC today."

"That's great. Thanks."

"You okay?"

"Yeah. I'm good."

Pike wondered why she still wasn't looking at him. It wasn't like her. She didn't seem angry and wasn't giving him attitude. She just wouldn't look at him when he was looking at her. Pike checked to see Cole was still working, then went to the girl. He stood so close she had no choice but look up at him.

She said, "What?"

"Don't worry about it."

"What?"

"Last night. Forget it. We're okay, you and me."

"I know."

She seemed even more uncomfortable, but made a smile as Cole called from the table.

"I found something."

Cole was tipped back in the chair, holding up the spiral notebook page.

Pike said, "You can make out what he wrote?"

"Not the words, but I got most of the numbers. Look—"

Pike went over, and this time the girl came with him. Cole smoothed the page on the table, and pointed out one of the numbers. 18185.

Pike said, "Like he started to write a phone number, but stopped."

818 was the area code for the San Fernando Valley.

Cole said, "This isn't a phone number. It looks like he started to write a phone number, but it's an address—"

Cole put one of his handmade maps over the spiral page, then looked at Larkin.

"This is your street. The number jumped out because I've been making my notes by address."

Larkin said, "I'm at 17922."

"You're three blocks north in the 17900 block. The numbers get larger as you go south. This is where you had the accident—"

Cole touched a place on the street where he had made a small X to mark the accident, then tapped the building next to it.

"—and this is 18185, right on the alley they were backing out of when you nailed them."

Cole had written each building's address in small block numbers. 18185 was the abandoned warehouse at the mouth of the alley.

Pike said, "When did Luis arrive in-country?"

Cole checked the dates on the airline ticket.

"Not until four days after the accident. The feds had already been all over the area. Larkin was back with her father in Beverly Hills, and the wreck was old news. If they were lining up on Larkin, they would want her loft and her home in Beverly Hills, but why would they care where the wreck happened?"

Pike knew Cole was right. Luis and his hitters would have had no reason to check out the accident site.

"So maybe he wasn't sent to the wreck. Maybe he went to the building."

"We should take another look."

Pike went for a long-sleeved shirt as Cole gathered up his work. When Pike was buttoning the shirt, he caught the girl watching him again. He had been thinking about what to do when he left her once more, but now he decided.

"You can stay here if you want. You don't have to come sit in the car."

The girl looked surprised, then glanced away again as if the weight of his eyes was painful. The Larkin he had seen dancing on the bar hadn't been awkward or uncomfortable, and neither had the Larkin in the desert, but this was a different Larkin. Pike sensed she wanted to say something, but hadn't made peace with what.

She said, "I'd like to come. If that's okay."

Not telling or demanding. Asking.

Pike said, "Whatever you want."

Five minutes later they went to the cars.

28

PIKE and Larkin followed Cole down from the hills, cruising silently along streets that were unnaturally clear. The girl wasn't sitting with her legs twisted beneath her and her shoes on the seat the way she had yesterday. She faced forward with her feet on the floor. Pike made no comment. If she wanted to speak, she would speak. Or not.

He watched her from the corner of his eye, and twice she seemed about to speak, but both times she turned away. They were crossing Sunset Boulevard when John Chen called.

"I couldn't call before now."

Chen was whispering so softly Pike had trouble hearing him. Other people were probably around.

"Can you call from a better location?"

"I'm at a homicide in Monterey Park. Some douche bag poured Drano down his mother's throat. Pinned her until she stopped kicking, then turned himself in. I been out here since six fuckin' o'clock, man. I'm in the bathroom."

"What do you have?"

"You were spot-on about those prints."

"Get an ID?"

"Two out of two through the South American database at Interpol. Shit, hang on—"

Chen's voice grew muffled, then louder, Chen saying, "I can't help how long—it was bad *carnitas*—"

Chen whispered, "Pricks."

"Tell me what you found."

"Jorge Manuel Petrada and Luis Alva Mendoza, Petrada having been born in Colombia and showing arrests all over Colombia, Venezuela, and Ecuador. Mendoza was born in Ecuador, but he managed to spread around his career, too. Both subjects have pulled prison time and are currently wanted on multiple counts of murder, with Mendoza showing wants on three counts of rape. Where'd you get those glasses, man?"

Pike ignored him.

"Who do they work for?"

"Says they're known associates of someone named Esteban Barone, part of the Quito Cartel out of Ecuador, ID'd by DEA as one of the groups who took up the slack after the Medellín and Cali cartels in Colombia were broken."

"Do they have associates or family here in L.A.?"

"Not listed here."

"Anywhere in the U.S.?"

"Nothing."

"What about gang affiliations?"

Latin gangs from L.A. like Mara 18 and MS-13 had spread to Central and South America.

"No, man. They were soldiers for this guy, Barone. Nothing suggests they've been here before."

Chen had confirmed what Pike learned from Jorge, but Pike wasn't hearing anything that would bring him closer to Meesh.

"Did you run the guns?"

"Can't until I get outta here, but listen—the feds confiscated the Malibu guns, too. Rolled into the Sheriff's lab like they did with us and cleaned them out—the guns, the casings, everything."

"Pitman?"

"The same kind of deal—no questions asked. Those stiffs from Malibu and Eagle Rock, are they part of this Quito group, too?"

"Yes."

"Here's what I think—I think the feds already know who they are. I think they just want us out of the picture."

"You're probably right, John."

"I don't get it. So they're drug dealers. Why would the feds care if we ID some assholes from Ecuador? Our people work with international agencies all the time. I know some narcotics guys, they spend so much time in Mexico they damn near live there."

Pike was wondering the same. Money laundering was money laundering whether the money came from Jersey mobsters or drug lords in Ecuador. The energy the feds were burning to cover their case against the Kings made less sense by the hour, and didn't require freezing out the police. Pike trusted none of it. He believed Pitman was covering something else, but he didn't know what.

Chen said, "You think if I ran the Eagle Rock and

Malibu prints through Interpol, I'd get a hit? That would be a major coup, bro. That would be excellent."

"Better to let it rest, John."

"Better?"

"Let it rest, we might find it's larger than we think."

"You're not telling me everything, are you?"

"I don't know everything yet. I know some, but not all. I'll tell you more when I know."

Chen grunted, the grunt saying he was okay with gambling on an even bigger payoff down the line.

"Let me ask you something—these guys from Ecuador, what are they doing up here?"

Pike gave the best answer he could.

"Dying."

Pike closed his phone, then glanced at the girl. She was watching him again.

"The full name is Esteban Barone."

"It still doesn't ring a bell."

"The men trying to kill you work for Barone."

"I thought they worked for Meesh."

"He's in business with Meesh. That's what Pitman claimed—that Meesh was up here investing South American money."

When she didn't respond, Pike looked at her. She was staring at him in the same thoughtful way she had all morning, but now she didn't look away.

She said, "I need to ask you something—what you said last night, that I want to be seen. Why did you say that?"

Pike thought it was obvious.

"You feel invisible. If no one sees you, you don't exist, so you find ways to be seen."

A soft line appeared between her eyebrows, but she didn't seem angry or insulted. Pike thought she looked sad.

"I've been in therapy since I was eleven. You've known me three days. Jesus, am I that obvious?"

"Yes."

"How? Because I was dancing on the bar? Go see what they do at Mardi Gras."

Pike thought about it to give her an example.

"In the desert. How you looked at your father. Not looking to see him, but to see if he was paying attention. He was focused on Bud and his lawyer and me, so you would say something outrageous to get his attention. You needed to have him see you."

She glanced out the window.

"I don't care if he sees me or not."

"Not now maybe, but once. You wouldn't need it so badly if you didn't care."

She looked back at him, and now the line between her brows had softened.

"And you can see all that by watching me?"

"By seeing you. There's a difference."

"And how is it you see so clearly?"

Pike thought about whether or not he wanted to answer. Pike was a private man. He never talked about himself, and didn't care much for people who did, but he figured the girl had a right to ask.

"My folks and I would be watching TV, my mom and dad and me, or we'd be eating, and something would set him off. My old man would knock the hell out of me. Or her. I learned to watch for the signs. How his shoulders bunched, the way his lips pressed together, how much booze he poured. Half an inch more in the glass, he was ready to go. Little things tell you. You see them, you're okay. You miss them, you go to the hospital. You learn to watch."

She was silent, and when Pike glanced over, her face was sad.

She said, "I'm sorry."

"Point is, I saw the play between you and your father. You needed something from him you weren't getting, and probably never had."

Pike glanced at the girl. She was still watching him.

She said, "Thanks for seeing me."

Pike nodded.

"Bud told Gordon and my father you would protect me. My father, he just looked at Gordon. Gordon, he just wanted to know how much. But Bud told him you were the one. I guess you are."

Pike continued driving.

"Bud say anything else?"

"Just that he had worked with you. That we could trust you. He said you would get the job done. He guaranteed it."

Pike took that in without comment or expression, hiding his sadness from the girl as he hid most everything else.

THE SHORTSTOP LOUNGE
0720 HOURS

The Shortstop was an LAPD tradition. Located on Sunset Boulevard in Echo Park, midway between Alvarado

*and Dodger Stadium, the Shortstop Lounge was conven-
ient to Rampart Station and the police academy. Birth-
day parties were celebrated between dark wood walls
lined with badges and department patches, as were
divorces, retirements, promotions, memorials, and the
supercharged hyper-life moments whenever an officer
survived a shoot-out. Careers began at the Shortstop.
Careers also ended.*

*At 0720 hours on his day off, Pike sat at a small
table, the only man seated alone, ignoring the tense
glances and comments. Pike had expected worse, but he
was good with it. He had chosen this place to see Bud
Flynn.*

*Pike now had three years, four months, and change
on the job. His boot year ended twenty-eight months
earlier. Of his academy classmates, Pike was the first and
only to kill another human being in the line of duty, a
distinction about which he held mixed feelings. Five
weeks ago, he had become the first of his class to kill a
second man. This second shooting occurred on a brutal
afternoon at the Islander Palms Motel, a ragged roach
trap where, by his own admission before an LAPD
Board of Review, Joe Pike caused the shooting death of a
decorated twenty-two-year LAPD veteran named Abel
Wozniak while defending the life of a pedophile named
Leonard DeVille. Abel Wozniak had been Pike's partner.
They had sat together at this same table many times, but
now that was done.*

BOARD OF REVIEW
Inquiry into shooting death of Officer Abel Wozniak

Timeline of events (from the findings):

0925 hrs: Ramona Ann Escobar (5 yr, female) abducted fm Echo Park Lake

0952 hrs: APB Escobar; suspct L. DeVille, knwn pedophile, in area

1140 hrs: Ofcs Wozniak & Pike learn loc. of DeVille, seen by wit w/ minor female child

1148 hrs: Ofcs Wozniak & Pike arrv Islander Palms Motel

1152 hrs: Ofcs Wozniak & Pike enter DeVille rm; question DeVille; find photographic evidence of Escobar, but child is not present
(note for record: evidence inclds photos of minor female Escobar sexually abused by DeVille)

1155 hrs: Ofc Wozniak threatens to kill DeVille unless DeVille produces girl; Ofc Wozniak strikes DeVille with service pistol
(note for record: examining ER physician confirms DeVille injuries consistent)

1156 hrs: Ofc Pike attempts to calm Wozniak with no success; Ofc Wozniak aims weapon at DeVille; Ofc Pike intervenes

1157 hrs: *Ofcs Wozniak & Pike struggle; weapon dis-*
              charges; Ofc Wozniak DOA at scene
(note for record: SID, CI & ME exam results consistent)
(note for record: Ofc Woz prior hist. w/ suspect DeVille;
              two arrests)

Finding: *Accidental Discharge. No charges brought*
              in above matter.

By seven-thirty that morning, the Shortstop was filled with night-watch officers anxious to burn off the street before heading home. Pike ignored the way they looked at him, the cop who had caused his partner's death protecting a pedophile.

Bud had the grim look of a gunfighter when he entered the bar, thumbs hooked in his belt. He was one of the few officers present who still wore his uniform; everyone else had showered and changed at the station. His jaw was tight, and his mouth was a hard, lipless crevice. Bud squinted around the room, searching the crowd until Pike raised a hand. They hadn't seen each other in weeks. Since before it happened.

When they made eye contact, Pike nodded.

Bud stared across the room, still with his thumbs in his belt, then spoke so loud every cop in the place turned to look.

He said, "There's the best damned man I ever trained, Officer Joe Pike."

An anonymous voice in the background spoke just as loud.

"Fuck him, and fuck you, too."

A few of them laughed.

Bud walked directly to Pike's table and mounted a stool. If Bud heard the comments, he did not react. Neither did Pike. It was like facing down a crowd in a riot situation.

Pike said, "Thanks for coming."

"Take off those goddamned sunglasses. They look silly in here."

Just like Pike was still a boot and Bud was still his T.O. Pike didn't take them off.

He said, "I'm leaving the job. I didn't want you to hear it from someone else."

Bud stared at him like Pike owed him money, then scowled at the men lining the bar. A division robbery detective was watching them and met Bud's eye.

Bud, maintaining the contact, said, "What?"

The detective returned to his drink, and Bud turned back to Pike.

"Assholes."

"Forget it."

"Don't let these bastards beat you. Just ride it out."

Pike spread his hands, taking in the bar and everyone in it.

"We're at the Shortstop, Bud. Somebody has something to say, they can say it to my face."

Bud made a ragged smile then, but it was pained.

"Yeah. I guess that's you. Asking me here instead of someplace else."

"I'm turning in the papers today. I wanted to tell you, man-to-man."

Bud took a breath, then laced his fingers. Pike thought Bud Flynn looked disappointed, and was sorry for that.

Bud said, "Listen. Don't do this. Put in for Metro. That Metro is an elite unit, the best of the best. After Metro, you could do whatever you want in this job. If you don't want to be a detective, you could put in for SWAT. Whatever you want."

"It's done, Bud. I'm out."

"Goddamn it, you're too good to be out. You're a police officer."

Pike tried to think of something to say, but couldn't. Not what he really wanted to say. Even with three years on the job, Pike still thought of himself as Bud's boot and wanted his approval, though he did not expect it now.

Bud suddenly leaned toward him again and lowered his voice.

"What happened in there?"

The Islander Palms Motel.

Pike leaned back and immediately cursed himself for it. Bud would read his move as being evasive. All through Pike's boot year, Bud had taught him to read people—the nuance of body language, expression, and action could save a cop's life.

Pike tried to cover himself by leaning forward again, but he already sensed it was too little, too late. Bud was good. Bud was a wizard.

Pike said, "You know what happened. Everyone knows. I told the review board."

"Bullshit. Struggle for the gun, my ass. I knew Woz, and I sure as hell know you. If you wanted that gun he would've been on his ass before he could fart."

Pike simply shook his head, trying to pull it in deep, trying to be empty.

"That's what happened."

Bud studied him, then lowered his voice still more.

"I heard he was into something. Was Woz being investigated?"

Pike could see Bud working on the read and knew any movement or expression would be a tell, so he cleared himself and answered with the fewest words.

"I don't know."

Bud placed his hand on Pike's arm. Digging deeper.

"I heard the M.E. had questions. Said the angle of entry was consistent with a self-inflicted wound."

Never looking away, Pike repeated what he told the review board.

"Wozniak pointed his weapon at DeVille. I grabbed it and we struggled. Instead of turning the weapon away from Wozniak, I turned it toward him. Maybe I could have done something else, but that's what I did. The gun discharged during the struggle."

Bud spoke slowly.

"You guys wrestling with the gun, I could maybe see it going off in his stomach or maybe his chest, but up at his temple?"

"Let it go, Bud. That's what happened."

Bud stared at him so hard it felt as if he were seeing inside Pike's head.

"So what happened in there, it has nothing to do with Wozniak's family."

Like Bud knew. Like he could read Pike's mind that Wozniak was being investigated for theft and criminal conspiracy, that Pike had been trying to make him resign for the sake of his family.

"No."

"It has nothing to do with his death benefits. That if he committed suicide, they would get nothing, but if he died fighting with you, they still get the checks."

Like everything Pike ever thought or felt was written on his face.

"Let it go, Bud. That's what happened."

Bud finally settled back, and Pike loved and respected him all the more. Bud seemed satisfied with what he had seen.

Bud said, "Tell you what. I know the sheriff out in San Bernardino. You could get on out there. Hell, I know some pretty good guys up in Ventura County. You could get on up there, too."

"I've already got another job lined up."

"What are you going to do?"

"Africa."

Bud frowned deeper, like why would any sane man give up being a cop to go over there?

"What's over there, the Peace Corps?"

Pike hadn't wanted to get into all this, but now he didn't know how to avoid it.

"It's contract work. Military stuff. They have work over there."

Bud stiffened, clearly upset.

"What's that mean, contract work?"

"They need people with combat experience. Like when I was a Marine."

"You mean a fucking mercenary?"

Pike didn't answer. He was already sorry he told Bud his plans.

"Jesus Christ. If you want to play soldier, re-up in

the goddamn Marines. That's a stupid idea. Why in hell do you want to go get yourself killed in a shithole like Africa?"

Pike had taken a contract job with a licensed professional military corporation in London. It was work he understood and at which he excelled, with the clarity of a clearly defined objective. And right now Pike wanted clarity. He would be away from Wozniak's ghost. And far away from Wozniak's wife.

Pike said, "I've got to get going. I wanted to tell you I'm glad you were my T.O. I wanted to thank you."

Pike put out his hand, but Bud did not take it.

"Don't do this."

"It's done."

Pike left out his hand, but Bud still did not take it. Bud slid off the stool, then hooked his thumbs in his belt.

Bud said, "Day we met, you wanted to protect and to serve. You quoted the motto. I guess that's over."

Pike finally lowered his hand.

"I'm disappointed, son. I thought you were better than this."

Son.

Bud Flynn walked out of the Shortstop, and they would not speak again until they met in the high desert.

Pike sat alone at the small table, feeling empty and numb.

I'm disappointed, son.

He listened to the men and women around him. They were like any other group of people with whom he had served—talking, complaining, laughing, lying; some he respected, others not; some he liked, others not; as different from each other as pebbles on the beach, but different from most other people in a way Pike admired—they were people who ran toward danger to protect and to serve. Pike loved being a cop. He couldn't think of anything he would rather be, but you played the cards you were dealt, and now this life was gone.

Pike left the Shortstop. He went to his truck, thinking about his first night with Bud Flynn, the night they answered the domestic call. Pike hardly thought about that night, just as he rarely thought about his combat missions or the beatings his old man used to give him. Pike flashed on scrapbook photos of Kurt Fabrocini stabbing Bud in the chest. He saw the Beretta's sights aligned at the top of Fabrocini's ear at the instant he squeezed the trigger; he saw the red mist. Then, after, Bud still shaking, saying, "Our job isn't to kill people—it's to keep people alive." Saying that about a man who had been stabbing him in the chest. What a man, Bud Flynn. What a police officer.

Pike said, "I'm going to miss you."

The father he never had.

Pike started his truck. He drove away. He played the cards he was dealt even when they were bad cards, and he lived with the result.

But sometimes he wished for more.

29

THE STREET grumbled with outbound trucks moving cargo up along the river toward the freeway. The same roach coach sat at the mouth of the alley, only today, this time of morning, the thinning crowd of sweatshop workers lingered on the sidewalk with breakfast burritos and plastic containers of orange juice. Pike smelled the chorizo and chili as they pulled to the curb behind Cole.

Pike studied the warehouse until he found the address, faded and peeling but still readable, like a shadow on the pale wall. 18185. Cole was good.

Pike glanced at Larkin.

"You sure you're okay with this?"

"I want to be here. I'm okay."

She started to open the door, but Pike stopped her.

"Wait for Elvis."

Cole got out of his car first. He scanned the surrounding roofs and windows like a Secret Service agent clearing the way for the president, then meandered around his car to the passenger side. He hefted a long green duffel from behind the seat and slung it over his shoulder. Pike saw him wince. From the way the bag pulled, you could see it was heavy.

Cole came back to the girl's side of the car.

"There's a little parking lot at the far end of the alley should work for us. Padlocked gate and a couple of doors. Let's go see what we see."

Larkin said, "Are we going to break in?"

Cole laughed.

"It's been known to happen."

They walked past the rear of the catering truck, then down the alley with the abandoned warehouse on their right and the sweatshop on their left, first Cole, then the girl, then Pike. The huge loading doors were still chained, but Cole continued past them and along the alley to the next street. At the corner, a small parking lot with another loading dock was cut into the building. The parking lot was littered with yellowed newspapers and trash, and brown explosions erupted from cracks in the tarmac where weeds had sprouted, flourished, and died. A loading dock lipped from one wall as high as Pike's chest, and a metal, human-size door was set at ground level on the adjoining wall. A realty sign covered with graffiti was wired to the gate, advertising the building for sale or lease.

Pike turned to watch the catering van as Cole peered through the fence, but Cole spoke almost at once.

"Yep. They were here."

When Pike turned back, Cole pointed at the corner of the roof. A pale blue alarm panel was mounted near the end of the building, but the cover was missing. Old wires had been cut, and new wires had been clipped to bypass the old. Whoever jumped the alarms hadn't bothered to replace the cover, as if they didn't care whether or not their work was discovered.

Pike glanced back at Cole.

"You still game?"

"Sure. Insurance companies make the owners carry security even when the buildings aren't used. Now we don't have to worry about the rent-a-cops. Makes it easier."

Cole pulled a three-foot bolt cutter from the duffel, snapped the padlock, and Pike pushed open the gate. Cole went directly to the door, and Pike followed with the girl, lagging behind to cover their rear.

The employee door was faced with metal and secured by three industrial-strength dead-bolt locks. Cole didn't waste time trying to pick the locks. He hammered them out of the door with a steel chisel and a ten-pound maul. Pike was proud of the girl. She didn't ask questions or run her mouth. She stood to the side with her arms crossed and watched Cole work.

When the door swung open, Cole returned his tools to the duffel, then passed a flashlight to Pike and kept one for himself. He also gave them disposable latex gloves.

Pike went in first, stepping into a gloomy office suite that had long since been stripped of furniture, equipment, and everything else of value. A heavy layer of dust and rat droppings covered the floor, and the air was sharp with the smell of urine. Pike snapped on his flashlight and saw a confusion of fresh footprints pressed into the dust.

Pike moved deeper into the room so Elvis and Larkin could follow, then squatted to examine the footprints.

Larkin said, "Ugh. It stinks in here."

Cole snapped on his light and walked it over the prints.

"What do you think?"

Pike stood.

"Three people. A week or so ago. Maybe ten days."

Pike traced his light along a trail of footprints to the corner of the room where a large stain mottled the floor.

Larkin said, "What's that?"

"One of our friends took a leak."

"Oh, that is *so* gross."

The footprints came from a second room beyond the first.

Pike said, "Back here."

Like the first room, this second room was empty, but a door and a window were set into the wall so the manager could keep an eye on things in the warehouse. An enormous empty space lay beyond the glass, murky with a dim glow from skylights cut into the roof. Pike shined his flashlight through the glass, but the empty darkness swallowed the beam. His view of the room was limited, but he saw more footprints beyond the glass.

Cole and the girl came up on either side of him.

Pike said, "They came here the one time. They looked around and haven't been back."

The girl cupped her eyes to the glass.

"What were they looking for? Why would this place have anything to do with me?"

Cole went to the door.

"That's what we want to find out. Tell me if you find a clue, okay?"

When Cole opened the door, a fresh spike of ammonia burned at Pike's nose, but a stronger smell was behind it; something earthy and organic.

Larkin covered her mouth.

"Ugh."

Pike followed Cole into the warehouse, with the girl coming out behind him. Their footsteps echoed loudly, and their lights swung through the murk like sabers.

The girl saw it first.

She said, "Ohmigod! That's the car!"

Pike and Cole saw it together after that. A silver Mercedes sedan was parked near the loading dock off the little parking lot, alone and obvious in the empty warehouse. The fender behind the left rear wheel was crumpled and bent.

Larkin said, "This is the car I hit. This is the Mercedes."

The girl walked over as if none of this were strange or frightening or not a part of her everyday life.

Pike said, "Larkin."

"This is the car!"

She walked directly to the car, looked inside, then clutched her belly and heaved.

Cole caught up to her and turned her away as Pike shined his light through the glass. A dead man in the front passenger seat was slumped across the center console. A dead woman was curled on her side in the backseat. Both were naked, with their ankles and knees and wrists bound by cord. Their bodies were discolored and swollen so badly their bindings had split the flesh. Each had been shot in the back of the head. Pike figured they were the Kings, but he had never seen the Kings. He turned back to the girl.

Pike said, "I think it's the Kings, but I don't know. Can you see?"

Larkin was breathing through her mouth. Her face had gone grey, but she came closer.

"It just surprised me, that's all."

Pike stood between her and the car.

"Don't look in the back. Just look at the man in the front seat."

Pike shined his light. The girl leaned past him enough to peer into the car, then turned away.

"That's him. That's George King. Ohmigod."

Pike glanced at Cole, and Cole nodded.

Pike said, "Go with Elvis. I'll only be a few minutes."

"No. I can stay."

"You don't have to stay."

Her face hardened, and Pike liked how she was pulling herself together.

"I can stay. I'm all right."

Pike turned back to the Mercedes and shined the light in again. The keys were still in the ignition, which meant the car wouldn't be locked. Pike looked back at the girl.

"Cover your mouth and nose. With a handkerchief. If you don't have a handkerchief, use your shirt."

She looked confused.

"What?"

"The smell. Cover your mouth and nose."

She pulled up her shirt and pressed it hard with both

hands over her mouth and nose, but now she backed away. Cole backed away, too.

Pike opened the driver's-side door. The gases from the bodies had been building for more than a week. The smell rolled over him with the rotten-egg stink of a body dissolving itself. Pike had smelled these things before, in Africa and Southeast Asia and other places; corpses left for days in buildings or along the sides of roads or in shallow open graves. Nothing smelled worse than the death of another human being. Not horses or cattle or rotten whales washed onto a beach. Human death was the smell of what hid in the future, waiting for you.

Behind him, the girl said, "Holy *Christ!*"

Pike took the keys from the ignition, then checked the man's body. George King had been shot behind the right ear. The bullet exited his left temple, taking a piece of his head the size of a lime with it. If he had been wearing a watch or rings or any other jewelry, those items had been taken. Pike found no other wounds. The lack of blood spatter and tissue fragments in the car suggested he had been shot outside the vehicle, then placed within it.

Pike checked the floorboard under the steering wheel, the area beneath the seat, and the sun visor. A California Vehicle Registration slip and a card offering proof of insurance were clipped to the visor, issued in the name of George King. Pike moved to the backseat.

The woman was in worse shape than the man. She had also been shot in the back of the head, but she had been shot twice, as if the first bullet hadn't killed her. Most of her right eye and cheek were missing, as was her jewelry. She was curled on her right side, but her left arm and hip were mottled deep purple where her blood had settled. This also suggested they had been killed at a location other than the warehouse, then transported here, giving time for the lividity to form.

Pike checked the floorboards and the seat beneath her body, but found nothing. He backed out of the car, opened the trunk, and found a layer of blood-soaked newspapers. This confirmed the story. They had been executed elsewhere, loaded into the trunk, then driven to the warehouse in their own car.

Pike put the keys back into the ignition, closed the car, then joined Cole and the girl. They were standing by the loading dock door, as far from the car as they could get. Pike was halfway to them before he took a deep breath. The smell was so bad his eyes were burning.

Cole pointed his light at the ceiling, then along the tire tracks on the dusty floor.

"They came through the skylight, opened the door from the inside, and drove right up the ramp."

The girl said, "I think I'm going to throw up again."

"Let's go. Let's get out of here."

Outside, they stripped off the latex gloves and breathed deep to flush out the smell, Cole coughing to get out the taste, then the girl coughing, too. Pike squinted at her through the brighter light, feeling angry for her because all of it was worse than either of them had known. She saw him watching.

"I'm okay now. It was the smell."

Cole said, "When Pitman and Blanchette first approached you, they came to your house?"

"Yeah."

She coughed again, still making a face from the smell.

"When you met them downtown, where did you meet?"

"The Roybal Building. That's where they have federal offices."

"Was it just Pitman and Blanchette, or were other agents present?"

"What difference does it make?"

Pike said, "He's trying to decide whether Pitman is really a federal agent. Everything else Pitman told you is turning into a lie."

She shook her head, not understanding.

"The room was filled with people. My father. Gordon brought two other attorneys from his firm. We don't do *anything* without our lawyers. Gordon negotiated my involvement every step of the way."

Pike said, "Why is Meesh trying to kill you?"

"So I can't testify against Mr.—"

She saw it and stopped herself, but Cole finished for her.

"Way Pitman explained it, Meesh wants you dead so you can't testify against the Kings. Everything that's happening to you was supposedly because Meesh was protecting the Kings."

Larkin shook her head.

"But the Kings are dead."

"Yeah, and it was Meesh's people who put them here. Meesh knows they're dead. It wouldn't matter to

Meesh if you testified against them or not. You can't indict dead people."

"Maybe someone else killed them. Maybe it wasn't Meesh."

Pike said, "Luis was wearing George King's watch. It was Meesh."

"Then why is he still trying to kill me?"

"I don't know."

Cole turned back to the warehouse.

"Wonder why his people put their bodies back here where you had the accident. Could've dropped them anywhere, but he put them here."

Pike said, "Tell her what else."

Larkin crossed her arms and paled.

"There's *more*?"

Cole turned back from the warehouse.

"The day after your accident—the next afternoon— two days before they saw you, Pitman and Blanchette and at least two other agents questioned people here. They flashed pictures of two men. One of those pictures matched your description of Meesh. Pitman knew or suspected Meesh was in the car even before they talked to you. They lied to you about what they knew."

Larkin raised her hands and pressed her palms to her head. She fought to control herself.

"Tell me this can't get any worse."

Pike said, "We'll figure it out. We'll talk to Bud. They haven't been lying only to you; they've been lying to everyone."

She sobbed, but it was more like a laugh.

"Please tell me it can't get worse."

Pike pulled her close and held her. He held her for what seemed like a long time, but wasn't really.

Pike led them back to their cars, though he noticed that Cole lingered behind, watching the building as if it was whispering, telling secrets none of them could hear.

30

Elvis Cole

THE BUILDING and the bodies within it bothered Cole. Here was this warehouse, exactly on the spot where the lives of Larkin, the Kings, and Meesh crossed like overlapping ripples, and now someone had murdered the Kings and taken an enormous risk by placing their bodies in that location. The location was the tell. The killer left them in this particular building to send a message. What Cole didn't yet get was who was sending the message, and who was supposed to receive it. He believed the building was the key.

Cole made good time in the lull between the morning rush and the lunchtime crunch. He dropped off the freeway at Santa Monica Boulevard, then headed west to his office. Pike and Larkin were returning to Echo Park to call Bud Flynn, but Cole didn't think they should bring in Flynn until they knew who they could trust, and right now Cole believed they couldn't trust anyone. He wondered whether Pitman and Blanchette knew about the bodies in the warehouse. He wondered if Pitman and Blanchette had put them there.

Donald Pitman and Clarence Blanchette had come to his home and identified themselves as special agents with the U.S. Department of Justice. Cole believed this much to be true. Credentials could be faked, but these guys had muscled LAPD, and LAPD didn't roll for a couple of fakes. Also, Larkin, her father, and their lawyers had numerous meetings with them and other federal employees in official federal offices, and these same people had set up the Barkleys with the United States Marshal's. Cole accepted that Pitman and Blanchette were real, but everything about their operation felt like a scam, and Cole wondered why.

Cole kept an office on the western edge of Hollywood, four flights up. He had gone in only a couple of times since he got out of the hospital, but now he climbed to his office again. He brought his notes, his maps, and the list of phone numbers and other information. Neither Pitman nor Meesh nor the hitters from Ecuador were waiting for him, which was disappointing and predictably normal. Bad guys rarely waited for you. You had to go find them.

Cole said, "Hey, blockhead. How's it going?"

Pinocchio grinned at him from the wall. Cole had found the clock at a yard sale. It had a big Pinocchio grin and eyes that moved back and forth as it tocked. Prospective clients were usually less than impressed, but thugs, bad guys, and police officers were fascinated. Cole had stopped trying to figure out why.

Cole liked his office, liked how he felt when he was

in it. He had an adjoining room for Joe Pike, though Pike's office had never been used. Two director's chairs faced his desk for those rare occasions when more than one client vied for his attention. Beyond the chairs, French doors opened onto a small balcony. On a clear day, he could step out onto his balcony and see all the way down Santa Monica Boulevard to the Channel Islands. On even better days, the woman who occupied the office next to his would sun herself wearing a bikini top the size of a postage stamp.

Cole opened the French doors for the air, then went to his desk. First thing he did was get to work on the building. He laid out his maps, then phoned a woman in Florida named Marla Hendricks who could—and would—track down the building's ownership history, along with all liens, litigations, settlements, and evictions pertaining to the property. Cole had used her services for years, as did other licensed investigators around the country. She was a three-hundred-pound wheelchair-bound grandmother in Jupiter, Florida, who made her nut by subscribing to and searching online databases. She did not have access to military, medical, or law enforcement sources that were sealed by law, but she could pretty much access anything else.

When Cole finished with Marla, he studied the list of phone numbers, then called his friend at the phone company.

First thing she said was, "I was beginning to think you didn't love me anymore."

"You just love me 'cause I get good Dodgers tickets."

"No, my husband loves you because you get good

Dodgers tickets. I love you 'cause your tickets make him happy."

"I think all three of us are about to feel the love."

Cole had helped a best-selling novelist convince an Internet stalker that his time was better spent in more positive ways. The novelist had killer seats in the exclusive Dodgers Dugout Club, and shared them with Cole several times each year. Gratis.

Cole said, "I have a list of phone numbers I need to identify."

"No problemo."

"Before you say that, let me warn you. Most of these numbers are probably registered to disposable phones, and four of the numbers are international."

"I might have a problem with the international numbers if they're unlisted."

"They're likely in Ecuador."

"They could be in Siberia, it wouldn't matter: Foreign providers are reluctant to cooperate unless we go through official channels, which I can't, considering I'm doing this for Dodgers tickets."

"I gotcha."

"The disposables—well, I'm just letting you know— if the phones were cash buys, I can't find out who owns them. That information won't exist."

"If you can't ID an owner for a particular number, could you get the call records for that number?"

"It's possible."

"Sooner or later these phones called real phones, and those phones have names. Maybe we can come at it backwards."

She didn't say anything for several seconds. Cole let her think.

Finally she said, "I'll try. It depends on the provider. Some of these little companies, well—give me the numbers. I'll see what I can do."

"It's a long list. Can I fax them?"

Cole copied her fax number, sent the list, then put on a pot of coffee. When it started dripping, he returned to his desk and reread the NCIC brief on Alexander Meesh. He wanted to see if he had missed anything that would explain the accent Pike reported, or connect Meesh to Esteban Barone or someone named Carlos. He hadn't. Only a single line connected Meesh to South America: ". . . *fled the country and currently believed to be residing in Bogotá, Colombia.*"

Cole decided the investigating agents must have developed evidence or statements that placed Meesh in Bogotá, else they would not have entered the statement into the record. Cole paged to the end of the report and noted the investigator's name—Special Agent Daryl Willis with the Colorado State Justice Department, a state agency. The FBI had probably come in later, but Willis was the point man because murder was a state crime. A phone number was listed under Willis's name. It was six years old, but Cole dialed it anyway.

A woman answered.

"Investigations."

"Daryl Willis, please."

She put him on hold for almost five minutes. Cole passed the time watching Pinocchio's eyes until a man's voice came on the line.

"This is Willis."

"Sir, this is Hugh Farnham. I'm a D-2 here at Devonshire Homicide with the Los Angeles Police Department. I'm calling about a homicide you worked a few years ago, a fugitive named Alexander Meesh."

Cole made up a badge number and rattled it off. He doubted Willis would actually copy it, but he knew it was the thing to do.

"Oh, yeah, sure. What do you need?"

Willis sounded no more interested than if Cole had asked what color car he drove.

"We pulled his brief off NCIC, and you have this alert here saying he fled to Colombia—"

"That's right. He was tied in with a boy down there about the time of the murders. Wasn't enough money up here for him in hijacking; he wanted to bring in drugs, so he worked out something with a—lemme think a minute—a boy named Gonzalo Lehder. Made a few trips down there working out the deal, and I guess they hit it off. When we put the indictments on him, that's where he went."

Cole wrote down the name. Lehder.

"Lehder was a supplier?"

"One of the fellas who popped up when the Cali and Medellín cartels fell. Little operations popped up all over down there, maybe thirty or forty of'm. Some of'm aren't so little anymore."

"Was Meesh hooked up with someone named Esteban Barone?"

"Sorry. I couldn't tell you."

"Barone is out of Ecuador."

"All I knew was Lehder."

Six years was a long time. Meesh probably started

with Lehder, then branched out to Barone and the other cartels. One hundred twenty million dollars was a lot of investment capital.

Cole said, "All right, then. Let's get back to Meesh. Did he have any dealings here in L.A.?"

"Can't say that rings a bell. Sorry."

"How about Lehder? L.A. ring a bell when you think about Lehder?"

"Farnham, listen, I haven't paid much attention to this in, what is it, five or six years? Can I ask what this is regarding?"

"Meesh is in Los Angeles. We believe he's involved in a multiple homicide."

Willis didn't say anything, so Cole watched Pinocchio's eyes. Waiting.

Willis said, "This is Alexander Meesh you're talking about?"

"That's right."

"Alexander Liman Meesh?"

"Yes, sir."

"Meesh isn't in Los Angeles, partner. Alex Meesh is dead."

Cole stopped looking at Pinocchio and dropped his feet to the floor. He wasn't sure what to say. A room filled with federal agents had interviewed Larkin over the course of a week, and were confident with her identification. Cole suspected they had also identified Meesh's fingerprints in George King's car, but Willis sounded absolutely certain, and now all traces of boredom were gone from his voice.

Cole said, "We have a confirmed identification from the Department of Justice."

"What are they basing that on? They got a fingerprint match? They got the DNA?"

Cole didn't know what they had, but if Meesh was Meesh, then Meesh was Meesh.

"Yes on both counts."

"Then those boys don't know a lab test from a hemorrhoid. Alexander Meesh is dead."

Willis had moved from bored to interested to angry, as if he was taking it personally.

Cole said, "Why do you say he's dead?"

Willis hesitated, almost as if he was deciding whether to answer, so Cole pressed him.

"I have a multiple homicide here, Mr. Willis. I've been told to find Alex Meesh, and now you're telling me the DOJ is wrong. How can you be sure?"

Willis made a grunt, then cleared his throat.

"The Colombians and the DEA were after Lehder in a big way. That's how we knew Meesh went down. The Colombian National Police called the DEA, and the DEA called me. Meesh had been down there about eight months by then, setting up a drug deal between Lehder and some Venezuelans, only Lehder turned on him. Killed him."

"If Meesh is dead, why haven't you closed the warrant for his arrest?"

"The DEA. We knew Meesh was down there through undercover agents in Lehder's operation. If we tagged the file with a note about Meesh's death, or named Lehder as a known associate, those agents would be compromised. Also, you can't confirm a death without a death certificate, and we're not likely to get one."

"Why is that?"

"Lehder found out Meesh was lying to him about how much dope the Venezuelans were going to sell. Meesh was lying about it so he could steal the difference for himself. Lehder found out, he played like he didn't know and sent Meesh up to Venezuela to pick up the dope along with three or four of his boys. Only Lehder's boys shot Meesh to death in the jungle. It's a big jungle. His remains were never recovered and aren't likely to be."

"Then how can you be sure he's dead? Maybe he escaped or survived. Maybe he bought off Lehder's men."

"DEA and Colombian UC agents were present when Lehder's boys got back. They brought Meesh's head so Lehder could see. Left the body, but brought back the head. Both agents were standing there with Lehder when these boys pulled the head out of a bag. Lehder says, Good work, fellas, and that was that."

Cole didn't know what to say. But then Willis went on.

"At the time, we all believed Lehder really had sent Meesh up there to bring back the dope. We expected Meesh to come tooling back with a couple hundred kilos of raw cocaine, so the DEA and the Colombians planned to arrest them. They didn't care about Meesh, but they wanted Lehder. I wanted Meesh for the murders up here, so they let me tag along. I was with'm in that room, Detective, I saw the head. Without the drugs present, the Colombians waved off the bust. They didn't even wanna try busting the fucker for killin' Meesh, so I hadda sit there and drink tea for another hour, makin' like nothing was wrong. I still don't know what Lehder's boys did with the head, but I saw it. I recognized him. It was Meesh. So whoever you got there in L.A., he's not Alexander Meesh."

Cole felt hollow, with a faraway buzz in his head like he had gone too long without eating.

"Can I ask one more question, Mr. Willis?"

"Kinda takes your breath away, don't it?"

"Yes, sir."

"What's your question?"

"Did Meesh have a speech impediment or maybe speak with an accent?"

Willis laughed.

"Why would he have a damned accent?"

"Thanks, Mr. Willis. I appreciate your time."

Cole put his feet up, leaned back, and stared at the Pinocchio clock. The only sound in his office was the tocking of its eyes.

The call to Willis should have been simple. Cole went into it hoping to learn something about Meesh's connection to Barone, and Barone's connections to Los Angeles, and maybe even whether or not Meesh spoke with an accent—but not this.

Is this the man you saw, Ms. Barkley?

Yes. Who is he?

His name is Alexander Meesh.

Cole stared at the Pinocchio clock, then a small ceramic figurine of Jiminy Cricket a client had given him. Let your conscience be your guide. Everyone needed a Jiminy.

He flipped through the NCIC brief, which did not contain fingerprints or photographs or DNA markers. Why would you need those things if you believed what you were told?

31

PIKE DROVE slowly when they left the warehouse. He rolled the windows down so the air would wash them, and took a long, meandering route through Chinatown, driving for more than an hour. They hadn't eaten breakfast, but she wasn't hungry. He stopped anyway and picked up Chinese for later. Pike hoped the drive and the air would help her leave the bodies, but the first thing she did when they got to the house was go to the table with his gun-cleaning things. She poured powder solvent onto the cotton cloth and pressed it to her nose like a huffer sniffing paint.

She said, "I can still smell them. They're in my hair. They're all over me."

The Kings.

He took the cloth from her.

"Take a shower and brush your teeth. Put on fresh clothes. I'll clean up after you."

Pike phoned Bud while she was in the shower, but Bud didn't answer. Pike considered leaving a message, but a message might be discovered by someone else, so he decided to call again later.

When the girl returned with new clothes and wet hair, Pike took care of himself. He scrubbed hard, massaging the soap in deep, then rinsed and washed again, running the hot water until none was left. When he finished, he wet his clothes, rubbed in the soap, then left them soaking in the tub. He would have washed the girl's clothes, too, but they were fancy. He didn't want to ruin them.

Pike dressed in his last set of clean clothes, then stepped out of the bathroom to find Cole and Larkin in the living room. Cole was holding a manila envelope.

"I missed you guys so much I had to come back."

Larkin said, "He just walked in. He says he can still smell them, too."

Pike knew something was wrong. The tension in Cole's body was as obvious as a corpse hanging from the ceiling. Cole was pretending to be fine for the girl.

Pike said, "What's up?"

"Got something here to show Larkin. Let's take a look."

Pike followed them to the table, where Cole opened the envelope. He put two grainy photographs that looked as if they had been run through a fax machine on the table. They were booking photos showing a dark-haired man with a round face, pocks on his nose, and small eyes. Cole stepped back so Larkin could get a good look, but Pike watched Cole.

"What do you think? Ever seen this guy?"

Conversational with a no-big-deal nonchalance. Would you like fries with that, ma'am?

"Uh-uh. Who is he?"

"Alexander Meesh."

Larkin shook her head as if Cole had made an innocent mistake.

"No, this isn't Meesh."

"It's Meesh. He was murdered in Colombia five
years ago. These are his booking photos from the Denver Police Department."

Pike put his hand on her shoulder. He felt the tension in her trapezius muscle. She didn't want to
believe it.

"Well, maybe he had plastic surgery. That's possible,
isn't it? Don't criminals do that?"

Cole shook his head.

"Larkin, I'm sorry. This is Meesh. The record Pitman
gave you, it's Meesh's record, but the man you saw with
the Kings wasn't Meesh."

"Then who was he?"

"I don't know."

"Why would they tell me he was *this* guy?"

Pike said, "Same reason they lied about everything
else."

Cole looked at Pike.

"Better talk to your friend Bud. See what else
they've been lying about."

Larkin suddenly stiffened under Pike's hand.

"Ohmigod, we have to tell my father."

Pike hesitated. Whatever Pitman was doing, they
had an advantage so long as Pitman didn't know they
were onto him. Pike didn't trust Conner Barkley and his
lawyers not to give them away.

"We can't tell your father. Not yet."

Larkin went rigid and flushed.

"I can't not tell him! These people have lied about

everything, and now Meesh isn't even Meesh! Who is he? Why are they lying?"

"Larkin—"

She grabbed his shirt.

"They're lying to him, too, and he still believes them! He's my father. If you won't tell him, I'll tell him myself!"

Pike studied her, seeing both fear and hope in her eyes. Conner Barkley was her father. She wanted to protect him. And maybe by protecting him, he might finally see her.

Pike took out his phone and punched in Bud's number. This time Bud answered. Pike told Bud they needed to see him and the girl's father as soon as possible. It was serious, Pike told him. Pike set the location, then ended the call before Bud could ask questions. When he lowered the phone, the girl squeezed his arm. She was calmer by then, though not particularly happy. Pike couldn't blame her.

Cole said, "When we were at the warehouse—"

Pike waited.

"I'm glad you didn't tell her things couldn't get worse."

Pike looked at the girl.

"Get your stuff. Let's go."

32

THE WAR in California between Mexico and the United States had ended in Universal City. Far from the skirmishes still being waged near Mexico City and the Texas border, the treaty to end local hostilities was signed in a small adobe mission known as Campo de Cahuenga at the top of the Cahuenga Pass. The mission was preserved, but it now stood invisible and unnoticed across the street from Universal Studios, hidden in plain sight by freeway ramps, parking lots, and two strange towers marking the entrance to an underground subway station. It was a good place to meet.

Pike and the girl were waiting with the engine running when the black Hummer turned in from Lankershim.

The Hummer made its way past the mission, then through the parking lot. The doors opened the moment it stopped, and Bud, Conner Barkley, and Barkley's lawyer, Gordon Kline, stepped out. Pike wasn't pleased to see Kline.

Pike said, "Let's do it."

They got out as Bud and the others came to meet them.

Her father said, "Larkin, it's about time—we've been worried sick. Let's get you out of here."

Larkin didn't move.

"I'm not going anywhere."

Her father seemed flustered, as if he feared she was about to explode.

"But you have to come home. We were so worried."

He looked at Kline.

"Tell her, Gordon. Tell her to stop this."

Pike was already tired of them. He faced Bud and spoke only for him.

"Pitman hasn't been straight. The man he named as Alexander Meesh is not Meesh. Meesh died five years ago."

Gordon Kline threw up his hands. Pike had seen plenty of that when he was a cop. Courtroom Theatrics 101.

"We're not going to listen to this. I will have you prosecuted for kidnapping. I knew you were a lunatic the moment I laid eyes on you."

Larkin raised her voice, and now it had a hard, angry edge.

"Shut the fuck up!"

Barkley was still looking at Kline. Larkin grabbed her father's arm.

"Will you *listen* to me? Will you please just *look* at me and *listen*? We came here to *warn* you."

Conner Barkley looked pained.

"Don't be like that, Larkin. Everyone's worried."

Kline said, "We're bringing you home—"

He reached for her, but Pike caught his hand and rolled it. Kline jumped back.

"You sonofabitch! Flynn! Do something—"

"He could have ripped it out by the root, Gordon. Let's see what they have."

Pike took the faxed booking photo from his pocket and gave it to Flynn.

"This is Meesh. This is not the man in the pictures Pitman showed Larkin."

Kline and Barkley both peered over Flynn's shoulder to see. Barkley seemed uncertain, but Kline was impatient and stepped away.

"No, it isn't, but so what? For all we know, you made this yourself."

Bud slowly looked at him.

"But why would he do that?"

"To milk us for more money."

Larkin was focused on her father.

"This isn't the man in their pictures. They told us that man was Alexander Meesh, but he isn't. They lied to us, Daddy."

Daddy. It didn't seem like a word she would use. Pike liked her for it, but her using it left him sad.

Kline took a breath, then softened his voice.

"We all saw those pictures, and I agree with you—the man in those pictures was not this man. But you're making it sound as if they misled us. Two people can have the same name."

Bud glanced through the attached pages.

"Same name, maybe, but not identical arrest records. This record matches what Pitman gave me when I came onboard."

Gordon raised his eyebrows.

"Really? Then here's what we need to do—we need to cut Pike loose here and now. Pike has to go. We need to get Larkin home and then we can ask Mr. Pitman. Believe me—I have plenty of questions. *Believe* me—if I don't like the answers, he'll regret the day he was born."

Conner's head bounced up and down as if all of this was the best idea he ever heard.

"Why don't we go home, sweetie? We'll see what this man Pitman says after we get you home."

"I'm not going home."

Kline stared at the ground as if he couldn't believe the trouble she was causing.

"Flynn. Would you please put her in the car?"

"No, sir. Not unless it's voluntary."

Pike said, "She isn't safe at home, Kline. Don't you get that?"

Gordon Kline gazed up at Pike from beneath bushy eyebrows, and his voice was still carefully soft.

"Are you sleeping with her?"

Pike's mouth twitched, but he watched Conner Barkley. Barkley did not react, and Pike felt even more sad for the girl.

Larkin said, "Fuck you, Gordon."

"This is obstructing justice. You're a witness in a federal investigation. This man, Pike, he's putting you in dangerous situations—"

"This *is* a dangerous situation."

"—and he's alienating the people trying to help you. All I'm suggesting is maybe Pitman has a good reason for doing what he's doing. We'll ask him, and he'd damn well better explain."

Pike said, "Ask him why he pretended he didn't know who was with the Kings the night Larkin hit them."

"Are you saying he knew?"

"He was flashing pictures of the man the day after the accident—two days before he approached Larkin. Ask him why the man he claims to be Meesh is still trying to kill Larkin even though the Kings are dead."

Kline glanced at Conner Barkley, then shook his head.

"I spoke with Agent Pitman this morning. He said they were still looking for the Kings."

"They've been dead more than a week. We just found them."

"I don't understand."

Larkin said, "We found them—as in, we looked, and we found them. Someone put their bodies exactly where I had my accident, Gordon. Would you like the address? 18185. I think it was a message. That I'm going to join them."

Kline wet his lips. He glanced at Barkley, then shook his head.

"You're sure it was the Kings? You are telling us now that George King is dead?"

Larkin's voice was brittle.

"And his wife. They were in the Mercedes."

Bud stared at Pike.

"How?"

"Head. Executed in another location, then brought to the warehouse. The vehicle was registered to George King."

Kline said, "So what's your point here, that Pitman murdered them?"

"I don't know."

"Do you believe Pitman is behind the attempts on Larkin's life?"

"I don't know. It would explain the leaks, but all we know for sure is everything he's told you are lies."

Larkin said, "You have to be careful, Daddy. You can't trust him."

Kline glanced at Bud.

"Will you check this out? Eighteen-eighteen-five."

"Right away."

Kline focused on Pike.

"The man in the picture—the man who isn't Meesh—do you have any idea who he is?"

"We might have his fingerprints. I don't know that we do, but we might. We might be able to identify him."

"As an attorney, I am telling you that if you withhold any evidence from the police, you can and probably will be charged with obstruction of justice and possibly as an accessory to the crime. I want you to know that."

Bud said, "He knows that. Jesus."

Pike said, "I'll take my chances."

Kline nodded.

"Just so you understand. You're fired. Is that clear, Bud? This man is no longer in our employ. He no longer works for you, nor will he receive money from us or from you so long as you are in our employ."

Larkin shouted over him.

"What is *wrong* with you? Haven't you paid attention?"

Her father said, "Larkin, honey, now he's breaking the law. We can't have that."

"We came here to *warn* you, Daddy!"

Kline interrupted.

"Conner, I have work. Let's get out of here."

He walked back to the Hummer.

Conner Barkley frowned at his daughter. His quizzical expression had frosted into something impatient.

"This puts me in jeopardy with the government, Larkin. We should never have been involved. We should have turned Pitman away, but you had to tell your story, and now here we are. Think of the exposure with the IRS. Think of the SEC. They could punish me, Larkin."

It wasn't about Larkin's safety. It was about her father. The company. The exposure.

Pike said, "Bud, for Mr. Barkley's record—I am not in your employ, nor his, and never have been."

Pike glanced at Larkin.

"I'm helping a friend."

Larkin ran to the Lexus, and Pike followed her.

"Officer Pike—"

Pike glanced back to see Bud make a tight smile. Kline and Conner Barkley were already at the Hummer.

Bud said, "Call if you need me."

Pike got into the Lexus and drove away fast. He turned out into traffic, watching his mirror, but the Hummer stayed in the lot. They would need a different car soon. Kline or her father might describe the Lexus to the police.

Pike knew they had lost an edge. They had lost the element of surprise. Gordon Kline was probably already on the phone with Pitman. They had to move even faster than before.

Larkin said, "What are we going to do?"

"Keep going."

She touched his shoulder. She rested her hand on his delt.

"We won't back up."

"We never back up."

Pike turned into a Safeway parking lot in Burbank and went into the trunk. The black backpack Pike took from the motel was inside along with their other things. Everything he had taken from Jorge and Luis was in it. Pike went through the maps and passports until he found the Baggie containing Larkin's picture. He closed the trunk, then climbed in behind the wheel and pulled back into traffic.

She said, "What's that?"

"Your picture. The guy who's after you, he gave it to Luis. He touched it, so we might have his fingerprints. It didn't matter when we thought he was Meesh. Now it matters."

Pike took out his phone. He was dialing when Larkin spoke again.

She said, "You know what's fucked up? I love him."

"Yeah. I loved mine, too."

Pike had never said those words to anyone. Not even Elvis Cole.

33

John Chen

SO HERE he was, after-hours yet again, working off the books and against the rules, flying low in a one-hundred-percent free-fire danger zone that would get his ass canned if Harriet found out, but John Chen loved it. He abso-fucking-lutely LOVED it! Maybe better than his Porsche. Maybe better than seeing his name in the paper. Maybe even better than the 'tang.

Okay, well, let's not get carried away. Nothing was better than 'tang.

Chen giggled when he realized what he was thinking, a kind of snurfling yuck-yuck-yuck. Chen had always hated his laugh. The other kids had made fun of it (along with everything else about him), but Chen no longer gave a rolling rat-fuck because—as of twenty minutes ago—John Chen was THE MAN!

Chen had this epiphany when Joe Pike called, Pike asking him to drop everything and run a fingerprint check.

His personal friend, Joe Pike—

—who *needed* John Chen.

—who *valued* Chen's knowledge and skill.

—who *trusted* him.

(And was not Joe Pike the baddest muhfuh kickin' the streets of this city? Was he not the bravest, toughest, most feared ex-cop to stride the Earth? The most brilliant investigator [Pike had been carrying Cole for years]? Was he not a superhero in Levi's [Chen thought they could make a mint selling Joe Pike action figures]? *Did he not get the most 'tang* [like that steaming hot babe waiting with Pike in the parking lot]?)

Joe Pike was THE MAN, and WHO did Pike call when he needed help?

John FUCKING Chen, that's who!

Harriet said, "John! Why are you still here?"

Snuck up right behind him, that bitch.

Caught by surprise, John ducked his head and hunched his shoulders even as the skin along his back crawled, cringing in that instant of panic like he had cringed so many thousands of times before—but then John Chen thought, No—THE MAN does not cringe.

Chen straightened and gave her his most confident smile. And, you know, he actually *felt* confident.

"Finishing some work from yesterday. Don't sweat it, Harriet. I punched out an hour ago."

Chen had already reached his overtime limit for the week.

Harriet peered past him into the glue box. The glue box was an airtight Plexiglas chamber where superglue and other toxic chemicals were boiled to enhance fingerprints. Currently, John had a picture of Pike's girlfriend soaking in poisonous fumes.

Harriet eyed the picture suspiciously.

"She looks familiar."

"Yeah, she has one of those faces."

"What case?"

"The Drano murder. The detectives think a third person might have been at the scene."

John had never felt such confidence in his lies. As if they were coming from a core of absolute truth.

Harriet eyed the photograph a moment longer, then stepped back and appraised him.

"Thanks for not hitting me up for the overtime. These budget cuts are killing us."

"I know, Harriet. Is there anything else?"

"No. No, thanks. Listen, how's that tooth?"

"I don't even feel it."

"I'm sorry I gave you a hard time about that. I didn't mean to be insensitive."

"It's not a problem, Harriet. Don't sweat it."

Harriet skulked away as if feeling ashamed of herself, and John smiled even wider. He had seen it in her eyes. She knew he was THE MAN.

Chen turned back to the box and examined the picture through the glass. White smudges were appearing on the front and back surfaces of the photograph, but he still had a long way to go. Fingerprints were nothing but sweat. After the water evaporated, an organic residue was left. The fumes from the superglue reacted with the amino acids, glucose, and peptides in the organics to form a white goo, but growing the goo took time. John figured he still had another ten or fifteen minutes before the prints would be usable.

A reflection moved in the glass, and Chen saw La-

Molla at the other side of the lab. She had edged to the door, hiding from Harriet. LaMolla waved him over, gestured toward the gun room, then disappeared.

Chen made sure Harriet was gone, then hurried out of the lab. LaMolla was waiting at the gun room, holding the door.

She said, "Get in here. I don't want anyone to see us together."

She damn near pulled him off his feet, then locked the door behind him.

Chen said, "You get anything?"

LaMolla glared at him.

"If you're setting me up, you fucker, I'll kill you in your sleep."

"Why would I set you up?"

"Trust no one, John. We work for the freakin' government."

LaMolla led him to her workbench as she told him what she found.

"The Browning was shit; it was stolen in 1982 from a Houston police officer named David Thompson. The BIN showed zip besides the Thompson hit, and nothing rang a bell."

The ATF maintained the National Integrated Ballistic Information Network—the BIN—logging data on firearms, bullets, and cartridge casings that had been recovered at crime scenes or otherwise entered into the system. LaMolla would have run both guns through the BIN, but computer hits were rare. Chen was far more interested in LaMolla's "bell."

LaMolla said, "But the Taurus was different. Look at this—"

She brought him to her computer. On the screen was a magnified picture of the base of a cartridge casing. The brass casing was a ring surrounding a round silver primer. A shadowed indentation in the center of the primer showed where the firing pin had struck the primer.

"You see it? Kinda jumps out at you, doesn't it?"

The casing looked like every other casing Chen had ever seen.

"What?"

"The pin strike. See here at the top where it's kinda pointy? I saw that, I thought, Gee, I know that pin."

The indentation looked perfectly round to John, but this was why firearms analysts were wizards.

LaMolla said, "Last couple of years, the Taurus was used in a couple of drive-bys and a robbery-homicide in Exposition Park. No arrests were made, but the suspects were all members of the same gang. MS-13. It's a pass-around, John."

A pass-around was a street gun, usually not owned by one person, but passed from user to user within the same gang.

LaMolla shook her head.

"Sorry, man—wish I could give you something more specific, but that's it. Doesn't seem like much."

"It's more than we had."

Chen left her to it and hurried back to the glue chamber. The latent prints had developed nicely, but so many prints covered the picture John wondered if any would be useful. Prints overlaid prints, one atop the other, because that's the way people handled things. No one ever grabbed a book or a cup or a magazine with a single firm grip; people picked something up, moved it around, passed it from hand to hand, put it down, then picked it up again, overlaying their prints until only a smudgy mess was left.

The girl's picture was no different.

Chen vented the chamber to blow out the fumes, then removed the picture using a pair of forceps and examined it under a magnifying glass. Smudged circular patterns were heaviest on the sides of the picture where people had held it with their thumbs, but the bottom and top were heavily smudged, too, and still more smudges were randomly scattered over the picture's glossy front. Chen saw several prints he thought would be usable, but the back of the picture was impossible to read. The white residue from the organics disappeared on the white paper.

Chen clipped the picture to a small metal frame, then gently brushed a fine blue powder over its back. When the back was covered, he used a can of pressurized air to blow off the excess powder, revealing clusters of dark blue smudges, some readable, but most not. He turned over the picture, repeated the process, then examined each of the singular prints.

Chen was pleased. He had twelve separate and singular prints, each showing defined typica. Typica were the characteristic points by which fingerprints could be identified—the loops and swirls and bifurcations that make up a fingerprint.

Chen lifted each print off the picture with a piece of clear tape, then pressed the tape onto a clear plastic backing. One by one, he set them onto a high-resolution digital scanner and photographed them. He fed the pictures into his computer, then used a special program to identify and chart the characteristic points. The FBI's National Crime Information System didn't compare pictures of fingerprints; it compared a numerical list of identifying characteristic points. It looked at numbers. After you had the numbers, everything else was easy.

Chen made the special request for an international database search.

John checked his watch again. Pike and the girl were sweating out in the parking lot, and he didn't want them to sweat too long. He didn't want Pike to lose faith in him. He wanted to come through.

Chen need not have worried.

The NCIC/Interpol logo flashed on his screen when the incoming files opened, and John Chen read the results.

John had positive matches on all twelve prints, identifying seven separate male individuals, two of whom Chen had earlier identified—Jorge Petrada and Luis Mendoza. Like Petrada and Mendoza, four of the remaining men were thugs from South America associated with Esteban Barone, but the seventh man was not.

Chen realized his mouth was dry when he had trouble swallowing.

He knew why the Department of Justice was involved.

He knew why Parker rolled.

John printed the seven files, carefully stapled them together, then cleared his computer so no one would see the downloads. He collected the fingerprint slides and the picture of the girl and sealed them in an envelope. He took the envelope and the files and walked out of the lab.

The sun was low in the western sky, searing the sky

with fire. The Verdugo Mountains were purple turning to black. Chen went directly to Pike's car, and he didn't give a damn if Harriet saw him because he knew this was bigger than that; this was bigger than anything he had ever worked on, and maybe ever would.

Pike and the girl watched as he approached.

John Chen gave Pike the files.

"Read it."

The girl saw the picture on the cover page and said, "That's him! That's the man in the pictures."

The girl scooted close to Pike, and they read it together. Chen didn't think about how hot she was, or how her hand rested on Pike's thigh as she read, or fantasize about the taste of her skin. He thought only about what they were reading.

The fingerprints belonged to a man named Khali Vahnich. Vahnich was a forty-two-year-old former investment banker from the Czech Republic who had been convicted of drug trafficking before leaving that country. His activities since that time included additional drug trafficking, illegal arms sales, and known associations with terrorist organizations in Europe and the Middle East. A large black alert warning appeared in the center of the page. John remembered it clearly and knew he would never forget it. The surface roiled. A monster appeared.

It read:

ALERT: THIS MAN IS ON THE TERRORIST WATCH LIST. NOTIFY THE FBI IF YOU BELIEVE HIM TO BE IN YOUR AREA. APPREHEND BY ANY MEANS.

Pike looked up at John when he finished, and Chen would always remember his expression. Pike's face showed nothing, absolutely nothing, but the gleaming black lenses smoldered with the fire in the sky. Chen felt so proud of Pike then, so terribly, awfully proud that this man had included him.

Pike said, "Thank you, John."

"Whatever you need. Anything I can do, I'll do it. I don't care what. I'll do it."

"I know."

Pike put out his hand, and Chen took it, and wanted never to let go, not ever, because John Chen felt he had something now, something that made him better than he had ever been or ever could have been; something Chen wanted to keep forever.

John Chen said, "Good luck, my brother."

34

LATER that night they made hot jasmine tea and ate the Chinese food while Larkin watched television, a comedy about a middle-aged couple who said ugly things to each other. Pike didn't find it funny, but the girl seemed to enjoy it. Pike phoned Cole, filled him in, and they made a plan for the next day.

When the show ended, Larkin went to her room, but returned a few minutes later wearing shorts and a different top. She curled up on her end of the couch and flipped through a magazine. The couch was small. Her bare feet were close to Pike. Pike wanted to rest his hand on her foot but didn't. He moved to the chair.

Pike didn't care about Pitman or Pitman's investigation or why Pitman had lied except for how it affected the girl. He didn't care if Pitman was a good cop or a bad cop, or in business with Vahnich and the Kings. He had been hunting a man named Meesh, but now he was hunting a man named Vahnich. If Pitman was trying to hurt the girl, Pike would hunt Pitman. Pike's interest was the girl.

Pike watched her reading. She caught him watching and smiled, not the nasty crazy-curved smile, but something softer. With just a touch of the other.

She said, "You never smile."

Pike touched his jaw.

"This is me, smiling."

Larkin laughed and went back to the magazine.

Pike checked his watch. He decided they had waited long enough, so he picked up the phone.

"Here we go."

Larkin closed her magazine on a finger and watched with serious eyes.

Pike still had Pitman's number from when Pitman left the message, and now Pitman answered.

"This is Pike."

"You're something, man."

"Heard from Kline?"

"Kline, Barkley, Flynn. What in hell do you think you're doing?"

"How about Khali Vahnich? You hear from him?"

Pitman hesitated.

"You have to stop this, Pike."

"Vahnich changes everything. Larkin wants to come back."

Pitman hesitated for the second time.

"Okay, that's good. That's the smart thing to do here. This is all about keeping her safe."

Pike said, "Yes. I'm keeping her safe."

The girl smiled again as Pike made the arrangements.

RULE OF LAW

35

AT 6:57 A.M. the next morning, Pike watched a metallic blue Ford sedan turn off Alameda Street into the Union Station parking lot. The sedan slowed for the hundreds of subway commuters emerging from the station, then crept to the far end of the lot.

Donald Pitman was driving, with Kevin Blanchette as a passenger. This was the first time Pike was seeing either man, but Cole had described them well, and Pitman had said they would be in the blue sedan. Both were clean-shaven, nice-looking men in their late thirties. Pitman had a narrow face with a sharp nose; Blanchette was larger, with chubby cheeks and a balding crown.

Neither they nor the seven other federal agents who were concealed in a perimeter around the station saw Pike. Pike assumed they were federal, but wasn't sure and didn't care. They had moved into position ninety minutes earlier. Pike had been in position since three A.M.

Pike watched them through his Zeiss binoculars

from the second-floor pantry of an Olvera Street Mexican restaurant owned by his friend Frank Garcia. The ground floor was being remodeled, so the kitchen was closed. Pitman was expecting Pike and Larkin to arrive at seven A.M., but this did not happen. Larkin and Cole were having breakfast about now, and Pike was in the pantry.

At 7:22, Pitman and Blanchette got out of their car. They studied the passing traffic and the commuters coming from the station, but Pike knew they were worried.

At 7:30, they got back into the car. It wouldn't be much longer until they accepted that they had been stood up.

Pike hurried downstairs to the employees' bathroom off the kitchen. It had a single window that looked out at Union Station. Pike had opened it when he first arrived so its movement would draw no attention.

At 7:51, the seven agents surveilling the area emerged from their hiding places and gathered at the north corner of the parking lot. Pitman had flagged the play. Pike left the restaurant and trotted to Cole's car, which was parked at the end of Olvera Street. Cole had swapped for the Lexus.

Pike followed the blue sedan south on Alameda toward the Roybal Building—the federal office building. The rush-hour stop-and-go was brutal, with only a few cars at a time spurting forward between grudging light changes, but Pike counted on this working for him.

The blue sedan was three cars ahead when the yellow went red, and Pitman was trapped. Pike maneuvered Cole's car into a loading zone, got out, and watched the crossing lights ahead. When the crossing light signaled the lights were about to change, Pike trotted forward, picking up speed.

Pike closed on the sedan like a shark tracking a blood trail and attacked out of their blind spot. Neither man saw him, and neither was expecting his assault. Pike reached Blanchette's side of the sedan just as the light turned green, and shattered Blanchette's window with his pistol.

Pike jerked the door open and pushed his gun into Blanchette's side, screaming to keep him confused.

"Your belt. Pop your belt—"

Pike stripped Blanchette's gun, dragged him from the car, and proned him on the street, keeping his gun on Pitman.

"Hands on the wheel! On the wheel or I'll kill you."

The cars ahead of them were gone. The lane was clear. Horns behind them shrieked as Pike slid into the car.

Pitman said, "Pike?"

Pike stripped Pitman's weapon and tossed it into the back. Outside, Blanchette was getting up.

"Drive!"

Pitman didn't move, maybe slowed by confusion, but his eyes flickered with anger.

"I'm a federal agent. You can't—"

Pike hit him hard in the forehead with his pistol, grabbed the wheel, and powered through the light.

36

THEY WERE under the First Street Bridge when Pitman woke, parked between towering concrete columns at the edge of the Los Angeles River. Abandoned vehicles impounded by the city were parked in even rows there in the dead space beneath the bridge, protected by a chain-link fence from everything but dust, birds, and taggers. Pike was parked at the end of the fence. Trucks passing overhead made the fence buzz like swarming bees. They were less than eight blocks from Cole's car.

Pitman jerked upright, trying to get away, but Pike had tied his wrists to the wheel with plastic restraints. Pitman twisted as far from Pike as possible.

"What are you doing? What in hell do you think you're doing, Pike? Let me go!"

Pitman looked younger now that Pike was close. His forehead was split where Pike hit him, leaking a crusty red mask over his face. Pike watched him, holding the pistol loosely in his lap.

Pitman said, "You assaulted a federal officer. You

fucking *kidnapped* me! Let me go! Cut me loose, and we'll forget about this. I can help you!"

Pike tapped the pistol.

"I'm not the one who needs help."

Pitman's face twitched and popped as if moving in every direction at once.

"You are in deep shit—*deep* shit! You are breaking major federal laws here! Walk away now, or you will be *under* the jail."

Pike said, "Khali Vahnich. A terrorist."

"I'm telling you, Pike—walk away!"

"A known terrorist."

"I'm not discussing this!"

Pike lifted the Kimber just enough to point it.

"We're talking about whether or not you die."

"I'm a federal officer! You would be killing a federal officer!"

Pike nodded, quiet and calm.

"If that's what it takes."

"Jesus Christ!"

Pike held up Pitman's badge. He had gone through Pitman's pockets for his credentials.

"This was never about the Kings, Pitman. This is about Vahnich. You put a target on her to bag the terrorist. Or protect him."

"That's insane. I'm not trying to protect him."

"You told her Khali Vahnich was Alex Meesh."

"We had to protect the case."

"You told her he was trying to kill her to protect his investment with the Kings, but the Kings were dead. There was no one to protect."

"We didn't know they were dead until yesterday,

Pike! We didn't know! We thought he was helping them—"

"There's no 'we' here, Pitman. It's on you. The Kings are dead, so why would Vahnich want to kill her?"

"I don't know!"

"I think you killed them and sold out the girl to help Vahnich."

Pike raised his pistol again, and Pitman jerked hard against the plastic.

"*We didn't know!* That's the God's honest truth! Listen to me—we knew they were in business, Vahnich and the Kings, but we didn't know Vahnich was in L.A. until just before the accident. Look in the trunk—my briefcase is in the trunk. *Look at it, Pike!* I'm telling the truth—"

Pike studied Pitman, getting the read, then took the keys and found an oversize briefcase in the trunk. The briefcase was locked. He brought it back to the front seat.

Pitman said, "Key's in my pocket—"

Pike didn't bother with the key. He slit open the case with his knife. Letters, memos, and files bearing Department of Justice and Homeland Security letterheads were jammed together in no particular order.

Pike said, "You aren't with Organized Crime."

"Homeland Security. Look at my notes—"

"Shut up, Pitman."

Many of the pages were marked CONFIDENTIAL. Pike saw memos about financial transactions and surveillances on the Kings, and other memos connecting Vahnich with Barone and numerous named and unnamed third parties in South America. Many of the memos described Khali Vahnich's movements both here and abroad.

Pike read until he understood.

"Vahnich makes money for terrorists."

Pitman nodded.

"That's the short version. The single biggest source of funding for organized terror outside of state-sponsored contributions in the Middle East is dope. They buy it, sell it, invest in it—and take the profit. These fuckers are rich, Pike. Not the lunatics blowing themselves up, but the organizations. Like every other war machine on the planet, they eat money, and they want more. That's what Vahnich does. He's an investment banker for these fuckers. Invests their funds, turns a profit, then feeds it back to the machine."

"With the Kings?"

"Economics works the same for everybody—Republicans and Democrats, drug lords and Al Qaeda. You limit your risk by diversification. The Kings are golden in real estate, and Vahnich wants to diversify. He put a hundred twenty million into play with the Kings—sixty from the cartels, but sixty was straight out of the war zone. My job is to isolate and capture that money."

"Money."

"Terrorist money. We don't want it going back to train suicide bombers."

"Where is it?"

"I don't know. The Kings accepted the transfer into a foreign account, but the money was moved that same day and we don't know where it went. Maybe that's why

Vahnich killed them. Maybe he wanted the money back."

"So all of this is about real estate."

Pitman laughed, but it was cynical and dry.

"Everything happening in the world today is about real estate, Pike. Don't you read the newspaper?"

Pike thought about Khali Vahnich and the Kings and all those boys come up from Ecuador. Outside, the bridge hissed with passing cars and the fence hummed. Pike thought about Larkin in the Echo Park house, cut off from her friends and her life, with a man like Khali Vahnich wanting her dead.

"Why is Vahnich trying to kill her?"

"I don't know. I thought I knew. I believed it was about the Kings."

"The Kings are dead."

"I didn't know Vahnich would try to kill her. How could I know that?"

"You should have told them the truth. The terrorists haven't taken over Los Angeles yet, Pitman—we're still the land of the free. You should have told those people who they were dealing with."

Pitman seemed as if he didn't understand, then shook his head.

"I told them."

"Told them what?"

"They knew it was Vahnich. The girl didn't, but her father did. He advised us not to tell her."

Pike must have looked confused because Pitman tried to explain.

"We had meetings about it, Pike—her father, his

attorneys, our people. You don't want to alienate a co-operative witness, but we needed discretion. Barkley said she couldn't deliver. They advised us not to identify Vahnich until just before the testimony."

"They advised you? Her father lied to her?"

"She isn't the most stable person. She would have used it to draw attention to herself."

Pike felt cool even in the morning's warmth. He flashed on the girl from the night before, desperate to warn her father. Demanding it.

Pitman said, "She's a freak, man. You gotta know that by now."

Pike looked at Pitman's badge again. He thought of his own badge. He had given it up to help Wozniak's family. He had loved that badge and everything it represented, but he had loved Wozniak's family more. Families needed to be protected. Families needed someone to be the protector. This was just how Pike felt.

Pike said, "She just wanted to do the right thing."

Pike put away his gun.

"We're finished here."

Pitman tugged at his restraints.

"Cut these things off. Bring her back, Pike. We can protect her."

Pike opened the door.

"You're tied to a steering wheel. You can't even protect yourself."

Pike got out with the keys and the badge.

Pitman realized Pike was leaving, and jerked harder at the wheel.

"What the fuck? What're you doing?"
Pike threw Pitman's badge into the river.
"Not my badge! Pike—"
Pike threw the keys after it.
"Pike!"
Pike left without looking back.

37

Elvis Cole

COLE STOPPED by his office that morning to pick up the calling logs before heading on to stay with the girl. His friend at the phone company had faxed twenty-six pages of outgoing and incoming phone numbers, some of which were identified, but many of which were not. Cole would have to go through the numbers one by one, but the girl would probably help. Cole liked the girl. She was funny and smart and laughed at his jokes. All the major food groups.

When he let himself in, she was stretched out on the couch, watching TV with the iPod plugged in her ears.

Cole said, "How can you watch TV and listen to that at the same time?"

She wiggled his iPod.

"Did they stop making music in 1990?"

You see? Funny.

"I have to make a couple of calls, then I want you to help me with something."

She sat up, interested.

"What?"

"Phone numbers. We have to build a phone tree tracing the calls to and from the phones Pike found. We'll trace the calls from phone to phone until we identify someone who can help us find Vahnich. Sound like fun?"

"No."

"It's like connect the dots. Even you can do it."

She gave him the finger.

Cole thought she was great.

He set her up at the table with the list of numbers, and identified which numbers belonged to Jorge, Luis, and the man they believed was Khali Vahnich, aka Alexander Meesh. He showed her what to do, then went to the couch with his phone. That morning at his office he had found a message from Marla Hendricks, informing him that 18185 was owned by the Tanner Family Trust, which also owned several other large commercial properties in downtown L.A., all of which were for sale. In typical fashion, Marla had been thorough. 18185 had been purchased by Dr. William Tanner in 1968, and placed in trust in 1975. No fines, violations, judgments, or liens had been placed on the property during that time. The executor of the trust was Tanner's oldest daughter, Ms. Lizabeth Little, a former attorney, who was overseeing the sale of the properties. Marla had included Lizabeth Little's Brentwood home address and three phone numbers.

Cole said, "You doin' okay over there?"

Larkin was busy with the numbers.

"It isn't calculus."

"I'm going to make my call. Don't interrupt."

She gave him the finger again.

Cole phoned Lizabeth Little and scored on the first try. Lizabeth sounded as if she was in a rush.

"Yes, this is Lizabeth Little."

"My name is Elvis Cole. I'm a private investigator who—"

"How did you get this number?"

"It's that private-eye thing. Ma'am, I'm calling about a property you have for sale. I represent an interested buyer."

The ol' greed ploy. Gets'm every time.

"Which property?"

"A warehouse space downtown. 18185."

"Oh, sure. That's my dad's. We're dissolving the trust. I'll try to answer your questions, but you should speak with our broker about the terms."

She sounded normal. Not like someone who would bag away a couple of bodies, or know a person who would.

Cole said, "I just want a little background on the property."

"You're working with a buyer?"

"That's right."

"Then you should know this up front. We'll consider offers, but any offer we accept will be in a backup position. Is your buyer okay with that?"

"A backup. Has the building been sold?"

"We have an option arrangement with a buyer for all seven of our properties. I don't think your buyer needs to worry about it, though. The option is about to expire."

"Someone is buying all seven properties?"

"The upside potential here is enormous with the way downtown real estate is booming. Would your buyer be interested in all seven?"

"What are we talking about, pricewise?"

"The low twos."

"Two million dollars?"

She laughed.

"Two hundred million."

"That was me being funny. I knew what you meant."

"I got it. Options are common in deals of this size. People need time to raise the money. Sometimes the deals happen, sometimes they don't. This one looks like it might not. If that's the case, we'll sell the properties individually. If your buyer is interested, we should still talk."

"I'll pass that along. How long was the option period?"

"In this case, four months."

"Uh-huh, and how much does a four-month option cost for two hundred million dollars' worth of warehouses?"

"In this case, six million."

"Which you keep when the option lapses?"

"Oh, yes. I think it lapses in, oh, let me think, I don't have my calendar—another four days. Three days, maybe. You can call the broker for the exact date."

"I'll pass that along. One more question: You mind naming the buyer?"

"Not at all. Stentorum Real Holdings. I don't have the number, but my broker will give it to you. Since they haven't been able to raise the money, maybe your buyer could help and leverage a partial position. We'd love to have this deal go through."

Cole copied the name onto his pad. Stentorum Real Holdings. He hung up as Joe Pike walked in.

Pike stopped inside the door and stood like a statue.

The girl chirped up.

"Hey, man!"

Cole said, "Yo."

Pike didn't move or speak. Pike always looked strange, but now he looked even stranger. Cole wondered what was wrong.

"You talk to the brother?"

Pike walked out of the living room and into the bathroom. Strange.

Cole picked up his phone again and dialed the information operator.

He said, "I need a listing for Stentorum Real Holdings, please. That's in Los Angeles."

Larkin looked up.

"What did you say?"

"Stentorum Real Holdings."

"That's one of my father's companies."

The information computer came on with the number. Cole copied it, but never looked away from the girl. When he finished, he went to the table. He put his pad on the table, then turned it so she could read it. Stentorum Real Holdings.

"Your father owns this?"

"I own it, too, technically. It's one of our family's companies."

The water stopped and Pike stepped from the bathroom. He was shirtless and scrubbed, as if he had come home needing to wash away wherever he had been or whoever he was with. A spiderweb of old scars draped his chest where he had been shot. He pulled on his sweatshirt.

Cole said, "We need you."

Cole waited until Pike joined them.

Pike said, "What?"

"Larkin's father owns something called Stentorum Real Holdings. Stentorum is trying to buy 18185, along with six other buildings from the same owner. They optioned the right to buy four months ago, but their option is about to lapse."

Cole stared at Pike, with Pike staring back, his face unknowable and empty. Larkin sensed it was bad, but didn't understand why because she didn't yet know what they knew. Cole was letting Pike make the call, what to tell her, what not.

Larkin shook her head.

"What does that mean? Are you sure? My father is buying the building where we found the bodies?"

Pike reached across the table and offered his hand. Larkin placed her fingers on his. Pike squeezed. Cole had seen Pike do push-ups on his thumbs; push-ups using only the two index fingers. Pike popped walnuts like soap bubbles, but not now.

Pike said, "Stay with me, okay? Harden up, because it's about to get worse."

Five minutes ago, Cole thought Larkin looked twelve. Now she looked one hundred years old. She glanced at Cole, then looked back at Pike and nodded.

"Bring it. Both barrels."

"Your father and Gordon Kline both knew Meesh was Khali Vahnich. They worked out a deal with Pitman to keep you in the dark. Pitman said it wasn't his idea. Said it was your dad's."

Cole watched her hand in Pike's. Her fingers tightened until the tendons stood out, but nothing showed on her face.

"Why would they do that?"

"Don't know."

"Were they in business together, these disgusting people and my father?"

"That's what it looks like, yes."

Larkin leaned back and laughed, but still she held on to him.

Cole said, "We're just guessing about these things. We'll ask."

"I grew up with this! I know a business dispute when I see it! They couldn't close the deal, so somebody has to eat the deposit. Vahnich killed the Kings. Now he wants me and my—"

She stared at the endless sheets of phone numbers before looking up.

"Was it my father?"

Cole didn't understand what she was asking, but Pike seemed to know and answered her.

"I'll find out."

Her face paled, her eyes showing the kind of pain you'd feel if you were being crushed, as if the last bit of love were being wrung from your heart.

She said, "I don't want to find out. Please don't find out. Please do not tell me."

Then Cole realized what she had asked of Pike—was

her father the person telling Vahnich where to find her?

Cole said, "We're guessing too much. Let's go be detectives."

Cole got up and went to the door. Pike lingered behind for a moment, then followed him out.

38

Larkin Conner Barkley

LARKIN WATCHED Pike leaving, and in the moment he stepped outside, he was framed in the open door of their Echo Park house like a picture in a magazine, frozen in time and space. A big man, but not a giant. More average in size than not. With the sleeves covering his arms, and his face turned away, he seemed heart-breakingly normal, which made her love him even more. A superman risked nothing, but an average man risked everything.

When he glanced back before he pulled the door, she saw the emptiness in his face, the gleaming dark glasses; then the door closed and she was alone.

"Make it right. Please make it right."

Said it to the empty house, then felt stupid and ashamed of herself for saying it.

She was more frightened now than even those times when the men from Ecuador were shooting. If her father had abandoned her, then she was truly alone, more alone than she had ever felt or known or believed could be possible. Larkin felt as if she were having an out-of-body experience. She felt outside her own body, yet the air seemed alive on her skin, and the house was so quiet the silence was noise. Like being in the same place twice at the same time, each overlaid on the other and not quite connected. Except for the fear, she felt nothing. She tried to make herself feel something else. She thought she should be angry or resentful, but a switch had been thrown and now she was empty.

Larkin went into the bathroom and looked at herself in the mirror. She wanted to see if the emptiness showed on her face the way she saw it on Pike's. She couldn't tell. Looking at herself, she saw her father. She had his eyes and ears and the line of his jaw. She had her mother's nose and mouth.

She said, "I don't care."

She didn't care what he had done. He was her father. If Pike could carry his father, she could carry hers.

Larkin went back to the table and studied the lists of phone numbers and the phone trees she had been tracing. She found Khali Vahnich's number, then searched for it through each of the twenty-six single-spaced pages. Each time she found it, she marked it. When she finished with the twenty-six pages, she went back to the beginning and picked out the numbers Vahnich had called.

She found it near the bottom of the second page. She saw the number and recognized it because it was so familiar.

Vahnich had called her company's corporate head-quarters. The Barkley Company.

Larkin saw the number and thought, Wow, this is bizarre, because all she felt was the strange out-of-body sensation with the air humming on her skin. Her vision blurred, so she knew she was crying, but she didn't gasp or sob and her nose didn't clog; it was as if someone else was crying, and she was watching it from the inside.

She wiped her eyes so she could see better, and kept searching through the list. She found the number twice more, then stopped because, really, what was the point?

Joe and Elvis were right. Her father was connected with these people, and now they were both in trouble. Vahnich was trying to use her to get something from her father or punish him, and either way, he was fucking it up.

Pike's father had been a monster. Her father was a fuckup. Didn't matter. She loved him.

"Make it right."

She was speaking to herself.

39

THE BARKLEY Company occupied the top three floors of a black glass fortress in Century City with enough armed guards, security stations, and metal detectors to secure an international airport. Pike called Bud to arrange the meet, expecting to see Barkley at home, but Bud told him Barkley had been called to his office. Pike did not explain why they wanted to see him, except that it was about Larkin. Bud agreed to meet them—they would need Bud to get through security.

Bud said, "No guns, Joe. I can't let you be armed."

Pike said, "Sure."

"You bringing Larkin?"

"You bringing Pitman?"

"I'm not going to tell Pitman a goddamned thing. I won't even tell Barkley. Just meet me in the lobby and I'll take you up."

Bud hung up.

Parking at Barkley's office was an adventure. When Pike and Cole arrived, attendants took their names and asked for identification, and guards with mirrors examined the bottom of Cole's car.

Cole said, "If we have to get out of this place fast, we're screwed."

Pike didn't play off Cole's bait for a joke. He was thinking about the girl. He wanted to hurt the people who were hurting her. He kept reading the pain in her eyes, that she was trapped by herself in a tortured world, alone with a pain no one could share and from which she would never escape. And each time he saw it in her he saw it in himself, and wanted to punish them. He wanted to punish them badly enough that he would become his father to do it, and they would be him. He wanted them to know it like that—for hurting this girl. For abusing their power. For their arrogance.

Cole said, "You're awfully quiet. Even for you."

"I'm good."

Bud was waiting in the lobby with two visitor passes they had to wear around their necks. Bud had already signed them in.

Bud said, "You want to tell me what this is about before we go up?"

"No."

Pike knew from Bud's manner that Pitman hadn't called. They passed through a metal detector, then boarded a special elevator that went directly to the top floor.

As they rode up, Bud said, "How's she doing?"

"Not so good."

"You just keep her safe. That's why you're here. I think there's a lot these bastards aren't telling us."

When the doors opened, Bud led them into a reception area where an older woman with curly blond hair sat at a desk. She recognized Bud and waved them past.

"He's back there somewhere. If he's not in his office, just ask. They're having some kind of problem."

Cole nudged Pike and whispered, "Already? We just arrived."

They followed Bud down a long hall that looked like an art gallery, then past empty cubicles that should have been occupied by people Bud described as assistants. They found Conner Barkley outside his office with a small group of well-dressed men and women. They were immaculately groomed in Brioni and Donna Karan, but Barkley looked as if he had just rolled out of bed. His hair was sticking out at odd angles and his eyes were nervous and red. He blinked when he saw them approaching, then ran a hand over his head as he frowned at Bud.

"I didn't know you were bringing these people."

Pike grabbed Barkley by the throat and pushed him backwards into his office.

Bud was caught off guard.

"Joe!"

Chaos exploded like incoming mortars, but Pike ignored it. The well-dressed people were shocked and shouting, and Cole told someone to back the fuck up. Pike pushed Barkley into the wall as Cole and Bud surged into the office behind him and slammed the door, Bud trying to pull him off Barkley.

"Are you crazy? Did you lose your mind?"

Pike squeezed Barkley's throat. Not so hard. A little. Pike said, "Stentorum Real Holdings."

Barkley's eyes floated in pink pools. He wheezed, and his words were gurgles.

"I don't know what you want."

Bud had Pike by the arm. Cole stepped up beside him.

Bud saying, "Let go. Jesus, they're calling the police! You want the police?"

Cole saying, "How about I do the talking?"

Pike stepped away. Barkley clutched at his throat, then coughed and spat on the floor.

"Why did you do that? Why are you so mad?"

Pike wondered if Barkley was insane.

Bud moved between Pike and Barkley, raising his hands.

"Let's take it easy. Jesus, what are you doing?"

Cole said, "Stentorum Real Holdings is a company owned by Mr. Barkley. Stentorum is trying to buy the building where we found the Kings' bodies. They've had an agreement to buy that building for four months. It's the building where Larkin had her accident with the Kings and Khali Vahnich."

Barkley was still rubbing his throat.

"What are you talking about? I don't know anything about that. I own Stentorum, yes, but I don't know what you're talking about."

Pike watched Barkley as Cole went through it. Pike read his eyes and his mouth, and the rubbery way Barkley held himself. He listened to the timbre of Barkley's voice, gauging its rise and fall against Barkley's shifting focus and the nervous movement of his hands. Pike decided Barkley was telling the truth.

Pike said, "Did you know Alex Meesh was a lie?"

Barkley flushed. His eye contact faltered, he glanced away, then his eyes rolled up and to the left. Pike saw he was ashamed of himself.

"We thought it was the only way."

Bud took Barkley's arm.

"You knew about Vahnich? Jesus, Conner. For Christ's sake."

Cole said, "What about the property? I spoke with the executor of the trust. She has an option-to-buy agreement with Stentorum Real Holdings."

"I don't pay attention to those things. I have people for that."

Pike said, "Kline."

Barkley passed his hands over his head again, pushing the lank hair from his face.

"Gordon left. He's gone. I'll show you—"

Barkley led them down the hall to the far end of the building to Gordon Kline's office. Pike understood why Barkley's side of the floor was empty; a crowd of people were at Kline's end of the floor, going through his files and computer, and the computers that were used by his assistants.

Barkley said, "We think he left last night. I don't know. Some things are missing—"

Bud said, "Money?"

"We think so, yes. There were discrepancies. He was living here. He moved into his office when this mess with Vahnich started. He said he was scared."

Cole went to Kline's desk where a team of people were working at his computer.

"Could he have used Stentorum to buy the property without your knowing about it?"

"Of course he could. I let Gordon take care of these things. I trusted him."

Cole spoke loud to the room.

"Who has his phone log? C'mon, you people must log the calls. Is someone checking the log?"

Two women sitting together on a couch looked as if they didn't know whether to answer, but Cole was with Mr. Barkley, so the older one raised her hand.

"We have it."

Cole went over.

"Start about a month ago, doesn't matter which day. These logs include his cell and personal?"

"Yes, sir."

Executives of a certain level often got free phone service as one of their perks. Companies would absorb their phone bills under the rationale their executives conducted significant business by phone.

The woman flipped through the pages until she found the right dates, and Cole followed his finger down the page. He skimmed down one page, flipped to another, then looked up.

"It's the same number we got off Luis's phone. Vahnich."

Pike moved closer to Barkley and lowered his voice.

"Was it Kline who suggested you lie to Larkin about Vahnich?"

Barkley nodded, then realized why Pike had asked.

"Was Gordon telling Vahnich how to find her?"

Bud looked sick now, almost as sick as Barkley.

"That sonofabitch. He was probably trying to buy himself time. Maybe blaming you for holding up the deal."

Barkley suddenly turned away and threw up. Most everyone in the room glanced over but quickly turned away; only one person moved to help. A well-dressed young man with spectacles went to a bar and hurried back with a napkin.

Barkley said, "I'm sorry."

Pike thought he looked sorry, and Pike felt sorry for him.

"Vahnich put a hundred twenty million dollars into an investment with the Kings, sixty from a drug cartel in Ecuador and sixty from his own sources. That means terrorists, Conner. It's likely the Kings brokered the deal and thought they were coming to you for the balance."

"Nobody came to me. I don't know anything about this."

"Came to your company, and your company was Kline."

Cole said, "They needed two hundred million for the purchase. Kline probably figured he could steal the balance from you, or use your company's position to raise what he needed, but not as an investor with the Kings. He needed to buy the properties through your company in order to hide what he was doing. So the Kings gave him the one-twenty, but he couldn't raise the rest. Maybe Vahnich got scared because it was taking so long and wanted his money back. Kline probably blamed you to stall."

Barkley listened to him like a dog waiting to be kicked. Everyone else in the room was listening, too.

Barkley wiped his mouth.

"My lawyers advised me to call the police and the banking commission. I should call Agent Pitman about this. We have to get some forensic accountants in here."

Pike said, "You have a bigger problem than what Kline took. Vahnich still wants his money."

Barkley took a gulp of air when he realized what this meant, and colored again.

"Is Larkin all right?"

"She's fine."

"Does she know—"

He wavered again, then got it out.

"Does she know I lied to her?"

"Yes."

"I want to see her. I want to be with her right now."

Pike glanced at Cole, and Cole nodded.

"We'll take you."

40

PIKE ROLLED with Bud and her father, and Cole trailed them alone. Bud drove, with Pike on the passenger side and Conner Barkley in the rear. Pike filled in Bud on everything he had learned from Chen about the identities of the men from Ecuador and their possible connection to the Mara Salvatrucha street gang, MS-13. Bud put in a call to a friend of his who worked the LAPD Gang Unit, and asked him to find out whether anyone named Carlos showed on the roster of the Los Angeles MS-13 clique. After Bud made the call, they drove on in silence.

Riding with Bud at the wheel held a strange familiarity Pike did not enjoy, as if he had been forced back to a place he'd made peace with leaving. Pike listened to Conner Barkley to avoid thinking about it. Barkley spent most of their drive on the phone, wheezing nervously as he filled in his managers and attorneys.

Bud said, "Been a long time, Officer Pike."

Pike glanced over and knew Bud was feeling it, too—the familiarity they shared in the car, working crime and bad guys. Bud seemed warmed by it, but nothing felt the same about those days for Pike. He pointed ahead.

"Here's where we turn."

Pike directed them up the winding streets to the little house. The Lexus was still in the drive, and the old people were still on their porch. The two youngest Armenian cousins were washing their BMW, Adam and one Pike hadn't met. They looked over when the Hummer parked behind the Lexus. Cole parked next door.

Conner Barkley finally closed his phone and leaned forward to look at the house.

"This is where you've been staying? Larkin must have hated it."

Pike got out without answering, waited for Cole to limp up, then went to the house. Pike hopped onto the porch and rapped hard on the door one time to warn her.

"It's me."

Pike slipped the key into the deadbolt as he said it, and knew by the feel that the deadbolt wasn't locked. Pike pushed open the door.

"Larkin."

Cole, Bud, and Barkley clumped up onto the porch, coming inside as Pike called out.

"*Larkin!*"

Barkley said, "Larkin, are you here?"

Pike glanced at Cole, then Cole went to the kitchen while Pike checked her room and the bath. Her things were untouched, nothing was amiss, no signs of a struggle—it was two nights ago all over again. Larkin was gone.

Barkley put his hands on his hips, frowning.

"I thought she was supposed to be here."

Pike was already heading to the door when a young voice called from outside—

"Yo, bro! Bro!"

Adam was on the front lawn, barefoot and wet from his car. He was shading his eyes from the sun, but Pike knew he had seen something, and knew it was bad.

"Everything right over here, yo? Mona, she okay?"

"She isn't here. You see where she went?"

Cole, Bud, and Barkley had all come out. They clustered behind Pike on the porch.

Adam said, "Off with some cats. Wasn't that stalker dude, was it?"

Barkley said, "What stalker? What's he talking about?"

Pike hopped from the porch. Bud joined him, and Cole gimped down the steps. The milky sky had grown blinding, even through Pike's shades.

Pike said, "Someone picked her up?"

"She seemed cool with it, yo? Else we woulda said something."

Cole worked to relax the boy.

"You didn't do anything wrong. Say what happened."

"We were right here. She didn't call out or act like anything was wrong. They just got in the car."

"How long ago?"

"Half hour, maybe, somethin' like that. We were just soapin' up."

Bud stepped in closer, looking like a street cop even in the nice suit, but Pike could see he was tense. The white air seemed electric now with Larkin's absence.

"You get a clear look at these people and their car? What about your friend?"

"Thas my cousin, Garo. Yeah, we both saw. Coupla Latin cats and a white dude. Real sugar ride. Not my style, but sweet—one of those big-ass American cars all chopped down with the low seats."

"A lowrider?"

"Yeah, like that. I don't know the make, but it was sweet. Midnight black, chrome dubs—"

Pike said, "You get the tag?"

"Sorry, bro."

Bud headed for Garo as Pike unfolded the Interpol photo of Khali Vahnich. Adam nodded.

"Thas him, yo. That the stalker dude?"

Cole made a soft hiss.

"Jesus Christ. How did he find her? How could he find her here?"

Pike felt as if he had failed. He thought back to the dance club. Maybe it happened then. Maybe she had been recognized, and he had missed the tail.

Barkley called from the porch.

"Does he know where she is or not? Can someone tell me, please?"

Pike looked at the little house he had shared with Larkin Barkley, then went to the center of the street. He did it without thinking and wasn't sure why. The black lowrider wasn't going to be at the end of the block, and visible tire trails weren't going to be scribed in the street, but maybe that's why he went. Something deep in the DNA pushing him forward. Something primitive making him hunt.

Pike closed his eyes. He had kept her safe for five days, but now he had lost her. Larkin Conner Barkley was gone.

Something touched his back.

Pike opened his eyes and saw Cole.

"We'll find her."

Pike stared into Cole's eyes and saw shadows behind the comfort. Two small reflections, Joe Pikes staring back.

Pike's cell phone buzzed. Pike checked the number, but didn't recognize it. He answered anyway. The timing was too damnably perfect for it to be anyone else.

"Pike."

"I want the money."

Pike had heard the soft accent before. It was Khali Vahnich.

41

PIKE KEPT his voice even. His heart rate gave a bump, but he did not want Khali Vahnich to know he was scared.

"My friend is alive and unharmed?"

"For a while. Then we will see. To whom am I speaking?"

Pike motioned to Cole it was Vahnich, then hurried back to the house. He wanted silence so he could hear Vahnich clearly, and a pen to make notes. Confusion and mistakes would kill her as quickly as panic.

Pike said, "Put her on."

Inside, Pike went directly to the papers and pens spread over the dining table. He copied the incoming call number.

Vahnich sounded offended.

"She is fine. I will only kill her if I do not get the money."

"This conversation ends unless I know she's alive."

Cole and Barkley had followed him inside, Barkley

hearing enough to realize what was happening. He stomped forward as if he wanted the phone.

"Is this about Larkin? Is she dead?"

Pike motioned for silence. Cole clamped a hand over Barkley's mouth. Barkley struggled, but Cole whispered into his ear and he calmed.

"Put her on, Vahnich. Put her on or go away."

Pike focused on the call. He covered his free ear and listened for background noises that might identify Vahnich's location. He heard voices, but nothing that suggested the location. Then Larkin came on the line. She sounded fine.

"Joe?"

"I'm coming."

"I'm okay—"

Pike heard a thump as if the phone had been dropped. Larkin shouted something Pike didn't understand, then shrieked, but the shriek cut off. Vahnich came back on the line.

"Are you pleased to hear her living? Is this what you wanted?"

Pike hesitated. Keeping his voice level was more difficult this time. He nodded to let Cole and Barkley know she was alive.

"Yes. We only talk if she's alive."

"To whom am I speaking?"

"Her bodyguard."

"Let me speak with her father."

"You'll speak only to me. Everything goes through me."

"No more of this, then. Her father will transfer the

money and we can be done. I will give you the account number and access codes."

"Wait—listen—Kline took your money. He transferred the money out of the country. We don't know where he is."

"This is not my problem."

The front door opened, and Bud burst in. Cole immediately motioned him silent. Bud nodded, but went to the table and began to scratch a note.

Pike watched it all, but stayed with Vahnich.

"The Kings must have told you what happened before you killed them. This was Kline's deal. Barkley had nothing to do with this."

"I will tell you something. This money, it is not mine. Dangerous people entrusted it to me, and they look to me for its return. They do not care where it comes from."

Vahnich had made a mistake. That was the problem with talking, and Vahnich had been talking a lot. He had been trying to persuade, which meant he did not feel he could command. Pitman had been wrong about everything, but Pike had been wrong, too—Vahnich and his hit teams had never been trying to kill the girl; they had been trying to kidnap her so she could be used as leverage. The people who fronted the money wanted it back, and Vahnich was trying to save his own life. His fear could be used to buy Larkin time or manipulate Vahnich into another mistake.

Pike said, "How about if we help you find Kline? We'll work together."

Vahnich laughed.

"Of course we would. No, I think that would leave me in a weak position. I think now I am strong."

Bud turned with his note and held it for Pike to see. *SHE CALLED HIM. USED NEIGHBOR PHONE.*

The list of call numbers was still on the table. Larkin had found the calls between Vahnich and Kline, and had called him. Pike pointed at her father for Bud to show him the note.

"Why did she call you, Vahnich?"

Pike was sure he already knew.

"She wants to help him, but she helps me instead. These young girls are foolish, are they not?"

Pike was staring at Conner Barkley. Barkley was looking confused.

Vahnich said, "Tell her father. He will not want to lose such a daughter."

Cole went to the table and also wrote something. *MEET HIM.*

Pike nodded.

"He loves her, Vahnich. He worships that girl. I think we can work this out—"

Bud's cell phone chimed, but he turned away fast, cupping his mouth. Pike continued with Vahnich.

"Let's get together so we can work out the transfer. Tell me where we can meet you."

Vahnich laughed.

"Will you bring the money in cash? How many trucks will come? Please. He will transfer the money. When the money is safe, I will release her. You and I will never meet, my friend."

"He's not stupid, Vahnich. He won't transfer the money until he has his daughter."

"Then neither of us will have what we want, and we will both be sad."

Pike wanted to buy as much time as possible. If Vahnich wouldn't meet, they would have to find him.

"I'll talk to him. I have to find him, but I'll talk to him. He wants her back safe."

Vahnich said, "Copy these numbers—"

Vahnich began rattling off a string of numbers, but Pike stopped him.

"I don't know how long it will take to—"

"Copy them and read them back to me."

Pike copied them, then read them back. They were transfer and account numbers.

Vahnich said, "Good. These numbers you have are correct. He will have the money in this account in two hours or I will cut off her hand—"

Pike said, "Vahnich—"

"No money thirty minutes after that, I cut off her head. We need not speak again."

The line went dead.

Pike held the phone tight, listening to the silence. Cole and Conner Barkley were watching him. Bud was on his phone in the background, scribbling notes on a pad. Pike finally lowered his phone.

"She's alive for now, but he won't meet with us. He knows better than that."

Barkley said, "What does he want?"

"The hundred twenty million. We have two hours."

"But I didn't take it. I didn't know anything about it."

Barkley dropped onto the couch and pressed the heels of his palms into his eyes. His face clenched into a frustrated knot.

"Did she actually call this man? She *gave* herself to him?"

"She did it for you. She probably thought she could work out some kind of deal or convince him not to kill you."

Barkley shoved himself from the couch as if taking command of the situation.

"All right, I'll pay him. I can't move that amount of funds in two hours, but I'll pay him. Get him back on the line."

"Money isn't the answer."

Cole said, "Paying him isn't smart, Mr. Barkley. As soon as he has the money he'll kill her."

"He wants money, I have money—what else can we do?"

"Find him."

Bud finished his call and rejoined them.

"Got something here—the MS-13 connection might have paid off. The book shows two *veteranos* named Carlos—one is incarcerated, but the other runs with a clique that's been bringing in South American dope for years—"

Cole said, "Sounds like our guy."

"That's also the bad news. One Carlos Maroto—he's OG with Mara and lives dead-center in a Mara-controlled neighborhood. Finding him won't be easy. Getting him to cooperate will be even worse."

Pike knew Bud was right. With enough time, they could find him, but time was short, and finding a gang-banger in his own barrio would be difficult. Gang membership ran in families and could span entire neighborhoods. No one would cooperate, and word would spread quickly. In a world where pride and family were everything, Latin gangbangers went down hard and would not roll on their friends. Especially not for three Anglo outsiders.

Speed was life.

Pike said, "We need his cooperation."

"Yeah, that'll happen."

"It might if the right person asked."

Cole's eyebrows went up when he realized what Pike was thinking.

"Frank Garcia. Frank could make this happen."

Bud said, "*The* Frank Garcia?"

Pike checked the time.

"Let's do it. I'll call him from the car."

Cole and Bud headed for the door. Pike started after them, but stopped to look at Barkley.

"I'll call you when we know."

Barkley said, "I'm coming with you."

"Mr. Barkley, this is—"

Barkley turned a deep red.

"She's my daughter, and I want to be there. This is what fathers do."

Pike thought Barkley was getting ready to hit him. Pike's mouth twitched.

He said, "After you, sir."

Pike followed him out the door.

42

THE DIRECTIONS led them to a narrow street on the
border between Boyle Heights and City Terrace, not far
from the Pomona Freeway in East L.A. Stucco houses
with flat roofs lined the street like matching shoe boxes,
separated by driveways one car wide; most with yards
the size of postage stamps. American cars lined the
curbs, bikes and toys had been abandoned in the drives,
and more than one yard sported a deflating swimming
pool, wilted and lifeless in the nuclear heat.

Bud let the big Hummer idle down the street; Pike
rode shotgun, Cole and Barkley had the back.

Conner Barkley leaned forward to see.

"Where are we?"

Bud said, "Boyle Heights. You should buy it. Build a
big fuckin' mall."

Pike knew Barkley was nervous, but Bud was nervous, too.

Bud said, "You see him? I don't see him."

"He'll come. He said wait in the car until he gets
here."

"I'm not getting out whether he's here or not, these friggin' punks."

Bud eased on the brakes as they reached the address, stopping outside a small home identical to all the others except for a boat in the drive and an American flag hanging from the eaves. A yellow ribbon was pinned to the flag, and both the flag and the ribbon had been there so long they were bleached by the sun. More than one of the homes they passed were hung with similar ribbons.

Hard-looking young guys were sitting in the parked cars or standing in small groups as if they were impervious to the heat. Most wore white T-shirts and jeans baggy enough to hide a microwave oven, and most were heavily tattooed. They eyed the Hummer with studied indifference.

Bud read their gang affiliations by their ink.

"Look at these guys—Florencia 13, Latin Kings, Sureños, 18th Street—Jesus, 18th Street and Mara kill each other on sight. They friggin' *hate* each other."

Barkley said, "Are they gangbangers?"

Cole said, "Pretend you're watching TV. You'll be fine."

Pike said, "Frank."

A black Lincoln limousine appeared at the far end of the street and rolled toward them. Its appearance rippled through the young gangbangers, who got out of their cars, craning to see. Barkley saw their reactions and leaned forward again.

"Is he the head gangbanger?"

Cole laughed.

Pike thought that was funny, too. He thought if he

lived through this, he would tell Frank, and Frank would also laugh.

Pike said, "He's a cook."

Bud smiled at Pike. When he realized Pike wasn't going to say more, he twisted toward Barkley to explain.

"You eat Mexican food? At home? I know you have cooks, but maybe it's late and you want something fast, you keep tortillas in the house?"

"Uh-huh."

"The Monsterito?"

"Oh, sure, that's my favorite."

Pike thought this was a helluva thing to be talking about.

Bud turned forward again to keep an eye on Frank's limo.

"You and everybody else. Me, too. The little drawing they have on the package, the Latin guy with the bushy mustache? That's Mr. Garcia forty years ago. These kids out here—Frank used to be one of them. That was before he went to work making tortillas for his aunt. Used to make'm in her kitchen, that whole family recipe thing. Turned those tortillas into a food empire worth, what—?"

Bud glanced at Pike, but Pike ignored him.

Cole said, "Five, six hundred mil."

Pike wished they would stop talking, but Bud turned to Barkley again.

"Not your kind of money, but nothing to sneeze at. Thing is, he never forgot where he came from. He's paid a lot of doctor bills down here. He's paid for a lot of educations. He gives back. There are men in prison—and, by the way, I put some of those bastards there—Frank's been supporting their families for years. You think those boys wouldn't do anything for him? He's rich now, and he's old, but they all know he was one of them and didn't turn his back when he made it."

Frank's limo stopped, nose to nose with the Hummer. The front doors opened, and two nicely dressed young men popped out, one Frank's bodyguard, the other his assistant. Pike knew them both from visits to Frank's house.

Barkley said, "How do you know him, Pike?"

Bud said, "Joe almost married his daughter."

Pike pushed open the door and got out, wanting to get away from Bud's story. Pike had met the Garcias when he was a young patrol officer, still riding with Abel Wozniak. Years later, when Karen Garcia was murdered, Pike and Cole found her killer.

Pike waited as Frank emerged from the car. Frank Garcia looked to be a hundred years old. His skin, burnished as dark as saddle leather, had the crusty texture of bark, and his hair was a silver crown. He was frail, and had to be wheeled through the endless rooms of his Hancock Park mansion, but he could walk a bit if someone steadied his arm. When his bodyguard was unfolding his chair, Frank waved it away. He wanted to walk.

A craggy smile cracked his face when he saw Pike, and he clutched Joe's arm.

"Hello, my heart."

Pike returned his embrace, then stepped away.

"Carlos inside?"

"Abbot spoke with the people who could make it so. He will not know why he is here. I thought that best. So this man Vahnich could not be warned."

Frank Garcia was a sharp old man, and so was his attorney and right-hand man, Abbot Montoya. They had grown up together, Montoya like Frank's little brother. They had been White Fence together, and risen above it together as well.

The bodyguard and the driver took the old man's arms and the four of them crept up the walk, moving at an old man's pace. The front door opened almost at once, revealing a burly man in his middle forties. He was short but wide, with a weight lifter's chest and thin legs. His face was round, and pocked so badly he looked like a pineapple; his arms were covered with gang tats and scars. He studied Pike, then looked at the old man and held his door wider.

"Welcome to my home, sir. I'm Aldo Saenz. My mother, Lupe Benítez, was married to Mr. Montoya's wife's cousin, Hector Guerrero."

Frank shook his hand warmly.

"Thank you for your indulgence, Mr. Saenz. You do me an honor today."

Pike followed Frank into a small living room not unlike the Echo Park house, with furniture that had seen much use but was clean and orderly. This was a family home, with photographs of children and adults surrounding a crucifix on the wall. The pictures showed children of different ages, one of a young man in a Marine Corps dress uniform.

Including Aldo Saenz, Pike counted six men, two in the dining room and four in the living room. Their eyes hit Pike the instant he entered, and two of the men appeared nervous. Saenz gestured impatiently at the men in the dining room.

"Chair. C'mon."

One of the men hustled a chair from the dining room for Frank.

Frank said, "Please sit. Don't let an old man keep you on your feet. I must introduce myself—Frank Garcia. And may I introduce my friend—"

Frank waved Pike closer and gripped his arm. Pike was always surprised how strong the old man was. Hand like a talon.

"When I lost my daughter—when she was murdered—this man found the animal who took her. And now, now he is my heart. This man is a son to me. To help him is to help me. I wish you all to know this. Now, may we speak with Mr. Maroto?"

Saenz pointed at one of the men in the dining room. Maroto was a younger man, maybe in his early thirties, and now he tensed as if he was about to be executed. Powerful people had ordered him to be here; people who might end his life without hesitation. Every man in the room was watching.

Frank said, "Carlos Maroto of Mara Salvatrucha?"

Maroto's eyes flicked around the room. He was afraid, but Pike could see he was thinking. He had been told to be here, so he was here, but now he was preparing himself to fight if he had to fight.

Maroto said, "I am."

Frank once more clutched Pike's arm.

"This man, the son of my heart, he is going to ask something of you. Here, in front of the other members of our home. Before he does, let me say I understand these are sensitive issues, that business arrangements of long standing between individuals and groups might be involved. What we ask, we do not ask lightly."

The old man released Pike's arm and made a little wave.

"Ask."

Pike looked at Maroto.

"Where can I find Khali Vahnich?"

Maroto narrowed his eyes to show he was hard, and slowly shook his head.

"No fuckin' idea. Who's that?"

It occurred to Pike that Maroto might not know Vahnich by his real name. He took out the page with Vahnich's picture and held it out. Maroto did not take it, which told Pike Maroto knew him.

"Your crew is in business with Esteban Barone. Barone asked you to take care of him and some boys from Ecuador. You're helping a friend. I get that."

Saenz said, "Answer him, homes. No one is on trial here."

Maroto was angry and feeling on the spot.

"What the fuck? Yeah, that's right, why is this anyone's business?"

Pike said, "I want you to give him to me."

Maroto shifted again, and now he wasn't looking at Pike. He was looking at the others.

"What is this? We don't know this fuck. For all we know, he's a cop."

Aldo Saenz crossed the big arms, and Pike could see he was trying to control himself. When Saenz spoke, his voice was a low rumble.

"You are here as my guest. I treat you with respect, but do not insult Mr. Garcia in my home."

"I meant no disrespect to Mr. Garcia, but my clique has business with Esteban Barone. A long-standing and profitable business. He asked a favor, we do it. What do you want me to say?"

Pike said, "Khali Vahnich is Barone's friend, but that isn't all he is."

Pike passed the Interpol sheet to Saenz.

"Read to the bottom of the page."

Pike watched Saenz reach the bottom of the page, then saw him frown.

"What does this mean? Terrorist watch list? What is this?"

Frank clutched Pike's arm again and pulled himself to his feet.

"It means he is my enemy. He feeds the people who want to kill us, and arms their lunatics, and now— right now while we are standing here in this house—he is in Los Angeles—our *barrio*! And I want that mother-fucker!"

Saenz was motionless except for the rise and fall of his massive chest. His face creased like layers of slate, with a fierce tic in his cheek. He passed the sheet to the nearest man, then stared at Maroto.

Maroto grew pale and shook his head.

"Barone said help the guy, we helped. You think we know something like this? You think he said, Here's my friend, the terrorist? What the fuck?"

The man with the sheet passed it to the next man, and he to the next. Pike remembered the flag outside and the yellow ribbon. Saenz was staring at the picture of the young Marine, and Pike knew Frank Garcia had chosen this house well.

Saenz cleared his throat, then looked at Frank.

"If you could give us a moment, please. I mean no disrespect. Just a moment."

The bodyguard and the driver helped Frank up, and Pike followed them out. They were only halfway to his car when Saenz caught up and told them where to find Vahnich.

43

VAHNICH WAS using a small house on a low rise in the elbow where the Glendale Freeway met the L.A. River. Orange orchards had once stretched as far as anyone could see, but the orchards fell to developers, and the low rises and rolling hills of Glassell Park were covered with houses. Withered orange trees still peeked between the older homes; original tenants with gnarled trunks as black as soot. Pike and Bud both knew the area well; it was directly across the river from the police academy.

Bud was still bitching.

"This fucking Hummer stands out like a tank. We might as well be coming up here with a big sign, Here we come."

Pike said, "Right at the next street, then up the hill. It should be on the left."

Maroto told them the house sat at the end of a long drive, hidden from the street by scrub oak and olive trees and neighboring homes. Vahnich didn't live in the house, but had wanted a place to meet with the men from Ecuador. Vahnich had liked the privacy.

Larkin's father leaned forward, trying to see.

"What if she isn't here? What if he took her some-where else?"

Cole said, "Then Maroto is gonna have a bad night. That's why Saenz and those guys kept him—so he couldn't warn this guy and to make sure he didn't lie."

Bud slowed.

"Coming up. Look to the left."

The drive curved down and away from the street, following the roll of the hill. Pike saw the near corner of the house and the tail of a blue car, and then they were past.

Cole said, "Saw a blue car, but that's it. He could have an army in there."

Pike didn't mind. If you couldn't see them, they couldn't see you.

Bud kept rolling.

"Let's call the police. We gotta bring in LAPD."

Pike turned to watch the drive to see if anyone came out to look.

"Let's make sure she's here."

"What are you going to do?"

"Go see. Wait up the street. I'll call."

Conner Barkley said, "I want to come."

"I'm just going to look."

Pike stepped out at a fast walk, then trotted up the neighboring drive. The homes on this part of the street stepped up the gentle rise, each house a few feet above the one below. Pike followed a low retaining wall along-side the house past plastic garbage cans and old rain gut-ters and unused bags of fertilizer so old they had erupted. He stopped long enough to make sure the backyard was empty, then crossed the yard between three ancient orange trees and stepped over the edge.

Pike side-hilled the slope through ivy and ice plants and more orange trees until he was below Vahnich's house, then worked his way up. From his present position, he saw a ranch-style house in need of paint, set on a dead yard littered with rotten oranges. The neighboring house was above it. The drive curved up to a carport at the front of the house. The blue car he glimpsed from the street was blocking the lowrider described by the cousins, and a new Chrysler LeBaron in the carport.

Two men stood at the front of the lowrider, a liquid black 1962 Bel Air that shone like burning coal. The hood was up, and both men were lost in the joys of the engine.

The way the house was cut into the slope, Pike knew a retaining wall and walkway would run along the opposite side of the house along its entire length. He was pretty sure he would find windows, and then he might find Larkin.

Pike started through the skeletal fruit trees toward the near end of the house, but as soon as his sight line changed, he saw her through the sliding glass doors cut into the back of the house. Larkin was sitting on the floor against the far wall in an empty room, facing the sliding doors. A man walked past her moving from left to right, heading for the front of the house. He wasn't Vahnich. Pike thought it through. At least six men were present—the five remaining Ecuadoreans, plus Vahnich.

Pike studied Larkin and felt an enormous sense of relief. He had lost her, but now had found her. She was sitting with her knees together, and her hands behind her back. Pike couldn't tell if she was tied, but he wanted to know; if she was bound, her movement would be limited. She didn't seem uncomfortable or injured. Her head was up, her eyes were open, and she was looking toward the front of the house. The choppy black hair made her look tough and good to go. Pike wondered if she would grow it out again and go back to the red. She was saying something to whoever she was looking at. Pike decided she was angry, which made his mouth twitch. He settled back, thinking, You are one damn fine young woman.

Pike opened his phone to dial Vahnich, and Vahnich answered immediately.

"Yes?"

"He'll transfer the money. He's setting it up now."

"This is a wise man. He has made the right choice."

"I'm supposed to make sure you didn't cut off her hand or hurt her. He wants to be sure. Put her on for a second."

Vahnich didn't object.

A man entered from the right, squatted beside the girl, and held a phone to her head. It was Vahnich, and now Pike knew Larkin was tied.

Her voice came to his ear.

"Joe?"

"I won't let him hurt you."

"He says to tell you he hasn't hurt me."

"Stay groovy."

Vahnich came to the glass with the phone. Pike wasn't alarmed. Vahnich was simply looking out over the Glendale Freeway toward the Verdugo Mountains. Pike could have killed him, but three other men were still inside with the girl.

Vahnich said, "She is well, you see? I am a man of my word. I will honor our agreement."

"His business guy says it's going to take another few minutes to compile this much money for transfer. They have it spread all over hell and back."

"I understand."

"I'll call you again. At that time, her father will want to personally hear her voice. Just to be sure. Then they'll hit the button."

"Of course. I have no problem with that."

"Good. You won't have any problems."

A reasonable terrorist. Polite and considerate.

Pike ended the call, then dialed Cole. While he was waiting for the ring, Vahnich turned away from the sliding doors and exited to the left. Pike didn't like it. Now he had Vahnich somewhere in the back of the house, another man in the front, and two men in unknown locations.

Cole answered.

Pike said, "She's here. Two men are out front by the cars. The girl is inside in what looks like a family room or den at the back. At least three more men are inside, but I can't say where."

"You see Vahnich?"

"That's affirm."

"So Vahnich is confirmed in the house."

"Yes."

"Bud says he's calling the police."

"Whatever. Where are you?"

"We're across the street."

"How about you come up from below to watch the front? Bud can coordinate with the police and stay on the drive—stand by—"

A big man Pike hadn't seen before came from the front of the house and pulled the girl to her feet. He shoved her toward the back. Pike didn't like the rough way he treated her, but he also didn't like it that she was being moved. Pike returned to the phone.

"They're moving her. I'm going to see what's up."

Pike closed the phone, then made his way back across the slope to the far side of the yard, then to the walkway behind the house. Pike edged to the window, listened, then took out his gun. Pike didn't have to jack the slide or check to see if it was loaded like they do on TV. Pike kept one locked in the box and good to go. He knew it was loaded because it was always loaded.

He raised up enough to peek in the corner of the window. Larkin, the big man, and Vahnich were in an empty bedroom. Larkin was back on the floor with the big man standing nearby. They were watching Vahnich, who had a laptop open. He was getting ready for Pike's call. He had the girl ready to speak to her father, and his computer to confirm the transfer. After the transfer was confirmed, Vahnich would kill her. Vahnich or one of his men would likely cut her throat or strangle her, then they would drive to LAX and immediately leave the country. Pike wondered if Vahnich would do it himself.

Pike continued on to the carport. As he got closer, he heard the two men. He looked past the LeBaron. The two men had closed the hood, but were still by the car, talking. These two, Vahnich and the big man with

Larkin, left two men who might be anywhere. Pike wondered if Cole could spot them from the other side of the house.

Pike drifted back a bit, then phoned Cole again, whispering.

"Where are you?"

"Front of the house. I'm in some holly, downhill from the drive. How about you?"

Holly bushes lined the property directly across from Pike.

Pike said, "You see the two men by the Bel Air?"

"Twenty feet in front of me."

"Look at the LeBaron. Now look past the LeBaron."

"Got you."

"Vahnich plus one with Larkin, plus these two are four. Can you locate the missing two from your side?"

"Stand by—"

The two men by the Bel Air suddenly straightened and looked up the drive. Pike knew something was wrong, but he couldn't see what they were looking at. He lifted the phone—

"What's on?"

"Dunno. I'll look."

Pike raised up to see for himself just as he heard Cole's reaction.

Cole said, "Oh, shit."

Conner Barkley stalked down the drive.

44

BARKLEY came down the drive with an expression of blustery outrage, but the men were confused. They probably thought he was a neighbor and would have to shine him on, but Pike knew their confusion wouldn't last.

Pike accelerated through the carport. He covered the distance silently and fast, knowing it would go bad. Barkley looked at him, and both men turned to see what Barkley was looking at. Pike hit the nearest man with his gun, but the second man lurched sideways, barking out a shout—

Something behind Pike exploded and another man shouted as Cole pushed through the hedges. The two missing men were at the front door, one behind the other, the first man firing again—bam, bam—when Cole shot him in the chest; the shooter crumpling even as the man behind him shoved the door closed on his dying friend. Pike knew he would run to the back of the house.

All of it happened in glimpses: Barkley striding closer on abnormally stiff legs; Bud Flynn appearing at the top of the drive; Cole moving on the second man in a two-hand stance—

—only now the second man was on his knees with his hands up, staring at Cole.

Pike started for the house—

"Larkin—"

Cole said, "Go—"

Pike ran back the way he had come. Inside, the front shooter would be screaming about what happened; Vahnich would be confused, then afraid; he would make one or both of his hitters return to see what was happening; and then Vahnich would make a decision—

Middle of the day, a bright sunny day, and the world was gone to hell. Their only choices were bad—bad for Vahnich, bad for the girl, and bad for Pike. Vahnich could shoot it out in a hostage situation, or run. Vahnich didn't know how many people were on him, whether he was surrounded, or whether the police were involved, but the hostage card was a loser; if Vahnich stayed he would be trapped. Running was the best of the bad choices, so they would run—out the back and into the neighborhood, run and gun if they had to, invade a home in broad daylight, steal a car, and pray—but it was their last, best, and only chance.

Pike ran hard for the end of the house, and heard more shots as he ran. One shot would have been an execution, but multiple shots gave him hope. They were shooting at the front door to stall off a breach; this meant they were going to run.

Pike believed Khali Vahnich would kill Larkin, but he wouldn't kill her until they were outside the house.

Vahnich didn't know what he would be facing and might need her as a shield. If the way was clear, he might kill her just before he went over the fence, but he wouldn't kill her before. He would kill her to punish her father, and he would kill her to punish Pike.

Pike took cover in the orange trees beyond the house just as the window came up. The big man climbed out first, dropped to a knee, then said something into the window. They pushed Larkin through; she fell straight down and landed with a sharp gasp. Vahnich landed on top of her, and then the final man came out, a short muscular guy with a bandana tied around his head, everyone tangled together, and then Vahnich pulled her close.

Pike steadied his gun against the orange tree.

When Cole came around the far side of the house, the bandana saw him, popped off one shot, and Cole fired back. The bandana went down with a high keening whine, but pushed to his knee and fired again. Cole dropped for cover as the sliding glass doors flew open, and Bud Flynn came out, gun up and ready. Bud must have forgotten himself.

He shouted, "Police!"

The bandana swung toward Bud, and Pike shot him in the head.

Vahnich and the big man saw Pike, and Vahnich jerked the girl in front of them for a shield as they scuttled backwards toward the slope. The big man fired at Flynn, then Cole, but the shots were wild and pointless.

Pike said, "You're done."

Bud was behind a heavy clay pot, shouting.

"Drop your weapons! Drop'm *now*!"

Conner Barkley came through the doors. He had no gun and did not look for cover. Maybe he didn't know that's what you were supposed to do. He stormed past Bud into the yard and stopped—out in the open, in front of Bud, and alone.

Spittle flew from his face when he shouted.

"You let her go! *Let my daughter go!*"

The big man shifted out from behind the girl to fire. He only moved an inch or two, but the sight picture was perfect, like a dot on top of an *i*. Pike shot him before he could fire, and the big man fell like a sack.

Bud was still screaming, but he had crabbed sideways so he wouldn't shoot Barkley.

"Drop your weapon, goddamnit! Put it down! You're done, you sonofabitch! Down!"

Barkley was screaming, too; screaming as if he was having a tantrum.

"You let her go. Let *GO!*"

Pike stepped out from behind the orange tree. Vahnich caught the movement and angled to watch him, keeping the girl between them. Vahnich had drawn himself as small as possible behind her, and peeked from behind her head. His gun was pressed hard into her neck, but Pike couldn't have that. He moved into the open, set himself, and lined up on Vahnich's eye. He found the rhythm of Vahnich's fear. The eye moved, the gun moved; the eye and the gun became one.

Pike said, "Dead man."

The first kiss of sirens whiffed up the hill. Bud and Barkley were still screaming. Pike did not see Cole but trusted he was on target. He did not look at Larkin because she might see his fear. Pike saw only Vahnich's eye and the eye looking back.

Vahnich dropped his gun. The gun fell, but nothing else moved. Vahnich had made his decision. He would take his chances with the courts.

Vahnich called from behind the girl.

"I dropped it. I'm giving up. I surrender."

Bud shouted the instructions Pike had heard a hundred times.

"Raise your hands above your head. Raise them high! Lace your fingers on your head!"

Vahnich raised his hands. He laced his fingers on his head. The girl still had not moved, and neither had Pike.

Pike said, "Larkin. Go to your dad."

She started toward Pike.

"Go to your father."

She ran to her father.

Vahnich said, "I give up!"

Bud had come out from behind the pot. Cole was covering the men they had shot. Pike crabbed sideways across the yard until he was between Vahnich and the girl, his gun never leaving the eye.

Behind him, Bud said, "Joe. Son, the police are coming."

Pike said, "Larkin, you okay? You good?"

"He was going to kill me. He was—"

"I know."

Bud said, "Officer Pike—"

Pike pulled the trigger. The gun made a loud pop that sounded hollow in the open air. The body fell.

Pike walked over to secure their weapons. He checked the bodies. All three were dead.

Bud was staring at him with his hands at his sides as if he had been drained of life. Conner Barkley was holding his daughter. Cole tucked his own pistol into his waist as he came over.

Cole said, "You okay?"

"Sure. How's that leg?"

"Better. At least we didn't get shot this time."

Pike went to the girl. Conner watched him coming, and Pike saw he was crying. Billionaire tears looked like everyone else's.

Pike placed his hand on Larkin's back and whispered.

"I won't let them hurt you. I won't let anyone hurt you."

She turned to him then and hugged him. She buried her face against his chest, and Pike rested his chin on her head. Bud was watching him. Bud looked sad and disappointed.

Pike said, "I still hate bullies. Live with it."

Pike was holding the girl when the police arrived.

45

OCEAN AVENUE was lit with smoky gold light that time of morning, there at the edge of the sea. Pike ran along the crown of the street, enjoying the peace and the rhythm of his body. It was three fifty-nine that morning. No cars had disturbed him for more than two miles, and the coyotes did not pace him. He was the only beast in the city, but this was about to change.

She turned onto Ocean at San Vicente and roared toward him through the darkness. He recognized her new car, so he stayed on the center line and did not break his stride.

Larkin zoomed past, swung around, and idled up alongside him. She had gotten a pearl white Aston convertible. The top was down. She had kept the short hair, but had gone back to red. She grinned the lip-curling smile. Pike was glad her confidence was back.

"Only a lunatic runs this early."

"Only a lunatic driving this early would find me."

"I asked your boy Cole. Since you won't return my calls anymore."

"Uh-huh."

"I think he wants to kiss me."

"Uh-huh."

Pike had stopped returning her calls. They had talked often in the weeks following the incident, but he didn't know what more he could say.

She said, "Can you talk while you run?"

"Sure."

She took a moment to get it together, then told him what she came to say.

"I'm not going to bother you anymore. Now, just because I'm not calling you doesn't mean you can't call me if you change your mind. You can call whenever you want, but I get it you want me to stop, so I'm going to stop."

"Okay."

The old flash of anger darkened her eyes.

"My friend, that was WAY too easy. The least you could do is pretend."

"Not with you."

The car idled alongside him. Pike caught a glimmer on the bluff, and wondered if it was a coyote.

After a bit, she said, "Do you believe in angels?"

"No."

"I do. That's why I go driving like this. I look for angels. They only come out at night."

That was something else Pike didn't know how to answer, so he said nothing.

She looked up at him.

"I'm not going to call anymore because that's what you want; not because I want to stop. You probably think you're too old for me. You probably think I'm too young. I'll bet you hate rich people."

"Pick one."

Larkin smiled again, and Pike was glad to see it. He loved her in-your-face smile. But then her smile faded and her eyes filled, and he didn't like that so well.

She said, "You probably think I'll get over it, but I won't. I love you. I love you so damn much I would do anything for you."

"I know you would."

"I'd even stop calling."

The Aston Martin roared away, its engine screaming with pain.

Pike watched her taillights flare. She turned east on San Vicente, and raced toward the city.

Pike said, "I love you."

He ran alone in the darkness, wishing the coyotes would join him.

THE LAST DAY

GOODBYE KISS

46

JON STONE gazed out over the azure gulf and dreamed of ships at sea. Sailing ships of the late 1700s; not these silicon-chip water-rockets any geek could sail, but wooden ships built by hands and sweat, and sailed by men who lived by their belief in monsters. Jon imagined his ship rounding the point, a forty-gun frigate, himself a lieutenant in the Royal Navy, bound to the mast by duty and honor here on the far side of the world. Those were days of beauty, and Jon Stone wished he had been part of it.

The dude's house had put him in the mood; top-of-the-line, no-expense-spared new, for sure, but with a wild, primitive freedom that screamed for those earlier times. The walls were these big plantation shutters that could be pushed aside so the inside and the outside were one, opening the house to the sea and the jungle and a warm breeze that smelled of flowers caught in a woman's hair: a neo-plantation tropical palace overlooking the Gulf of Thailand—the beautiful chaos of the jungle bowling away to a coconut orchard, the orchard giving way to an immaculate white beach and the blue-on-blue sweep of ocean and sky, all of it like a rich boy's fantasy of Tarzan's tree house, maybe, or one of those African manors where British admirals retired.

Jon so totally dug it.

Jon Stone was thinking about the ships when a single muffled *wump* from the far side of the house broke the silence, just the one sound, like a baseball bat smacking onto a bed.

Stone sighed, knowing his time here was short.

He said, "I dig this house, man. I could live here."

Jon spoke clearly but did not expect an answer. It was a big-ass house with no one around to hear.

Jon walked through the open wall to the edge of a beautiful limestone deck and squinted down at the beach. Another three or four days, the beach would be jammed with bands and insane women.

"Full moon parties, bro. Cat in Big Buddha, he said they have'm every full moon. Seven, eight thousand people show up, all these bands and shit—food, booze, whatever. It's these tourist chicks. The chicks go wild, he said; just the one night, these crazy chicks thinking, What, what happens here stays here? Oh, man. We should stay, bro."

But no one answered, not way up there in the jungle. It was a long way to town.

The latex gloves made his hands sweat, so his hands were itching. Jon checked his watch, then started back through the house.

A staff of four usually worked at the house. A cook, some butler dude, a maid, and a full-time gardener. The gardener had two extra guys come to help with the big stuff every Tuesday. Every Friday a pool guy came to bleach the infinity pool, and an extra housekeeper came to help with the floors. Jon had patterned their movements for three weeks and arranged events so none of them would show up today.

No visitors, no employees, no witnesses.

Gordon Kline had been calling himself George Perkins when Jon's boy caught the scent. Told the locals he retired after selling off thirty-two McDonald's franchises up in Alberta. Cats down in town were used to stories like that from rich Europeans and Norte Americanos, most of them perverts come down to scarf the little Thai boy toys, and that's what they figured for the man who was calling himself George Perkins. Only Perkins had been keeping a way more dangerous secret than pedophilia.

Jon took the long way back to Kline's office, like walking with the MTV crew who let rap assholes and overpaid jocks brag about their cribs. Sixty-inch plasmas in every room, a beaten copper bar that had to be twenty feet long, a temperature-controlled triple-glazed wine room the size of Jon's bedroom; this monster saltwater aquarium drifting with neon fish. Jon had always wanted a big-ass aquarium like that. Dude had a black Hummer, a maroon Bentley Continental, and a pale green

Maserati Quattroporte right outside the double-wide front doors. Jon grooved on the Maserati. He could see himself tooling down to the beach in that bitch. Tooling back to the house with a couple of crazy-ass Aussie chicks.

Jon took out his gun, letting it dangle at his side.

A hundred twenty million could buy damn near anything, but not everything.

Jon found the office. Dude's body was facedown on a beautiful leather couch, an arm and a leg dangling over the side. A single round in the side of the neck had almost decapitated the sonofabitch. Blood was still pooling on the floor.

Jon said, "All set, Mr. Katz?"

"Almost."

Pike was using a passport that identified him as Richard Katz of Milwaukee, Wisconsin. Jon's own passport showed the name Jon Jordan, also of Milwaukee. Business partners on holiday together, let the locals think what they want.

Pike was behind the dude's desk, adding a laptop to a cardboard box already filled with computer CDs, papers, and a couple of hard drives. Account information where he had stashed the Vahnich money. A hundred million and change.

Stone looked at the body and lifted his pistol.

"Piece of shit."

Jon Stone fired two shots into what was left of the head. Pike kept going through the desk even with the shots loud as bombs.

Pike, over his shoulder, said, "Stop."

"Fuck him. You should have let me have him. I could have kept him alive for weeks, traitorous fuck."

Stone shot the body again.

Pike said, "Jon, please."

Stone lowered his gun. He tapped it against his leg, irritated because he was frustrated. Jon would have skinned the sonofabitch alive, a fuckin' American doing business with terrorists; snipped off the fucker's fingers and toes a joint at a time, then carved the living meat right off his bones. Well, okay, maybe not—Jon wouldn't have done those things, but it was fun to think about, and he had thought about it every day since Pike told him to find the sonofabitch. Jon Stone had been a soldier, a mercenary, a private military contract broker, and even an assassin, but he was also a patriot.

Pike's gun was on the floor by the couch. Pike had popped the fucker, then tossed his gun, which was how they planned it. Their weapons were local junk Jon picked up for the job; use'm then lose'm, which was easier than sneaking firearms into the country.

Pike came around the desk with the box.

Jon said, "Got everything?"

Pike grunted. What passed for a yes.

Stone kept thinking about the incredible view and how much he liked the house. Every full moon, the beach filling with out-of-control chicks.

Stone tapped his pistol.

"What the fuck, bro? Let's keep it. Wouldn't be like we're stealing it from worthwhile people."

Pike studied the room to make sure he hadn't missed anything.

"It's going home. Pitman might be able to do something with the hard drives."

Stone tapped his pistol again, then glanced at Pike's gun, thinking it would be easy—double-tap center-of-mass, and the box would be his. Spend the rest of his life in this fine, fine house.

Stone said, "Fuck it."

He raised his pistol and shot the body again, a single shot, square up the dude's ass. Then he tossed his gun onto the body.

Wouldn't be right, keeping this money, but it was fun to think about. Jon had made a fortune off Pike's contract anyway, and Pike hadn't taken a dime. Wouldn't. Though he made Jon help him find Kline. For free. That part of it sucked.

Pike said, "Hold this."

Pike pushed the box into Stone's hands, then went back to the desk. Pike took something from his pocket. Stone wondered what in hell Pike was doing, then saw it was a snapshot of the girl. Larkin Conner Barkley. Pike propped the snapshot against the dude's humidor so she was facing the body. Pike was a strange cat.

Back when Stone was a combat troop, the boys dealt business cards on their KIAs. Called'm Death Cards. Let the enemy know who they better not fuck with.

Pike touched the picture to make sure it was just right, then came back for the box.

"Okay. We're done."

They drove back through paradise along a winding road to the airport. They turned in their rental, then headed to the terminal, all the disks and computer stuff now packed in their bags. It was a small terminal: one low, flat building surrounded by sand, shells, and coconut trees.

Stone said, "I'm gonna grab a smoke. Wanna hang with?"

"Meet you at the gate."

Stone lit up as Pike disappeared into the terminal. He waited a few moments, then strolled to the end of the building and sat back to enjoy the moment. The sun was pure and bright in the very best way, and the air so clean Jon Stone wanted to stay there forever.

Stone had one of those cell phones you get to call home when you travel abroad. He dialed a U.S. number, then waited for the man to answer.

Stone said, "Over and out. We're coming home."

"Thank God. Thank Christ for that. He's all right?"

"Thanks for asking about me."

"You know what I mean."

"Pike's fine. He did what he had to do, just like you knew he would. That boy's a bulldog."

"I didn't have any choice."

"I know, I know."

Jon thought, Jesus, shut up already! The sonofabitch had been apologizing for months like he felt guilty for turning Pike loose. Jon suspected the man knew what Pike would do and how he would do it from the beginning.

The man was still going on.

"I didn't know how else to protect that girl. I knew what it took, but I wasn't up to it. He was."

"Listen, I gotta get goin'—"

"He's a good man."

"Yeah, he is, Mr. Flynn. That's why he's Pike."

"You boys get home safe."

Stone turned off the phone. He finished his cigarette, enjoying the clean sky and sensuous air until they called for his flight. Then he went inside to find Joe Pike at the gate.

Read on for a preview of
the next thrilling book in the
Elvis Cole series

by

Robert Crais

Coming soon in hardcover from
Simon & Schuster

Prologue

Beakman and Trenchard could smell the fire—it was still a mile away, but a sick desert wind carried the promise of hell. Fire crews from around the city were converging on Laurel Canyon like red angels, as were black-and-white adam cars, Emergency Services vehicles, and water-dropping helicopters out of Van Nuys and Burbank. The helicopters pounded by so low overhead that Beakman and Trenchard could not hear their supervisor.

Beakman shook his head, cupping his ear to indicate he had not heard. *"What did you say?"*

Their supervisor, a patrol sergeant named Karen Philips, leaned into their car and shouted again. "Start at the top of Lookout Mountain. Emergency Services is already up, but you gotta make sure those people leave. Don't take any shit. You got it?"

Trenchard, who was senior and also driving, shouted back, "We're on it."

They jumped into line with the fire engines racing up Laurel Canyon but quickly turned up a cut in the canyon's west wall, climbing Lookout Mountain Avenue up the steep hill. Once home to rock 'n' roll royalty from Zappa to Neil Young to Marilyn Manson, Lookout Laurel Canyon had been the birthplace of country rock in the sixties. Crosby, Stills, and Nash had all lived there. So had Jim Morrison, Don Henley, and Glenn Frey. Beakman, who banged away at a Fender Telecaster in a cop band called Nightstix Blues, thought the place had to be musical magic.

Beakman pointed at a small house.

"I think Joni Mitchell used to live there."

"Who gives a shit? You see that sky? Man, look at that. The frakkin' air is on fire!"

A charcoal bruise smudged the sky as smoke pushed toward Sunset Boulevard. Beginning as a house fire at the crest of the Hollywood Hills, the flames had jumped to the brush in Laurel Canyon Park, then spread with the wind. Three houses had already been lost, and more were threatened. Beakman would have plenty of stories for his kids when he returned to his day job on Monday.

Jonathan Beakman was a level II reserve officer with the Los Angeles Police Department, which meant he was armed, fully sworn, and did everything a full-time uniformed officer did, except he did it for free and only two days per month. In his regular life, Beakman taught high school algebra. His kids weren't particularly interested in the Pythagorean theorem, but they bombed him with questions after his weekend ride in the car.

Trenchard, who had twenty-three years on the job and didn't like music, said, "Here's how it goes down:

We get to the top, we leave the car and work down five or six houses on foot, me on one side, you on the other, then go back for the car and do it again. Should go pretty quick like that."

The fire department had been through the area, broadcasting the order to evacuate over their public address system. A few residents already had their cars piled high with clothes, golf clubs, pillows, and dogs. Others stood in their front doors, watching their neighbors pack. A few were on their roofs, soaking their homes with garden hoses. Beakman worried the hosers might be a problem.

"What if somebody won't leave?"

"We're not here to arrest people. We have too much ground to cover."

"What if someone can't leave, like an invalid?"

"First pass, we want to make sure everyone gets the word. If someone needs more help, we'll radio down or come back after we reach the bottom."

Trenchard, ever wise for a man who didn't like music, glanced over.

"You okay?"

"A little nervous, maybe. One of these houses, you watch. Some old lady's gonna have fifteen pugs waddling around. What are we going to do with fifteen pugs?"

Trenchard laughed, and Beakman found himself smiling, though his smile quickly faded. They passed a little girl following her mother to an SUV, the girl dragging a cat carrier so heavy she couldn't lift it. Her mother was crying.

Beakman thought, *This is awful*.

When they reached the top of Lookout Mountain, they started the door-to-door. If the inhabitants weren't already in the act of evacuating, Beakman knocked and rang the bell, then pounded on the jamb with his Maglite. Once, he hammered at a door so long that Trenchard shouted from across the street.

"You're gonna knock down the goddamned door! If they don't answer, nobody's home."

When they reached the first cross street, Trenchard joined him. The cross street cut up a twisting break in the ridge, and was lined with clapboard cabins and crumbling stone bungalows that had probably been built in the thirties. The lots were so narrow that most of the houses sat atop their own garages.

Trenchard said, "Can't be more than eight or ten houses in here. C'mon."

They split sides again, and went to work, though most of the residents were already leaving. Beakman cleared the first three houses easily enough, then climbed the steps to a rundown stucco bungalow. Knock, bell, Maglite.

"Police officer. Anyone home?"

He decided no one was home and was halfway down the steps when a woman called from across the street. Her MINI Cooper was packed and ready to go.

"I think he's home. He doesn't go out."

Beakman glanced up at the door he had just left. He had banged on the jam so hard the door had rattled.

"He's an invalid?"

"Mr. Jones. He has a bad foot, but I don't know. I haven't seen him in a few days. Maybe he's gone, but I don't know. He doesn't move so well, that's why I'm saying."

Now she had the irritated expression of someone who wished she hadn't gotten involved.

Beakman climbed back to the door.

"What's his name?"

"Jones. That's all I know—Mr. Jones. He doesn't move so well."

Beakman unleashed the Maglite again. Hard.

"Mr. Jones? Police officer, is anyone home?"

Trenchard, finished with his side of the street, came up the stairs behind him.

"We got a holdout?"

"Lady says the man here doesn't move so well. She thinks he might be home."

Trenchard used his own Maglite on the door.

"Police officers. This is an emergency. Please open the door."

Both of them leaned close to listen, and that's when Beakman caught the sour smell. Trenchard smelled it, too, and called down to the woman.

"He old, sick, what?"

"Not so old. He has the bad foot."

Down on the street, she couldn't smell it.

Beakman lowered his voice.

"You smell it, right?"

"Yeah. Let's see what's what."

Trenchard holstered his Maglite. Beakman stepped back, figuring Trenchard was going to kick down the door, but Trenchard just tried the knob and opened the door. A swarm of black flies rode out on the smell, engulfed them, then flew back into the house. Beakman swatted at the flies. He didn't want them to touch him. Not after where they had been.

The woman shouted up, "What is it?"

They saw a man seated in a ragged club chair, wearing baggy plaid shorts and a thin blue T-shirt. He was barefoot, allowing Beakman to see that half the left foot was missing. The scarring suggested the injury to his foot occurred a long time ago, but he had a more recent injury.

Beakman followed Trenchard into the house for a closer look. The remains of his head lolled backward, where blood and brain matter had drained onto the club chair and his shoulders. His right hand rested on his lap, limply cupping a black pistol. A single black hole had been punched beneath his chin. Dried blood the color of black cherries was crusted over his face and neck and the chair.

Trenchard said, "That's a damned bad foot."

"Suicide?"

"Duh. I'll call. We can't leave this guy until they get someone here to secure the scene."

"What about the fire?"

"Fuck the fire. They gotta get someone up here to wait for the CI. I don't want us to get stuck with this stink."

Trenchard swatted futilely at the flies and ducked like a boxer slipping a punch as he moved for the door. Beakman, fascinated, circled the dead man.

Trenchard said, "Don't touch anything. We gotta treat it like a crime scene."

"I'm just looking."

A photo album lay open between the dead man's

feet as if it had fallen from his lap. Careful not to step in the dried blood, Beakman moved closer to see. A single picture was centered on the open page, one of those Polaroid pictures that develop themselves. The plastic over the picture was speckled with blood.

The flies suddenly seemed louder to Beakman, as loud now as the helicopters fighting the flames.

"Trench, come here—"

Trenchard came over, then stooped for a closer look.

"Holy Mother."

The Polaroid showed a female Caucasian with what appeared to be an extension cord wrapped around her neck. The picture had been taken at night, with the woman sprawled on her back at the base of a trash bin. Her tongue protruded thickly from her mouth, and her eyes bulged, but they were unfocused and sightless.

Beakman heard himself whispering.

"You think it's real? A real woman, really dead?"

"Dunno."

"Maybe it's from a movie. You know, staged?"

Trenchard opened his knife, then used the point to turn the page. Beakman grew scared. He might have been only a reserve officer, but he knew better than to disturb the scene.

"We're not supposed to touch anything."

"We're not. Shut up."

Trenchard turned to the next page, then the next. Beakman felt numb, but excited, knowing he was seeing a darkness so terrible that few people would ever imagine it, let alone face it. These pictures were portraits of evil. The mind that had conceived of these things and taken these pictures and hidden them in this album had entered a nightmare world. It had left humanity behind. Beakman would have stories for his kids when he returned to school, but this story would not be among them.

"They're real, aren't they? These women were murdered."

"I dunno."

"They look real. He fucking killed them."

"Stop it."

Trenchard lifted the album with his knife so they could see the cover. It showed a beautiful sunset beach with gentle waves and a couple leaving foot-prints on the sand. Embossed in flowing script was a legend: *My Happy Memories*.

Trenchard lowered the cover.

"Let's get away from these flies."

They left the album as they had found it and sought solace in the smoky air.

PART ONE

LOOKOUT MOUNTAIN

1

Joe Pike waited without making a sound. He had not spoken or moved in more than twenty minutes. This was nothing for Pike. I have known him to go soundless for days.

My office—our office; he owns it, too—was a good place to be that morning. There was only the tocking of the Pinocchio clock, the scratch of my pen, and the hiss of the air conditioner fighting the heat. Pike had stopped by to pick me up. After I finished the paperwork, we were going to work out at Ray Depente's dojo in South-Central Los Angeles. Nothing like bruises to top off the morning.

Pike said, "We're burning."

I glanced up from the work. Pike was framed in the French doors that open onto my balcony with its view across West L.A. to the Pacific.

"Where?"

"Hills west of the 405. Twenty klicks."

Klicks. Pike was into the military thing.

"I'm almost finished here. Warn me if it gets within ten miles."

Like that could happen. I went back to work. It was fire season, when fires erupted across the Southland like pimples on adolescent skin.

Pike said, "It's beautiful."

"The fire?"

"The city. We are never more beautiful than when we are burning."

Only Pike would say something like that.

Then Pike cocked his head toward the door, and everything that had been good about that morning changed.

"Listen—"

The door pushed open, and the first cop strode in like he was storming a bunker in Faluja. He was a stocky guy with a high and tight haircut and a wilted tan sport coat. He showed me his badge as if he expected me to dive under my desk.

"Welcome to hell, shitbird."

I looked at Pike.

"Did I hear a knock?"

The second cop wore a blue business suit with a shoulder bag slung on her arm, and a silver and gold LAPD detective shield. She looked tired, and the heat had played hell with her hair.

"Stop with the language, Charles. Let's just do this."

I was still blinking at Pike.

"Did he really call me a 'shitbird'?"

Charles tipped his badge toward me, then Pike, but he talked to the woman.

"This one's Cole. This one's gotta be his bun boy, Pike."

The corner of Pike's mouth twitched, which is as close as Pike comes to an expression. Pike was six-one, a bit over two, and could kill you just by thinking real hard. He was suited up with a sleeveless gray sweatshirt and shades. When he crossed his arms, the bright red arrows inked on his deltoids rippled.

The woman pushed hair from her brow as she showed her badge.

"Detective Connie Bastilla, LAPD. This is Charlie Crimmens. Are you Elvis Cole?"

I am a professional investigator. I run a professional business. Police officers did not barge into my office. They also did not call me shitbird.

"Did you make an appointment?"

Crimmens said, "Answer her, shitbird."

I gave Crimmens a nice smile, and stood.

"Say it again I'll shove that badge up your ass."

Bastilla took a seat in one of the two director's chairs facing my desk.

"Take it easy. We have some questions about a case you once worked."

I stared at Crimmens.

"You want to arrest me, get to it. You want to talk to me, knock on my door and ask for permission. You think I'm kidding about the badge, try it out."

Pike said, "Uh."

Crimmens smirked as he draped himself over the file cabinet. He studied Pike for a moment, then smirked some more.

Bastilla said, "Do you recall a man named Lionel James?"

"I didn't offer you a seat."

"C'mon, you know Lionel James or not?"

Charlie said, "He knows him. Jesus."

Neither of them moved to leave, and neither offered to apologize. Something about Crimmens was familiar, though I couldn't quite place him. I knew most of the Hollywood bureau detectives, but these two were new.

"You aren't out of Hollywood."

Bastilla placed her card on my desk.

"Downtown. I'm with Homicide Special. Charlie's attached out of Rampart. Now, c'mon. Lionel James."

I had to think.

"We're talking about a criminal case?"

"Three years ago, James was bound over for the murder of a twenty-seven-year-old prostitute named Yvonne Bennett, a crime to which he confessed. You produced a witness and security tape that supposedly cleared him of the crime. His attorney was J. Alan Levy, of Barshop, Barshop, and Alter. We getting warmer here?"

The facts of the case returned with the slowness of surfacing fish. Lionel James had been an unemployed mechanic with alcohol problems and a love/hate relationship with prostitutes. He wasn't a guy you would want to know socially, but he also wasn't a murderer.

"Yeah, I remember. Not all the details, but some. It was a bogus confession. He recanted."

Crimmens shifted.

"Wasn't bogus."

I took my seat and hooked my foot on the edge of my desk.

"Whatever. The video showed he was here in Hollywood when Bennett was murdered. She was killed over in Silver Lake."

Behind them, Pike touched his watch. We were going to be late.

I lowered my foot and leaned forward.

"You guys should have called. Joe and I have an appointment."

Bastilla took out a notepad to show me they weren't leaving.

"Have you seen much of Mr. James since you got him off?"

"I've never seen him. I never met the man."

Crimmens said, "Bullshit."

"He was your client. You don't meet your clients?"

"Levy was my client. Barshop Barshop paid the tab. That's what lawyers do."

"So it was Levy who hired you?"

"Yes. Most of my clients are lawyers."

Lawyers can't and don't rely on the word of their clients. Often, their clients don't know the whole and impartial truth, and don't have the facts. Often, their clients lie. Since lawyers are busy lawyering, they employ investigators to uncover the facts.

Bastilla twisted around to see Pike.

"How about you?"

"Not my kind of job."

She twisted farther to get a better look.

"How about you take off the shades while we talk?"

"No."

Crimmens said, "You hiding something back there, Pike? How 'bout we get a look?"

Pike's head swiveled toward Crimmens. Nothing else moved, just his head.

"If I showed you, I'd have to kill you."

You never know if he means these things or not. I stepped in before it got out of hand.

"Joe didn't help on this one. Some cases, he works; others, not. This thing was Detective Work 101. I must pull thirty cases like this a year."

Crimmens said, "Oh, that's sweet. You must take great pride in that, Cole, helping shitbirds like James get away with murder."

Crimmens was pissing me off again.

"What are we talking about this for, Bastilla? This thing was settled three years ago."

Bastilla opened her pad and studied the page.

"Are you acquainted with a man named Lonnie Jones?"

"No."

"Do you recall the name Adam Tomlinson, Tomlinson being a person you interviewed during your investigation?"

"Yeah, kinda."

Tomlinson was a coffee shop barrista who had been the last person to see Yvonne Bennett alive.

"Have you had any contact with Mr. Tomlinson since the time of your investigation?"

"No."

"Would you know how to reach him?"

"He worked at a coffee shop on Sunset in Silver Lake. I might have a couple of numbers, but I'd have to look them up."

"How about you do that and call me?"

"Sure, fine, but why do you care about Tomlinson?"

She flipped the page again, ignoring my question.

"So you are telling us you have never met Lionel James?"

"Yes."

"And you've had no contact subsequent to his release?"

"Where are you going with this, Bastilla? Have you re-arrested him?"

Bastilla scribbled a note. When she looked up, her eyes were ringed with purple that cut down to the corners of her mouth like bruises. She looked as tired as a person can look without being dead.

"No, Mr. Cole, I wish we could arrest him, but we can't. The day we had the fires up Laurel Canyon, he was found during the evacuation. Head shot up through the bottom of his chin. He'd been dead about five days."

I shook my head.

"I didn't kill him."

Crimmens laughed.

"Wouldn't that be funny, Con? Wouldn't that be too perfect? Man, I would love that."

Bastilla smiled, but not because she thought it was funny.

"He committed suicide. He was up there under the name Lonnie Jones. Know why he'd be using an alias?"

"I got no idea. If the man's dead and you don't think I killed him, why all the questions about whether or not I've seen him?"

"Lionel James murdered seven women. We believe he murdered one woman every year for the past seven years. Yvonne Bennett was his fifth victim."

She said it as matter-of-factly as a bank teller cashing a check, but with a softness in her voice that spread seeds of ice in my belly.

I shook my head. It was all I could think to do.

"He didn't kill Yvonne Bennett. I proved it."

Bastilla put away her pad. She got up, then slung her bag on her shoulder, finally ready to go.

"Material linking him to the murder was found in his home. He killed her. He murdered a sixth woman the summer after his release. His most recent victim was murdered thirty-four days ago. Now he's killed himself. We've been going back through the time line to make sure all seven fit, and, so far, it's solid."

The crystals spread a fine coldness that even the devil's wind couldn't touch.

Crimmens licked his lips as if he wanted to eat me alive.

"How do you feel now, Mr. Thirty-a-Year?"

I shook my head and looked back at Bastilla.

"I don't believe it."

She shrugged as if she didn't give a damn either way.

"What does that mean, you found material?"

"We're not at liberty to say."

"You tell me the man killed seven people, but you won't tell me what you have?"

"You want to know what we have, tune in tonight; there's going to be a press conference. In the meantime"—Bastilla nodded toward her card—"anything you remember about him might help us figure out how he got away with it for so long."

She left without waiting, but Crimmens made no move to follow. He stayed on the file cabinet, staring at me.

I said, "What?"

"Escondido and Williams."

"Why are you still here, Crimmens?"

"You don't recognize me, do you?"

"Should I?"

"Think about it. You must've read my reports."

Then I realized why he was familiar.

"You were the arresting officer."

Crimmens finally pushed off the cabinet.

"That's right. I'm the guy who arrested James. I'm the guy who tried to stop a killer. You're the shitbird who set him free."

Crimmens glanced at Pike, then went to the door.

"Lupe Escondido and Glenda Williams are the women he killed after you got him off. You should send the families a card."

Crimmens closed the door when he left.

Not sure what to read next?

Visit Pocket Books online at
www.simonsays.com

**Reading suggestions for
you and your reading group
New release news
Author appearances
Online chats with your favorite writers
Special offers
Order books online
And much, much more!**